Other books by Victor Kelley

**HOW TO GET INTO THE BUSINESS
OF PHOTOGRAPHY**

SHOOTING
Confession... ...oter
(Pho... ...s)

RUMINATIONS FROM A RETIRED RECLUSE

HUBRIS FROM A NOT-SO-HUMBLE HERMIT

FRESH NOSTALGIA

THINGS I FORGOT TO REMEMBER

DIARY OF A DILETTANTE

"...AND THEN WHAT HAPPENED?"

Victor Kelley

authorHOUSE®

AuthorHouse™
1663 Liberty Drive
Bloomington, IN 47403
www.authorhouse.com
Phone: 1-800-839-8640

Published by AuthorHouse   06/14/2013

ISBN: 978-1-4817-5792-8 (sc)
ISBN: 978-1-4817-5791-1 (e)

Library of Congress Control Number: 2013910987

DEDICATION

To Louis "Studs" Terkel, American-born journalist of historical genius whose expertise was extracting fascinating stories in interviews with a wide spectrum of American people, be they destitute, wealthy, blue collar, street people, homeless, drunk or sober, or just trying to exist in America.

And after they were done telling their stories, Studs would add, ". . . And then what happened?"

"And then what happened" would come pouring forth the real tales that enriched his interviews because people realized they could trust him, and revealed their souls in words telltale of their real lives.

Studs Terkel's radio and print interviews are a bonanza legacy he gave to America in defining the character and wisdom of common folk who lived here.

TABLE OF CONTENTS

Ship High in Transport 1
Legitimate Ruminations & Judgments 4
Quotable Quotes 10
Saturday Night Specials 35
Ghostbuster Alert! 39
My Walter Mitty Marriages 43
Hand-Me-Down Religions and Politics 49
Truth and Consequences 51
You Don't Even Want to Know About This! 52
Choices 56
Morbidity Report 59
Off the Wall 63
A Better Mousetrap – Sort Of 70
Welcome to Kvorka! 74
The "Funnies" 76
Cues to Keep Everyone Off Balance 88
History You Missed 91
Games People Play 94
Disparate Dispatches 97
   Annals of Law 97
   The Perfect Squelch 101
   Palliatives 103
   Gospel or Gossip 105
   Remembering When 110
Out of the Mainstream 113
Once Upon a Time 118
Papal Fun and Games 120
Death by a Thousand Slices 123
Confession 126
"Throw All the Bums Out!' 130
Reconstruction 135
Chiliheads 136

What Will They Think of Next!.............................. 141

Salient Trivia 143

   Salient Facts of Little Importance...................... 143

   Ode to the Dimpled White Ball.........................145

   Little Known Facts 146

   Men for All Ages...................................... 148

   Pallbearers 149

Studs... 150

Potpourri 155

   Ratted Out.. 156

   Unknowns... 157

   What's in a Name?..................................... 158

   39 Things You Should Have Learned by Now 160

   Distractions... 163

Bureaucracy at Its Best................................... 166

Orientations.. 169

Pending Release from Hell 172

Off the Wall 176

   Things to Tell Your Grandchildren 177

   Chivarees Exposed 179

   Recycled Beverage..................................... 180

Godammit Redux... 185

Awards That Went Awry 188

How to Create and Eat a Salad............................ 192

Who Fired That Round? 196

Choosing Next-of-Kin Sale................................ 200

Encore 201

Anomalies.. 204

Things You Never Knew 'till Now 208

Conundrum..215

Stuff... 220

   Bar Story Memoirs..................................... 222

   Longevity Anyone? Have a Banana!.................... 225

Acts of Kindness 229

Wikileaks.org...233

"I Was Fired" 239
Radio Codes 240
Name Your Seduction 243
  Assessment 244
Famous Comments from Guess Who? 246
Curiosities 249
Dates of Disasters and Deliverance 256
Congressional Rough & Tumble 260
Uncle Sam Needs You! Now! Who Are These
Congressmen? 264
What Don't You Want to Know 267
Don't Even Go There Smorgasbord 273
  Political Correctness 273
  A Sex Story 273
  Beef Up the Grief! 276
Sundry Ruminations Wear and Wherefore of
Underwear 279
Heavenly Voices 283
Crosses to Bear 290
So You Wanna Be a Chef 292
Priests, Pederasty, and the Catholic Church 297
Birth of Religions 301
My Name Is Ota Benga 302

SHIP HIGH IN TRANSPORT

Fertilizer has always been a commercial commodity throughout the world. Manure has always been the prime source of it. In figuring out how to ship it to foreign ports became a lesson in trial and error, giving us the etymology of a favorite English expression (if not expletive) that has become the most used word as a noun, verb, adjective, and adverb in our language.

It all began when 16th and 17th century entrepreneurs figured out that shipping raw manure abroad in quantity was too heavy to be profitable. By allowing it to dehydrate, however, removed the heaviness of its moisture and its aroma, shrinking it in mass some 90%, and allowing it to be bundled cargo of extreme value.

It was on a ship headed for the colonies that a situation developed that required a dramatic change in just how and where in the ship it had to be stored.

On an early voyage, one vessel, whose hold was full of the dried product, was rocked by high waves at sea to the point that seawater spilled into the hold itself. As the packages mass in the hold absorbed the moisture (and grew exponentially), fermentation began to produce a by-product of manure: *methane gas.* When an inspector went below deck at night to check on his load, using an oil lamp for light, an explosion of some magnitude destroyed the ship. After a few others boats suffered the same consequences, merchants figured out that future payloads should be stored in areas that would not be subject to immersion by ocean waves and set off the volatile cargo with its ability to manufacture methane gas.

Thereafter, notices of bundled dry manure were labeled "Ship High In Transport" when loading a cargo vessel. Thus was born the acronym SHIT. It's not exactly a prosaic term for what has become the most functional English word.

For example:
- You can get shit-faced, be shit-out-of-luck, or have shit for brains.
- With a little effort, you can get your shit together, find a place for your shit, or be asked to shit or get off the pot.
- You can smoke shit, buy shit, sell shit, lose shit, find shit, forget shit, and tell others to eat shit.
- Some people know their shit, while others can't tell the difference between shit and Shinola (the shoe polish.)
- There are lucky shits, dumb shits, and crazy shits. There is bullshit, horseshit, and chicken shit.
- You can throw shit, sling shit, catch shit, shoot the shit, or duck when the shit hits the fan.
- You can give a shit, or serve shit on a shingle.
- You can find yourself deep in shit or be happier than a pig in shit.
- Some days are colder than shit, some days are hotter than shit, and some days are just plain shitty.
- Some music sounds like shit, things can look like shit, and there are times when you feel like shit.
- You can have too much shit, not enough shit, the right shit, the wrong shit, or a lot of weird shit.
- You can carry shit, have a mountain of shit, or find yourself up shit creek without a paddle.

- Sometimes everything you touch turns to shit, and other times you fall in a bucket of shit and come out smelling like a rose.
- You could pass this along to your friends if you give a shit, or not if you don't give a shit.
- And remember, once you know your shit, you don't need to know anything else.
- Well, it's time to end this shit. Just wanted the reader to know that the author gives a shit, and hopes you have a nice day without a bunch of shit.
- But if you happened to catch a load of shit from some shit-head, well SHIT HAPPENS!

LEGITIMATE RUMINATIONS & JUDGMENTS

Throughout history, legitimate births are less memorable than illegitimate ones. Notoriety becomes the vehicle for fame when we realize that bastard birth was no deterrent to success for hundreds (thousands?) of men and women who were manufactured "love" children, intentional or not. One wonders what choice those born out of wedlock would make given an opportunity before coming into this world. Of similar importance would be their thinking once they discovered that their parents violated social and legal conventions en route to producing offspring.

Thanks to the Internet, an "A List" of famous persons, who arrived in the world as illegitimate or bastard issue of long-forgotten or obscure parents, has been compiled. Here are a few:

Alexander The Great – world conqueror
Sarah Bernhardt – actress
Cesar Borgia – Catholic Cardinal (son of Pope Alexander VI)
Aleksandr Borodin – composer
Pope Clement VII – spiritual head of Catholic Church
Leonardo da Vinci – artist
Alexandre Dumas – novelist and playwright
Alexander Hamilton – U.S. Secretary of the Treasury
Jenny Lind – singer
Marilyn Monroe – actress
Oprah Winfrey – television personality
Francesco Pizarro – conqueror of Peru
James Smithson – chemist and founder of Smithsonian Institute
Ella Fitzgerald - singer

August Strindberg – playwright
Richard Wagner – composer
William the Conqueror – first Norman ruler of England
Lucrezia Borgia – daughter of Pope Alexander VI
Louis Armstrong - musician

Of all the occupations that are pre-disposed to generate babies out of wedlock, one would be hard-pressed to eclipse that of millionaire athletes, most notably football, basketball, baseball, boxing and hockey. Their collective accomplishment in populating the world has no known peers. Just those in the United States almost boggle the mind in enumerating the progeny born by them in dalliances just in the last generation. Here are some of the more productive names of progenitors who have *allegedly* admitted paternity for their sextraordinary achievements:

And in the HEAVYWEIGHT COLUMN there are:

- Calvin Murphy: 14 illegitimate kids by 9 women. He is the current champion!

- Travis Henry: 9 kids by 9 women – all by the time he was 28!

- Willie Anderson: 9 illegitimate kids (if only his field goal percentage had been as high as his impregnation rate.)

- Evander Holyfield: 9 illegitimate kids (has more kids than brain cells left in his mottled head.)

- Jason Caffey: 8 illegitimate kids by 7 women

- Shawn Kemp: 7 illegitimate kids by 5 women. (They didn't call him the Reign Man for nothing.)

- Derrick Thomas: 7 illegitimate kids by 5 women. He died at 33 – enough said for that!

And now for the MIDDLEWEIGHTS

- Ray Lewis: 6 kids by 4 women

- Marshall Faulk: 6 illegitimate kids by 3 women. (No wonder he pondered coming out of retirement.)

- Larry Johnson: 5 kids by 4 women (3 are illegitimate.)

- Charles Rogers: 5 illegitimate kids

- Vlad Guerrero: 4 kids by 4 women

- Santonio Holmes: 3 illegitimate kids by 2 *women before leaving college.*

- Greg Minor: 3 illegitimate kids

- Ricky Williams: 3 illegitimate kids (is that why he smoked so much weed?)

- Priest Holmes: 3 illegitimate kids (love that first name!)

- Chad Johnson: 3 illegitimate kids

- Shannon "Horseface" Sharpe: 3 illegitimate kids

- Mike Bibby: had 2 illegitimate kids before he left "Zona."

And now, the LIGHTNING FAST GROUP

- Willis McGahee: 3 illegitimate kinds in 2 years in Buffalo (not too much to do in Buffalo besides making babies.)

GUYS YOU'D LEAST EXPECT TO HAVE ILLEGITIMATE KIDS

- Walter Herrmann
- Peja Stojakovic
- Wizards coach Eddie Jordan
- NHL player Daniel Alfredsson
- NHL player Richard Zednik
- Mike Miller
- Marvin Harrison
- Tracy McGrady

The famous OLD TIMER'S GROUP

- Steve Garvey: 2 illegitimate kids by 2 women
- Larry Bird
- Isiah Thomas
- Jim Palmer
- Darryl Strawberry
- Pete Rose
- Tug McGraw

The HEAD-START group

- Gary Sheffield: had 2 illegitimate kids by age 17. Added a few more later in life.

The THAT'S JUST WRONG Group

- Elijah Dukes: impregnated his foster child along with 4 more illegitimate kids.

The QUARTERBACK KIDS GROUP

- Matt Leinhart
- Tom Brady

Guys WITH AT LEAST ONE ILLEGITIMATE KID

- Antawn Jamison
- Chipper Jones
- DeShawn Stevenson
- Cliff Floyd
- Mark Messier
- Brian Urlacher
- Rae Carruth
- Oscar De La Hoya
- Juan Gonzalez
- Andre Rison
- David Justice
- Andruw Jones
- AlonzoSpellman
- Dave Meggett
- Gary Payton
- Stephon Marbury
- Jason Kidd
- Allen Iverson

- Latrell Sprewell
- Kenny Andersoon
- Scottie Pippen
- Hakeem Olajuwon
- Patrick Ewing
- Randy Johnson

These figures reflect *at least* 149 illegitimate kids (and counting) from their irresponsible athlete millionaire fathers. So much for hero-worshipping.

After viewing this rogue's gallery of spreading their sperm around, consider this: *None of these millionaires thought that the women they impregnated was even worth the price of a condom.* God only knows what they think of the children that were stuck with such derelict fathers.

QUOTABLE QUOTES

"A person who aims at nothing is sure to hit it."
... Anonymous

"Effort and courage are of no value without purpose and direction."
... John F. Kennedy

"Because I like the odds that one in four vice-presidents becomes Presidents. . ."
... Answer given by Lyndon Johnson to reporter's question why he accepted being JFK's choice for vice-president in 1960.

"There isn't any dress too small enough that I can't fit into."
... Dolly Parton

"Bull sessions produce only what bulls produce."
... Richard Nixon

"I've taken showers with people most Republicans have never met."
... NFL Quarterback, Republican Congressman, and Vice-Presidential Candidate Jack Kemp.

"I am confident that there truly is such a thing as living again and that the living springs from the dead."
... Socrates (at the end of his life)

"Tact is the ability to see others as they see themselves."
... Abraham Lincoln

"The most heinous and the most cruel crimes of which history has record have been committed under the cover of religion or equally noble motives."

. . . Gamtano Kanye Gulal

"When two people come under the influence of the most violent, most delusive, and most transient of passions, they agree to live in this highly excitable state until death do them part."

. . . (On marriage) George Bernard Shaw

"To become a spectator of one's own life . . . is to escape the suffering of life."

. . . Oscar Wilde

"Troubles come not as single spies, but in battalions."

. . . Anonymous

"He had delusions of adequacy."

. . . Critic Walter Kerr

"He can compress the most words into the smallest idea of any man I know."

. . . Abraham Lincoln

"One of the very difficult parts of the decision I made on the financial crisis was to use hardworking people's money to help prevent there to be a crisis."

. . . President George W. Bush

". . . We will extend a hand if you are willing to unclench your fist . . ."

. . . Barack Obama (2009 Inauguration speech.)

"He who learns and learns and yet does not what he knows, is one who plows yet never sows."

       . . . Alfred Korzybski

"I shall keep divorce legal in France, if only so I can leave that woman."

       . . . Napoleon (emperor-in-waiting, bemoaning
         his marriage to spendthrift Josephine)

"Success is just another one of those ABC's – Ability, Breaks, and Courage."

       . . . Charles Luckman

(On the morality of chess) "If your adversary is long in playing, you ought not to hurry him, or even express uneasiness at his delay; not even by looking at your watch, or taking a book to read, you should not sing, nor whistle, nor make tapping sounds with your feet on the floor, or with your fingers on the table, nor do anything to distract his attention."

       . . . Benjamin Franklin

"A good wife always forgives her husband when she's wrong."

       . . . Milton Berle

"I didn't attend the funeral, but sent a nice letter saying I approved of it."

       . . . Mark Twain

"I hope Obama fails."

       . . . Comic Rush Limbaugh

"I must go home periodically to renew my sense of horror."

    . . . Carson McCullers

"I would rather have newspapers without a government than a government without newspapers."

    . . . Thomas Jefferson

"Pops, music is music. All music is folk music. I ain't never heard no horse sing a song."

    . . . Louis Armstrong (answer to a question of what he thought of Country and Western music and folk music.)

"The reason white people don't have rhythm, they've never been beat."

    . . . Composer Billy "Sweet Pea" Strayhorn

"Never underestimate the intelligence of the American people."

    . . . H. L. Mencken

"If I had only followed CNBC's advice, I'd have a million dollars today, provided I started with $100 million."

    . . . Comedian Jon Stewart to CNBC's money guru Jim Cramer following the 2008 financial crash

"Those that can make you believe absurdities, can make you vomit atrocities."

    . . . Voltaire

"All books are written by men – not God."

. . . Thomas Paine, 1737-1809 (on the bigotry of religion)

"I never threw an illegal pitch. The trouble is, once in a while I toss one that ain't been seen by this generation."
              . . . Leroy "Satchel" Paige (1907-1982)

"A lie can travel half-way around the world while the truth is still putting on its shoes."
                    . . . Mark Twain

"The unexamined life is not worth living."
                    . . . Socrates

"I need to focus my attention on being a better husband, father, and person."
      . . . Tiger Woods, before revelations of his multiple
        sexual infidelities were revealed in the news.

"You've got to be very careful if you don't know where you're going, because you might not get there."
              . . . Lawrence "Yogi" Berra

"I'm so unlucky, if the last woman on earth were cut in half, I'd get the half that talked."
                    . . . Rodney Dangerfield

"Pain is a way for Mother Nature to talk to us. And when our invented process for understanding [i.e., MRI's] is at odds with what Mother Nature is telling us, we had better listen to Mother Nature." [Message: seek another opinion.]
      . . . Dr. James Thrall, chairman of the board of
      chancellors of the American College of Radiology

"The difference between a successful person and others is not lack of strength, not lack of knowledge, but rather in a lack of will."

. . . Vince Lombardi

"A human being is first a human being before he or she becomes infected with the virus of religious ideology and superstition."

. . . Jeffery, from New Jersey, letter to the editor of *The New York Times* commenting on the origin of religions.

"It's not the road you travel; it's your choices along the way."

. . . Joe Biden

"The first (and most important) item to pack in a suitcase is toilet paper."

. . . Victor Kelley

"He has no enemies, but is intensely disliked by his friends."

. . . Oscar Wilde

"Kissing a smoker is like licking an ashtray."

. . . Tony Randall

"Victory belongs to the most persevering."

. . . Napoleon

"The person, who knows something no one else knows, will be a success."

. . . Aristotle Onassis

"You never get a second chance to make a first impression."

. . . Anonymous

"Liberals feel unworthy of their possessions; Conservatives feel they deserve everything they have stolen."
. . . Mort Sahl

"By and large, jazz is the kind of man you wouldn't like your daughter to associate with."
. . . Wynton Marsalis

"He has the attention span of a lightning bolt."
. . . Robert Redford

"His mother should have thrown him away, and kept the stork."
. . . Mae West

"If I owned hell and Texas, I'd live in hell and rent out Texas."
. . . Sam Houston

"Trust no man living with power to endanger the public liberty."
. . . John Adams (1772)

"The harder I work, the luckier I get."
. . . Sam Goldwyn

"The job of Presidents is to confront problems, not to pass them on to future presidents and future generations."
. . . George W. Bush

"No man can resist checking a claim that 'Your fly is open'."
. . . Victor Kelley

"Men never do evil so completely and cheerfully as when they do it from religious conviction."
. . . Blaise Pascal, 17th century scientist

"Behind every great fortune there is a crime."
. . . Honore de Balzac

"Women are only children of a larger growth."
. . . Earl of Chesterfield

"The trouble with people is not so much with their ignorance as it is with their knowing so many things that are not so."
. . . William Alanson White

"What this country needs are more unemployed politicians."
. . . Edward Langley

"All I can say for the United States Senate is that it opens with a prayer and closes with an investigation."
. . . Will Rogers

"Everybody is entitled to his own opinion but not his own facts."
. . . Senator Daniel Patrick Moynihan

"A government big enough to give you everything you want, is strong enough to take everything you have."
. . . Thomas Jefferson

"The only difference between a tax man and a taxidermist is that the taxidermist leaves the skin."
. . . Mark Twain

"I contend that for a nation to try to tax itself into prosperity is like a man standing in a bucket and trying to lift himself up by the handle."
. . . Winston Churchill

"If you have some daily anguish from some cause that's not really your fault – a rotten family, bad health, nowhere looks, serious money problems, nobody to help you, minority background, rejoice! These things are your fuel."

> . . . Helen Gurley Brown, longtime
> editor of Cosmopolitan Magazine.

"A government which robs Peter to pay Paul can always depend on the support of Paul."

> . . . George Bernard Shaw

"Never pass up the opportunity to have sex or be on television."

> . . . Gore Vidal

"You can't no more teach what you ain't learned than you can come from where you ain't been."

> . . . Mark Twain

"Giving money and power to government is like giving whiskey and car keys to teenage boys."

> . . . P. J. O'Rourke

"Just because you do not take an interest in politics doesn't mean politics won't take an interest in you."

> . . . Pericles (430 B.C.)

"Democracy must be something more than two wolves and a sheep voting on what to have for dinner."

> . . . James Bovard

"It does not require money to be neat, clean and dignified."

> . . . Mahatma Gandhi

"How can 59,054,087 people be so dumb?!"
   . . . Headline of UK newspaper London Daily Mirror
the day after George W. Bush was re-elected in 2004.

"If you don't read the newspaper, you're uninformed. If you do read the newspaper, you're misinformed."
                    . . . Mark Twain

"Foreign aid might be defined as a transfer of money from poor people in rich countries to rich people in poor countries."
          . . . Douglas Casey

"No one can make you feel inferior without your consent."
          . . . Eleanor Roosevelt

"I've had a perfectly wonderful evening, but this wasn't it."
          . . . Groucho Marx

"I don't make jokes. I just watch the government and report the facts."
          . . . Will Rogers

"Jazz is like knowing the most you ever will."
          . . . Wynton Marsalis

"Of course I believe in luck. How else do you explain the success of those you dislike?"
          . . . Jean Cocteau

"Government's view of the economy could be summed up in a few short phrases: if it moves, tax it; if it keeps moving, regulate it; and if it stops moving, subsidize it."
          . . . Ronald Reagan

"No man's life, liberty, or property is safe while the Legislature is in session."

> . . . Mark Twain

"Talk is cheap – except when Congress does it."

> . . . Anonymous

"Taxes are the price we pay for civilization."

> . . . Thomas Jefferson

"The ultimate result of shielding men from the effects of folly is to fill the world with fools."

> . . . Herbert Spencer

"There is no distinctly Native American criminal class – save Congress."

> . . . Mark Twain

"I do understand power, whatever else may be said about me. I know where to look for it, and how to use it."

> . . . Lyndon Baines Johnson

"No man's life is uninteresting."

> . . . Mark Twain

"Anybody can make a mistake. To repeat that mistake signifies stupidity."

> . . . Anonymous

"You can't step into the same river twice."

> . . . Heraclitus

"The more you do what you've always done, the more you'll get what you always got."

> . . . Albert Einstein

"The discipline of writing something down is the first in making it happen."

. . . Lee Iaococca

"We should be careful to get out of an experience only the wisdom that is in it – and stop there; lest we be like the cat that sits down on a hot stove lid. She will never sit down on a hot stove lid again – and that is well; but also she will never sit down on a cold one anymore."

. . . Mark Twain

"Only those who will risk going too far can possibly find out how far one can go."

. . . T. S. Eliot

"One test is worth a thousand expert opinions."

. . . Anonymous

"It is commonly, but erroneously, believed that it is easy to ask questions. A fool, it is said, can ask questions a wise man cannot answer. The fact is that a wise man can answer many questions that a fool cannot ask."

. . . Cassius J. Keyser

"To a mouse, cheese is cheese. That's why mousetraps work."

. . . Wendell Johnson

"Cowards can never be moral."

. . . Mahatma Gandhi

"Nothing so needs reforming as other people's habits."

. . . Mark Twain

"We cannot command the wind, but we can adjust our sails."

> . . . Anonymous

"You can't make me what you call me."

> . . . Al Fleishman

"A great many people think they are thinking when they are merely rearranging their prejudices."

> . . . William James

"It ought to be remembered that there is nothing more difficult to take in hand, more perilous to conduct, or more uncertain in its success, than to take the lead in the introduction of a new order of things. Because the innovator has for enemies all those who have done well under the old conditions, and only lukewarm defenders among those who may do well under the new."

> . . . Machiavelli

"Laughter is the only thing that'll cut trouble down to a size where you can talk to it."

> . . . Dan Jenkins

"Why do you sit there looking like an envelope without any address on it?"

> . . . Mark Twain

"He is a self-made man and worships his creator."

> . . . John Bright

"He is not only dull himself; he is the cause of dullness in others."

> . . . Samuel Johnson

"If you aren't getting flak, you aren't over the target."
. . . Gifford Pinchot

"More than any other time in history, mankind faces a crossroads. One path leads to despair and utter hopelessness. The other, to total extinction. Let us pray we have the wisdom to choose correctly."
. . . Woody Allen

"He who rejects change is the architect of decay. The only human institution which rejects progress is the cemetery."
. . . Harold Wilson

"Never do well that which you don't want to do again."
. . . Steve McGonigle

"The mass of men lead lives of quiet desperation."
. . . Ralph Waldo Emerson

"A self-indulgent man lives to eat; a self-restrained man eats to live."
. . . Mahatma Gandhi

"Get over it!"
. . . Supreme Court Justice Antonin Scalia's remark when questioned about the Court's decision to award George W. Bush the 2000 Presidency after illegally snatching the case from the Florida Supreme Court that had jurisdiction over Florida's disputed vote count in that election.

"Who can figure out the French? Their money dissolves in your hand, but you can't tear the toilet paper."
. . . Alexander King

"Fake it till you make it."
>. . . Hillary Rodham Clinton

"Do you feel lucky, punk? Well, do ya?"
>. . . Clint Eastwood as "Dirty Harry"

"All religions have their origins in collective hallucinations by male human beings."
>. . . Victor E. Kelley

"Let's just say, like Yogi Bear used to say, I'm smarter than the average bear."
>. . . Dwight "Mad Dog" White, Pittsburgh Steeler defensive end, and one of the quartet of the football team's 1970's Steel Curtain (along with Joe Green, L.C. Greenwood, and Ernie Holmes.)

"I don't want to be just Spam in a can."
>. . . Chuck Yeager, test pilot (X-15)

"The first thing you do when you find yourself in a hole is to stop digging."
>. . . Bob Herbert (columnist, NYT)

"We now know the number of stars in the universe is something like 1 followed by 23 zero's. Given that number, how arrogant to think ours is the only sun with a planet that supports life, and that it's in the only solar system with intelligent life."
>. . . Edward J. Weiler, NASA astrobiologist

"Without friends, nobody would choose to live."
>. . . Aristotle

"There's nothing wrong with you that reincarnation won't cure."

   . . . Comedian Jack E. Leonard

"The party that claims credit for the rain refuses to accept credit for a drought."

   . . . Anonymous

"I knew her before she was a virgin."

   . . . Oscar Levant's opinion of Doris Day's
Goody Two Shoes movie image

"Be fearful when others are greedy and greedy when others are fearful."

   . . . Warren Buffet

"A man I do not trust could not get money from me on all the bonds of Christendom."

   . . . J. P. Morgan

"You don't ever want a crisis to go to waste. It's an opportunity to do important things you would otherwise avoid."

   . . . Rahm Emanuel

"These are the times in which a genius would wish to live. It is not in the still calm of life, or the repose of a pacific station, that great characters are formed. The habits of a vigorous mind are formed in contending with difficulties. Great necessities call out great virtues. When a mind is raised, and animated by scenes that engage the heart, then those qualities which would otherwise lay

dormant, wake into life and form the character of the her and the statesman."
                    . . . Abigail Adams, in a letter written
                        to her son, John Quincy Adams.

"Marriage was designed for men who went to sea at 25 and women who died in childbirth."
                    . . . Thomas Detre (professor of Psychiatry,
                        University of Pittsburgh)

"Welcoming a penis just seems more womanly to me than baking chocolate chip cookies or doling out money for a grandchild's college tuition."
                    . . . Helen Gurley Brown, editor of
                        Cosmopolitan Magazine.

"The first clergyman was the first rascal who met the first fool."
                    . . . Voltaire

"No, we don't need them."
                    . . . General George Custer, reply to offer of
                        adding three Gatling guns for his troops
                        headed into battle with Indians.

"The worst thing I could imagine is being tortured for information I didn't have."
                    . . . Dr. Jonathan Miller

"Coffee to me always tasted like a chemical experiment."
                    . . . Agatha Christie

"An intelligent man is sometimes forced to be drunk to spend time with fools."
                    . . . Ernest Hemingway

"I still can't believe in this day and age an adult would go to a baseball game."

    . . . Michael Savage (Radio talk-show host)

"Gin and beef."

    . . . Answer to reporter Tom Sietsoma's
    question to Julia Child what she would
    like to have as her last meal.

"I want 6,000 Jews reported deaths every day."

    . . Nazi Buchenwald Commandant,
    Karl Otto Koch, April, 1945.

"I am a single, straight billionaire in Manhattan. It's a wet dream."

    . . . New York Mayor Michael Bloomberg.

"We're heading into nut country today."

    . . . JFK to wife, preparing to fly to Dallas, 1963.

"Ladies and gentlemen, President Hoobert Heever."
. . . Harry Von Zell, radio broadcaster in the 1930's introducing President Herbert Hoover, a verbal blooper that Zell never lived down.
"It is difficult to get a man to understand something when his salary depends on his not understanding it."

    . . . Upton Sinclair

"My specialty is being right when everyone else is wrong."

    . . . George Bernard Shaw

"Our beds are empty two-thirds of the time. Our living rooms are empty seven-eighths of the time. Our office buildings are empty one-half of the time. It's time we gave this some thought."

. . . R. Buckminster Fuller, architect

"I think that when statesmen forsake their own private conscience for the sake of their public duties, they lead their country by a short route to chaos."

. . . Sir Thomas More

"It was so quiet; you could hear a rat piss on cotton."

. . . Anonymous

"I hold the distinguished gentleman in minimum high regard."

. . . Ultra-polite1960's House Speaker John McCormick's most wrathful criticism when he became angry at a colleague. [Translation: "You're a shit!"]

"The only thing we learn from history is that we learn nothing from history."

. . . Hegel

"Every great man has his disciples, and it is always Judas who writes the biography."

. . . Oscar Wilde

"I hope that long after my marches have been forgotten, the clarion call of America which I tried to make the keynote of my compositions will continue to inspire her children with undying loyalty."

. . . Composer John Phillip Sousa

"I think the outcome would be much as when Christopher Columbus first landed in America, which didn't turn out very well for Native Americans."

> . . . Stephen Hawking, British astro-
> physicist in an interview on the possible
> consequences of aliens visiting earth.

"The termites have got me."

> . . . Baseball great George Herman "Babe" Ruth,
> comment made on his imminent death.

"He has, more than any man, the gift of compressing the largest amount of words into the smallest thought."

> . . . Winston Churchill, referring to Ramsay MacDonald

" . . . An amiable dunce."

> . . . Opinion of Ronald Reagan, offered by Clark
> Clifford, a political advisor to seven presidents.

"Sure I played. Did you think I was born at the age of 70 sitting in a dugout trying to manage guys like you?"

> . . . Charles "Casey" Stengel, Yankee Team
> Manager, when asked by Mickey Mantle
> if he'd ever been a baseball player.

"I have a spotless record of being in the wrong place at the wrong time."

> . . . NBC Edwin Newman, reflecting on
> his long career as a TV newsman

"To me, there's no real difference between a fortune teller or a fortune cookie and any of the organized religions. They're all equally valid or invalid, really. And equally helpful."

> . . . Woody Allen

"The poor have sometimes objected to being governed badly; the rich have always objected to being governed at all."

        . . . Gilbert Keith Chesterton

"Anger is never a management strategy."

        . . . British inventor James Dyson

"Life without music is like never having desserts"

        . . . Victor Kelley

"The right to showing my fist ends where the other man's nose begins."

        . . . Justice Oliver Wendell Holmes, Jr.

"Let's do it!"

        . . . Last words of convicted killer Gary Gilmore to his firing squad, inspiring The Nike Corporation advertising agency motto, "Just do it!"

"Some of the worst things in my life never happened."

        . . . Mark Twain

"Doubt is the father of invention."

        . . . Galileo

"DNA is the software of life."

        . . . J. Craig Venter

"As democracy is perfected, the office of President represents, more and more closely, the inner soul of the people. On some great and glorious day the plain folks of the land will reach their heart's desire at last and the White House will be adorned by a downright moron."

        . . . H. L. Mencken

"It got so quiet that you could hear a rat piss on cotton."
. . . Charles Robinson

"Don't ever put into writing what you wouldn't want to see on the front page of *The New York Times.*"
. . . Advice given to aspiring politicians

"No one ever went broke underestimating the taste of the American public."
. . . H. L. Menken

"I like your Christ. I do not like your Christians. Your Christians are so unlike your Christ."
. . . Mahatma Gandhi

"Room for your ass, and a gallon of gas."
. . . Description of Ford's 1955 revolutionary Thunderbird auto

"High School teaches you to learn. College teaches you to understand. You can forget what you learn, but you never forget what you understand."
. . . Victor E. Kelley

"The only way to get rid of temptation is to yield to it."
. . . Oscar Wilde

"Doubt is the beginning of wisdom."
. . . Aminus Darrow

"Marriage is a wonderful institution, but who would want to live in an institution?"
. . . H. L. Mencken

"Ossifer, I'm not half as trunk as thinkle peep I am."
. . . Words never to be uttered by erratic
drivers when stopped by policemen.

"You can always expect the Americans to do the right
thing – after they've tried everything else."
. . . Winston Churchill

"The only reason that they say 'Women and children first'
is to test the strength of the lifeboats."
. . . .Jean Kerr

"I've been married to a Communist and a Fascist, and
neither would take out the garbage."
. . . Zsa Zsa Gabor

"You know you're a redneck if your home has wheels and
your car doesn't."
. . . Jeff Foxworthy

"When a man opens a car door for his wife, it's either a
new car or a new wife."
. . . Prince Philip

"The best cure for sea sickness is to sit under a tree."
. . . Spike Milligan

"What Washington needs is adult supervision."
. . . Barack Obama

"Having more money doesn't make you happier. I have
50 million dollars, but I'm just as happy as when I had
48 million."
. . . Arnold Schwarzenegger

"Wood burns faster when you have to cut and chop it yourself."

   . . . Harrison Ford

"In hotel rooms I stay, I can't be the only guy who sits on the furniture naked."

   . . . Jonathan Katz

"You can tell a lot about a fellow's character by the way he eats jelly beans."

   . . . Ronald Reagan

"Home cooking – where many a man thinks his wife is."

   . . . Jimmy Durante

"The first piece of luggage on the carousel never belongs to anyone."

   . . . George Roberts

"It wasn't my finest hour. It wasn't even my finest hour and a half."

   . . . Bill Clinton"

"If this were a dictatorship, it'd be a heck of a lot easier, just so long as I'm the dictator."

   . . . George W. Bush

"Finishing second in the Olympics gets you silver. Finishing second in politics gets you oblivion."

   . . . Richard M. Nixon

"I'm the president of the United States, and I'm not going to eat any more broccolis."

   . . . George H. W. Bush

"Our growing softness, our increasing lack of physical fitness, is a menace to our security."

. . . John F. Kennedy

"I have kleptomania, but when it gets bad, I take something for it."

. . . Robert Benchley

"I'm not a paranoid, deranged millionaire. Dammit! I'm a billionaire.

. . . Howard Hughes

SATURDAY NIGHT SPECIALS

Asked about his choice of sexual orientation, comic writer and actor Woody Allen admitted that being bi-sexual seemed to him to have the best of both worlds. After all, he commented, "Think about Saturday nights, when you could double your chances of having a date."

For whatever reason, bi-sexuality doesn't seem to carry the social stigma that homosexuality does. Perhaps it reflects a suggestion of envy in people who go through life uncertain of their own sexual orientation and leery of being mislabeled by their peers, if word got out as to their preference. What isn't general knowledge about bisexuals is the degree of desire they have for male or female trysts – are they 50/50, 30/70, or 20/80, etc., either for men or women? Understandably, very few have been forthcoming to confess their variegated hormonal urges, unless, of course, it might be to a psychiatrist.

Truth to tell, the general public has shown no interest in bi-sexuality unless it involves people they know or read about. Celebrities draw the most interest since the revelation of their dalliances involves public perceptions as to the esteem, positive or negative, in which they might be held. Needless to say, this situation is always a nightmare for press agents, political parties, or religions, the three most popular segments of society that seem to provide the most fodder for bi-sexual revelations.

The list of more famous bisexuals, and those whose penchants for such diversity is known or suspected, has been compiled over the years and represents quite a cross section of society. Here are some of them:

Christina Aguilera – musician
Hans Christian Andersen – writer
Elizabeth Arden – cosmetic queen
Joan Baez – singer
Josephine Baker – cabaret singer
Tallulah Bankhead – actress
Drew Barrymore – actress
Alan Bates – actor
Sarah Bernhardt – actress
Leonard Bernstein – composer, conductor
Marlon Brando – actor
Louise Brooks – actress
Lord Byron – poet
Calamity Jane – scout
Caligula – Roman emperor
Nell Carter – actress and singer
Giacomo Casanova – traveler and writer
Jack Cassady – actor
John Cheever – writer
Patricia Cornwell – writer
Joan Crawford – actress
James Dean – actor
Emily Dickinson – poet
Marlene Dietrich – actress and singer
Daphne du Maurier – writer
Isadora Duncan – dancer
Greta Garbo – actress
Judy Garland – singer, actress
Farley Granger – actor
Cary Grant – actor
Alec Guiness – actor
Ted Haggard – televangelist preacher
Katharine Hepburn – actress
Billie Holiday – singer
Xaviera Hollander – writer

Judy Holliday – actress
Rock Hudson – actor
Jenna Jameson – porn star
Angelina Jolie – actress
Janis Joplin – singer
Danny Kaye – actor
John F. Kennedy, Jr. – lawyer, journalist
Jack Kerouac – writer
Billie Jean King – tennis pro
Alfred Kinsey – biologist, scientist
D. H. Lawrence – writer
Gertrude Lawrence – actress and singer
Beatrice Lillie – actress
Lindsay Lohan – actress, singer
Madonna – singer
Robert Mapplethorpe – artist, photographer
Carmen McRae – singer
Carson McCullers – writer
Margaret Mead – anthropologist and writer
Herman Melville – writer
Edna St. Vincent Millay – poet, playwright
Vincente Minnelli – film director
Marilyn Monroe – actress
Kathy Nijimy – comedienne, actress
Martina Navratilova – tennis pro
Laurence Olivier – actor
John Gielgud – actor
Anthony Perkins – actor
Edith Piaf – singer
Cole Porter – composer, songwriter
Ma Rainey – blues singer
Michael Redgrave – actor
Tony Richardson – film director
Jerome Robbins – choreographer
Eleanor Roosevelt – former first lady

George Sand – writer
Anna Nicole Smith – model
Bessie Smith – singer
Liz Smith – gossip columnist
Susan Sontag – writer
Dusty Springfield – singer
Sharon Stone – actress
Jacqueline Susann – writer
Alice Walker – writer
Ethel Waters – singer
Vanna White – television personality
Emlyn Williams – actor
Virginia Woolf – writer
Babe Zaharias - athlete

GHOSTBUSTER ALERT!

You, too, can be a ghostbuster! Look around you – there are many indications and signals that you have probably ignored, but are real apparitions or evidence that your abode could be housing spirits of past occupants that steadfastly refuse to leave (after all, it was theirs before *you* arrived!)

There are certain things people have to know about ghosts before they can actively seek them out, let alone drive them out. Here are some vital signals:

- Verify if anyone died in your domicile. If so, determine sex and age of dead person and date of death. You will need to know the cause of death and which room was the death chamber. Take extra caution of s/he was a child (under ten years of age.) If more than one person died, you will probably need professional help to convince the ghost(s) to re-locate elsewhere. The real estate person who handled your transaction is a good place to start. Don't be surprised if that person expresses shock right away and denies such a possibility, especially if the denial is immediate, after all, some research should be ethically mandatory after such a request.

- Most indications of ghost inhabitance of a household, warehouse, or church come from reports that such occurrences only happen after dark. Nobody has yet come up with any rationale for this time of day, other than it makes physical appearances more difficult to perceive against a variety of backdrops. There are records of some ghosts whose power to infuse themselves into a household result in taking a visible form akin to what they looked like in real life. Keep in mind, ghosts generally eschew disguising themselves as total unknowns in the habitat they choose to lurk or haunt.

- Traditionally, evidence of the existence of spirits in a home derive from areas least visited by the occupants of it. For example, attics, basements, pantries, fruit cellars, walk-in closets, roofs, fallout shelters, sheds, and toilets. (There is something curiously bedeviling about bathrooms that ghosts find uninviting. Perhaps an aversion to foul smells or aromatic toilet papers might influence their choice.) For some odd reason, reports of ghosts appearing in kitchens are few, with ghostbusting professionals bewildered for apparitions avoiding this area of a household.

Do-it-yourself ghostbusting, or going about it alone, is not recommended by The American Ghost Society. This organization was formed way back in 1996 by researcher Troy Taylor. Dedicated to seeking out allegedly haunted locations and assisting those who are experiencing problems with the paranormal, group members look for authentic evidence of the paranormal and try to determine if the location is haunted.

Mr. Taylor, the author of several books on the paranormal, avers working with psychics or conducting investigations using metaphysical methods. He also doesn't claim to be an expert on the supernatural since none exist, regardless of others who maintain such a talent. He does present, however, a close-knit tangible organization and network of followers dedicated to exchanging stories and tales of their adventures dealing with the paranormal (near-death experiences accepted.)

Troy Taylor's books and letters from readers, who confessed to haunting of their own, morphed in to an industry which he named the *American Ghost Society,* a membership organization structured by eight different levels, contingent on just how serious the applicant(s) is in active participation in advancing the aims and tenets of his business. These memberships to wit are:

1. ACTIVE MEMBERSHIP, Price $45 annually. Members must follow the standards of investigation set forth for the group and are encouraged to become Area Representatives for the AGS in their region. If they remain active in their region, they will be invited to renew their membership at the end of the year. Membership includes: New member packet with new member booklet and investigation forms; Member ID Card (with expiration date); Access to all meetings and seminars; One-Year subscription to Weekly Newsletter; Ghost report; regular email updates; Access to the AGS Members Only Mailing List; Special book discounts for members only and a copy of the *AGS Manual, The Ghost Hunter's Guidebook!* All for $45.00 a year.

2. COUPLES MEMBERSHIP PRICE: $55.00 for married (or otherwise), living at the same address. Benefits: same as above.

3. INVESTIGATOR MEMBERSHIP: $60.00. An additional membership in the group for Active Investigators and those actively researching the paranormal. Benefits: same as above.

4. *DELUXE* INVESTIGATOR MEMBERSHIP: $85.00 these members receive all of our Ghost Research Titles. Benefits: same as above.

5. RESEARCHER MEMBERSHIP: $110. Members receive FREE admission to the AGS National Conference. Benefits: same as above.

6. *DELUXE* RESEARCHER MEMBERSHIP: $150.00 Members receive FREE admission to the AGS National Conference and ALL OF OUR GHOST RESEARCH TITLES, plus special book discounts only for members. Other benefits: same as above.

7. GROUP AFFILIATE MEMBERSHIPS (Five or more) $30.00 per person. Any local ghost research group can now become members and an affiliate of the American Ghost Society. Benefits: same as above.

Avid ghost hunters are advised to hurry to take advantage of these annual membership fees before they increase without notice. For further information, check our website.

MY WALTER MITTY MARRIAGES

Trying to alibi my way through life admitting that I had not succumbed to the temptation of tying the nuptial knot *(and having to thus confess that while I was under the influence of the most violent, the delusive, and the most transient of passions that I'd agree to live in that highly excitable state until death did me and my girlfriend part)*, had an air of inadequacy about it trying to explain away why I was exempt from the hormonal urges of everybody else including the deafness that comes from negative advice from friends.

The embarrassment I suffered from not being able to discuss my previous marriages and how I finally came to my senses (after the 4th one) kept me from membership in the inner circle of people at my club, gatherings, and peers at the workplace. The situation worsened when presidential and congressional candidates and their ex-wives seem to dominate the news at the water cooler, and I was bereft of participating to the point that I was steamrollered in conversations, and, *de facto*, sustained benign neglect. The 4th wife seemed to make a course correction where I finally got the recognition I deserved. But it wasn't an easy path to achieve. 4th wife stories posed a problem to recount because of the hazard that, perhaps, I might be perceived as the one responsible for all my breakups. God forbid that my bad choices for past nuptials would reflect on my wisdom being blamed for such misfortunes. I didn't want to come across as a garden-variety dummy.

I decided that my first wife would have a typical profile of most first wives: the kind chosen by politicians other

Victor Kelley

acquaintances, a high school sweetheart that roiled my hormones to the extent that I felt I couldn't live without her. Somehow, I didn't seem to care that she was also being courted by most of the football team (more about that later.) At parties, Sally and I were standouts; she with her enormous breasts, and me as her gracious consort with a barely-controllable overt grin.

So the story went, two months after she graduated we got hitched and settled down in a third-floor rental apartment. I had secured a job bagging groceries at the local Kroger store, and realized I'd have to quickly upgrade my income to satisfy the non-stop department store invoices that began to appear regularly in our mailbox.

The first sign of difficulty in our marriage came when I suggested that my bride might want to get a job to neutralize the bills brought daily by our mailman. Not having a résumé, Sally ended up waiting tables at an all-night truck stop diner. At first I didn't complain, but when it interrupted our bedtime, I had second thoughts. Visiting her one evening on the job was a real awakening when I saw a booth with four guys ogling her. They were all too familiar – the same football players that had dated her when we were in school together. Trusting soul that I was, it took several months before it dawned on me, especially after a couple of impromptu visits to the diner, that the same guys had always been there when I popped in to see how Sally was adopting to her waitress job.

On one of the days she had to work overtime, I stopped to give her a key to a new door lock the landlord had installed "for security purposes", he said. Sally wasn't there. "She left with one of her cousins," her boss told me. "Something about an emergency at home," he added.

When I called her mother, she didn't know anything about any emergency. Sally was exhausted when she got home just as I was going out the door to my supermarket job.

Nothing was said about any emergency at the truck stop until I mentioned it a day later. She blew it off as "no big deal," her mother's cat had gone into convulsions and she took it to a vet to get it checked out.

When Sally's paychecks never reflected overtime work, and her bedtime enthusiasm for me seemed to wane, our marriage drifted into boredom. The girls in her carpool going and coming from the diner changed to all guys whom I recognized as the same football players that hung around the restaurant.

Well, two and two made four, and Sally and I split within a year. We're still friends, but no longer lovers. There was no estate to divide in our divorce. Our checking account was down to 37¢.

The imaginary breakup coincided with my draft notice. Boot camp left little time to dwell on the ashes of my first marriage. Nothing stirred in my sex life until I was transferred to Texas.

I met Lu at an NCO Club in San Antonio when I was stationed at Fort Sam Houston. She was a hostess with a heart-shaped mass that attracted every wandering eye of servicemen dropping in after work hours. I didn't really pick up on just how my attraction to her mimicked my romance with Sally. But it did. I liked being the envy of guys in my unit when Lu spent an inordinate amount of time with me. She had a tiny apartment off base with a circular bed that teased the imagination on picking a sleep position after sexual forays that I never dreamed existed before. It took a stretch in the Army and Lu's circular bed to awaken my dormant sex life – for which I am eternally thankful.

When I suggested nuptials, Lu was hesitant, but a sense of propriety supported by military benefits of housing triple the size of her apartment, made her come around. It was a real shock, though, to discover on our marriage license that her real name was *Ludmilla.* I had thought Lu was short for Louise, Mary Lou, or even Louella. It had never come up before in our relationship. To me, *Ludmilla* was an 18th century old maid's name, something out of a Charles Dickens novel, somebody who came from West Virginia coal-mining towns. I never introduced her to anybody as anything other than "Lu." There was an embarrassment factor built into her Christian (?) name. When we divorced after my stint in the military, an enormous weight was lifted from my psyche from the guilt I felt by never mentioning her real name to anyone during our four years of sharing the circular sex bed.

Oh! And I should mention I wasn't the only Corporal on the base that shared that roundhouse mattress. It seems that I was cuckolded by some of my buddies who just happened to play on our intramural touch-football team. History strikes again. It had repeated itself before my very naïve eyes – again.

On the day I mustered out of the Army, I met Blanche, my third phantom wife, at the San Antonio train station that was transporting me back to Pittsburgh. We had exchanged lingering glances waiting in line for tickets. I was pleasantly surprised when she boarded the same train I got on, and delighted when, of all things, she sat down next to me. The trip was longer than I thought, but her habit of leaning her head on my shoulder when tired (or napping) was an unexpected reward for the next two days aboard our car that clicked along the rails in a rhythmically sonic pattern that made it pleasurable (along with Blanche's head now perched closer to my cheek during her frequent naps.)

By the time we got to Pittsburgh, she seemed like an old friend from a high-school reunion – comfortable and cheery, even telling jokes that brought belly laughs from both of us. It cemented our friendship even more so when we learned that staying with relatives in the city (me with my brother; she with her aunt) was less than a couple of miles apart.

Blanch had been married before, no kids, to a guy twice her age. She confessed that it was her only way to escape a dysfunctional home with both parents whose only mutual attraction was sharing weekends with *Jack Daniels* followed by noisy bedroom cavorting. She was the oldest of nine kids that had come at ten-month intervals.

The guy she married turned out to have a thing for teenage girls, and she was just the latest in his history of child wives.

I decided to dream up a fourth wife after feeling some discomfort explaining away my first three. Nobody seemed to have any sympathy for any of them, let alone me, in discussions when I tried to keep pace with other guys stories that trumped me every time ex-wives dominated our barroom tales.

This time, her name would be Hermione, an English gal, whose nickname was "Herman", a clever moniker that allowed me to ultimately reveal that Hermione was transgendered, thought to be a male when born, was actually named "Herman", but chose the female counterpart name once s/he decided which gender she preferred in her adult life. I must say, this wife brought me more attention among my peers than any of the others. I began to hear comments like "bizarre", "wow", and have other guys tell their buddies about my wives.

I loved the attention, finally, having arrived at a point in my life that made me feel fulfilled, and with a history that now had other people talking about me as often as they did about themselves. A side effect that I hadn't counted on was the barrage of questions I got from people I didn't even know. They had heard about *Herman* from friends and plied me to expand on details that included our sex life. The stories I had to make up not knowing doodly squat about trans-gendered anything amazed even me, a real test of my imagination in the Walter Mitty world that I had used for social acceptance to explain away my covert life as a hermit.

As I got older, however, I began to feel a pride that I survived four wives, and began to feel at home, sympathizing with ambitious politicians whose marriage failures took their toll the same as mine did.

HAND-ME-DOWN RELIGIONS AND POLITICS

Throughout the ages, children of parents are heavily influenced by everything that surrounds the daily life of their families and those adults in close supervision of them. These include the clothes they wear, the foods that they consume, the schools they attend, the customs of the society in which they live, their manners, and, early on, the religions or beliefs that are practiced by the mothers and fathers of their offspring.

Just how devout the parents are to a particular religion or sect will be transferred to their progeny to be *unquestioned* during a child's formative years. The assumption that prevails in the family is that children would never be exposed to the why and wherefore people choose one variety of religion over another. In effect, what is happening is a hand-me-down event that the parents went through when they were growing up, to be repeated *ad infinitum* in future generations.

If there is a void in education of children in their teens or a curriculum that doesn't even suggest explaining why people make the choices that they do, the child will advance into adulthood ignorant of thought processes that advance mankind's status in a civilized society.

The one single "untouchable" that parents have practiced over the centuries is explaining to their children why and how they decided to belong (or not to belong) to a particular religion or sect. The reason they don't is because they, too, never thought to wonder or investigate their faith or whatever creed was inherited from *their* mothers or fathers. It seemed that to doubt what they had been taught from youth was tantamount to sacrilege, a serious infraction of the faith, and "sinful" in its very concept. The very act of *doubting* was itself wrongful. The very fact that a particular creed had been passed down from generation to generation gave it an authenticity, if not a tyranny, that it was exempt from any intellectual scrutiny by younger generations.

The only break in this chain of events happens when maverick's surface in a generation who are dissatisfied with the status quo of the hand-me-down religion force-fed them by their parents or guardians while advancing into maturity. What is even more confounding is the extreme lengths that some sects will go to control designer religions that sprout and splinter from yet other creeds.

That there are more than 35,000 religions in the world is testimony to the evolution under which faiths have gone over the past millennia. Four of the more predominant theological doctrines have been the major derivatives of such a varied landscape of them.

TRUTH AND CONSEQUENCES

Never in the history of the United States was truth in this country so disguised as lies as in President George W. Bush's administration 2003 preemptive war on Iraq, bolstered by a personally chosen inner circle of advisors, most on a Cabinet level, and some of whom will live in historical infamy as wholesale betrayers of the truth to the American people.

This is not to say, though, that the country was not forewarned when the 43rd president told the American public that he was "the Decider." It was to alert everybody that the old canard, *Forewarned Is Forearmed,* would be resurrected and alive again for the balance of his term – and then some.

Sharing the blame for support of this war was an obsequious incurious press media cowed into reporting what this Republican president spoon-fed them daily with unproven allegations to rationalize his invasion of this middle-eastern country. To do otherwise, the threat of being "unpatriotic" was being held over the press's head by presidential aides akin to a Sword of Damocles. Only a pity few members of Congress with safe constituencies dared to challenge Mr. Bush head-on. They would prove to be right as the war sank into a quagmire that had no future plans other than toppling Iraq's dictator, Saddam Hussein.

YOU DON'T EVEN WANT TO KNOW ABOUT THIS!

In the last half century that virologists have studied the connection between viruses and genetics, a stunning revelation has surfaced that deadly viruses have been around for millions of years, wiping out forms of life wholesale before consuming themselves into near-extinction and then mutating into states of impotent fragmentation. The same age-old viruses have re-appeared from time to time as evolution has produced mutations of living forms whose genes become vulnerable to another round of susceptibility to these killer afflictions.

Scientists know that the quicker a virus spreads, the weaker it becomes because of changes that naturally appear when reproducing so rapidly. Certain dissipation is always innate in an accelerated virus and some forms of life begin to develop immune systems able to overcome the weakened variety attacking them.

The classic example given of mutant change is the five-million year old variance between the appearance of humans and chimpanzees that share 98% of the same genetic makeup and have the closest origins on the same ancestral evolutionary tree.

In essence what the bio-scientists have discovered just happens to be a strengthened link to the credibility of Darwin's theory of evolution, and a setback for advocates of biblical creationism. The very evolution of deadly viruses and their effect on victims ultimately changed the defenses and appearances of those infected, and in doing so made the newer forms of life again vulnerable to other ancient viruses seeking hosts to replicate their deadly missions.

Ultimately, viruses that wiped out a generation or species of life ended up self-destructing themselves, leaving a residue of fractured remains in the affected, millions of which still exist today. They lie dormant until, by chance, connect with other similar fragmented diseases that activate their deadly sortie into the genes of victims unable to fend off these newer forms of foreign invaders.

The influenza virus that wiped out 50 million people worldwide toward the end of World War I is a classic example of a virus revisited. It was a repeat of the same "Black Death" that took the lives of 25 million men, women, and children around the globe from 1348 to 1350 AD, again in the 6th century, and centuries before that.

Genetic biologists in the early 21st century discovered these "fractured" bits of virus that still occupy living forms in humans and laboratory animals. Although benign in that status, they are still able to be transferred to others when their hosts reproduce, and pose a potential for an outbreak of re-generated activity in the future should they link up with other separate fractures lingering in a body's genetic makeup.

In a sense, every virus has the potential to rise from its ashes (like a Phoenix) and wreak its deadly mission on living forms whose immunity is unable to overcome a genetic invasion. Small pox and influenza are typical of the more virulent strains of diseases that have been controlled by vaccines. HIV that appeared on the planet in the 1970's, has yet to respond to anti-virus drugs because of its constant mutating even though partially responding to a series of cocktail medications that also have to be changed from time to time to meet the complex mutation rate of the disease. The frightening aspect of HIV is the possibility that a single vaccine may *never* be discovered despite a wholesale effort of pharmaceutical labs around the world dedicated to find a cure or a drug to permanently neutralize it.

As if the HIV threat that hangs over human life like a Sword of Damocles doesn't frustrate epidemiologists, an emerging avian virus, heretofore unknown, appeared in the early 21st century first appearing in disparate fowl from swans to chickens, pigeons, ducks, and birds raised for human consumption, and finally to humans themselves worldwide. Isolating this particular bird-virus was easy enough, but drugs or vaccines that counter its deadly effects have proven elusive as of the published date of this book.

Adnovirus 14 first appeared in the Western Hemisphere in 2006. It is just one of 51 known strains of adnoviruses, ubiquitous germs causing many illnesses including colds, pinkeye, bronchitis, stomach flu and respiratory infections (often called "bootcamp flu" because it plagued soldiers for decades.) Having first appeared in Holland in 1955, it spread to outbreaks in Asia and China before receding into an imperceptible microbe within the bodies of those infected.

When Adnovirus 14 surfaced again in 2006, a genetic analysis of it by the Center of Disease Control in Atlanta revealed that a mutated version of it had made it more virulent, suddenly causing pneumonia deaths almost overnight in people regardless of age or physical condition. Few were immune to this strain of the microbe. Outbreaks in Texas, San Diego, and areas around Chicago and Georgia also seem to emanate from cities with military installations nearby. From these, it then spread aggressively across the United States.

Since the discovery of ancient fractured viruses was identified independently by four laboratories in four different countries, and the realization that they existed millions of years ago (millennia before the age of dinosaurs), the very possibility that one virulent strain may suddenly emerge in the future that could wipe out civilizations (akin to the Mayan cultures of the past) before modern medicine could react, is a mind-numbing reality unthinkable to ponder.

CHOICES

Just when you think you know everything there is to know about yourself, another person, a lover perhaps, a sibling, a neighbor, a parent, a bartender, your dog, your mechanic, lawyer, doctor, insurance man, and accountant, you discover that you really know next to nothing about them.

Some examples:

The brand of toilet paper preferred by your father.

Your mother's first lover.

The make and model of the car owned by your mechanic.

When your dog is the most hungry?

Your girlfriend's best date?

The date your grandmother (either one) was born.

What brand of tires is on your brother's car?

The age of your parents (separately) on their first date.

Your first neighbor's names.

The name of the kid who sat three desks behind you in any grade of elementary school.

What was the first seafood dish you really liked?

What was the first food you refused to eat?

Your first theft.

The biggest lie you ever told.

The first person you ever hated.

Your worst regret.

The most unethical thing you did in your life.

The first thing taught in Law School court procedure preparation for a lawyer is never to ask a witness a question without knowing what answer will be forthcoming.

Too many lawyers believe that their instinct is such that this *caveat* can be bypassed, simply because they are seasoned attorneys and longtime veterans in courtroom savvy. Recently, in Mississippi, one such Southern prosecutor, questioning a grandmother on the stand, ventured to ask her a simple question to ease any tension she might have experienced having to testify before a courtroom full of people, let alone a jury and a judge listening attentively to the case in progress.

The prosecuting lawyer approached the elderly witness, smiled, and asked her, "Mrs. Jones, do you know me?"

"Why, yes I do know you, Mr. Williams," she responded. "I've known you since you were a boy, and frankly, you've been a big disappointment to me. You lie, you cheat on your wife, and you manipulate people and talk about them behind their backs. You think you're a big shot when you haven't the brains to realize you'll never amount to anything more than a two-bit paper pusher. Yes, I know you."

The lawyer was stunned, and momentarily speechless. Not knowing what else to do, he pointed across the room and asked, "Mrs. Jones, do you know the defense attorney?"

She again replied, "Why, yes I do. I've known Mr. Bradley since he was a youngster, too. He's lazy, bigoted, and has a drinking problem. He can't build a normal relationship with anyone, and his law practice is one of the worst in the entire state. Not to mention he cheated on his wife with three different women. One was your wife. Yes, I know him."

The defense attorney nearly died.

The judge immediately asked both attorneys to approach the bench, and, in a very quiet voice, said, "If either of you idiots asks her if she knows me, I'll send you both to the electric chair."

MORBIDITY REPORT

Few Americans can list the eleven wars that were fought since the Revolutionary War of 1776. The official number of American lives lost in these wars by government accounting reveals statistics that might amaze those interested in the historical value of such records. In particular, few realize that *the Civil War claimed more American lives than those in World War II.*

Here is a summary of the mortality of American human lives in those eleven wars:

1. American Revolution – 6,188 killed
2. War of 1812 – 4,505 killed
3. Mexican War – 4,152 killed
4. American Civil War – 498,332 killed (North and South)
5. Spanish-American War – 2,455 killed
6. World War I – 116,516 killed
7. World War II – 405,399 killed
8. Korean War – 54,246 killed
9. Vietnam War – 58,167 killed, and 2,000+ missing in action
10. Persian Gulf War – 293 killed, and 19 missing in action
11. War in Iraq – 4,042 killed (as of April 2008)

Total deaths to date, as of October, 2007:
    1,154,043 (and counting)

American lives lost to terrorist attacks:
    September 11, 2001, attack – 2,983 killed
    Bombing of U.S.S. Cole – 17 killed

On June 3, 1942, a contingent of the Imperial Japanese military invaded Alaska, a U.S. territory at the time, occupying two of the most western Aleutian chain of atolls extending some 1,300 miles from the Alaska mainland, Attu and Kiska Island, imprisoning the few Aleut natives that inhabited them. The shock of the Japanese presence on American soil (only the second occurrence since the War of 1812) was never made public until 1944, becoming a top secret for the Roosevelt administration lest Americans perceive that this country had been occupied, let alone actually under siege by a foreign power, and create a psychological doubt about the outcome of the war that had begun seven months earlier at another U.S. territory, Pearl Harbor in Hawaii.

A year passed before any U.S. retaliatory effort was made to regain control of the islands. The Japanese army was under the command of the fabled Admiral Isoroku Yamamoto whose reluctance to accept the assignment he voiced in his prophetic quote, "I fear we have awakened a sleeping giant." Threatened with veiled hints of assassination at home, Yamamoto added, "If you insist on my going ahead," he told the Prime Minister, "I can promise to give them hell for a year or a year and a half, but guarantee nothing after that."

Admiral Yamamoto was very familiar with the United States, having traveled extensively throughout the country prior to the war. His mission in the Aleutians was to divert the U.S. Pacific Fleet from the central Pacific Theater and to largely gain a psychological foothold on American soil. These he did with a minimum commitment of 5,300 men and materials.

Both Kiska and Attu islands were formed from volcanoes, mountainous and snow-covered, with valleys and plains of tundra grass atop volcanic ash that turned to sludge during the warm weather rainy months.

Mechanical ground equipment got bogged down with a frequency and frustration that often brought troop advancement and supply lines to a standstill.

American and Canadian troops began their assault on Attu on May 11, 1943, after heavy naval shelling and aerial bombing of the entrenched enemy that had fortified themselves in the high ground of the mountains akin to what the Japanese soldiers did on Iwa Jima and Tarara islands later in the war. Allied troops had to literally climb snow-covered ridges from below to rid the enemy snipers whose aim was more deadly than Allied generals had figured in their timetable to regain control of the island. Hampering the soldiers attacking from below was a shortage of equipment unable to come ashore because of the terrain and rough weather that alternated cloudy, rainy, and foggy with winds of hurricane force that appeared out of nowhere. In a matter of minutes, all of the above meteorological conditions could appear out of nowhere. In short, the soldiers were not geared for cold weather wet battle, causing many cases of frostbite, slippage down the mountainside from flat-soled leather boots instead of rubber ones, and missing cold-weather gloves to handle their weapons.

To give the reader an idea of how ill-prepared the battle plan ordered by the Allied generals was, a single day that was predicted by them to capture Attu took nineteen days to accomplish, despite 144,000 Allied soldiers pressed into action. When the Japanese commander on Attu realized that all was lost, he gathered all his remaining soldiers, some five hundred men, and told them they had to fight to their death. There would be no surrender. Hundreds of the enemy bunched together on the barren tundra plains, strapped hand grenades to their chests and exploded them after realizing imminent defeat, blowing holes in their abdomens and beheading most of them. Military photographers revealed massive piles of Japanese bodies strewn haphazardly next to each other on the forbidding landscape. Thirty Japanese soldiers elected to dishonor themselves by refusing the kamikaze order.

U.S. forces on Attu alone suffered 3,929 casualties: 549 killed 1,148 injured, 1,200 had severe cold injuries, 614 died of disease, and 318 of miscellaneous causes (largely from booby traps and friendly fire due to heavy fog.)

Massive trench burials for both Allied and Japanese dead followed the nineteen-day battle that ended the skirmish. It had started on May 11, and ended May 29, 1943. The "Secret War" was not declassified until October 14, 1944.

OFF THE WALL

Few websites get as much traffic as CRAIGSLIST.ORG/. It provides a myriad of sources for people advertising jobs, people looking for jobs, people looking for other people who are compatible (or otherwise) to their sexual needs, people providing services, and people looking to scam as many as they can before being ousted by complaints to the Internet's website owner. It lists a diversity of entries including Community, Housing, Personals, Jobs, For Sale, Services, Discussion Forums, Gigs, and even Resumes.

Craigslist also provides entertaining reading because censorship of naughty words is limited – people can say whatever they want to without being arrested (up to a certain point without advocating the overthrow of the government.)

The area of the website that gets the most hits can be found in *Personals:* lovers looking for lovers, often describing in fascinating detail, and without mincing words, specific traits and qualities they demand to satisfy their urges and passionate longings.

One listing in October, 2007, comes to mind that expresses an example of the above features that involved a 25-year-old female gold-digger in New York City asking to meet a man making over $500,000, complaining that men making just $250,000 "just don't cut it."

"Okay, I'm tired of beating around the bush. I'm a beautiful (spectacularly beautiful) 25 year old gal. I'm articulate and classy. I'm not from New York. I'm looking to get married to a guy who makes at least a half a million a year. I know how that sounds, but keep in mind that a million a year is middle class in New York City, so I don't think I'm overreaching at all. Are there any guys who make 500K or more on this board? Any wives? Could you send me some tips? I dated a business man who makes an average around 200-250. But that's where I seem to hit a roadblock. 250K won't get me to Central Park West. I know a woman in my yoga class who was married to an investment banker and lives in Tribeca, and she's not as pretty as I am, nor is she a great genius. So what is she doing right? How do I get to her level?"

One man responded, admitting he worked on Wall Street and made over 500K. Then he put her in her place, suggesting, "In economic terms, you are a depreciating asset, and I am an earning asset."

The word *testimony* has a very interesting ancient etymology. It refers to statements given by man as the truth in a court of law *while clutching the testes of a wild animal.*

Some advertising agencies are loaded with creative people who take pride in the ideas that emerge from brainstorming sessions that can give birth to campaigns that delight the mind or neutralize the competition.

A small Canadian agency in Vancouver, British Columbia, hatched a wonderfully devious plan to offset a long ballyhooed promotion by local major businesses to siphon Black Friday (the day after Thanksgiving) buyers prematurely into their stores the day after Thanksgiving. A group from its creative department took umbrage at the barrage of print and television commercials who were annoyed at some department stores opening their doors ranging from midnight to the early hours of Black Friday. Dominant merchants in the area joined in the hoopla by advertising "Christmas specials" at highly discounted prices, hoping that crowds would show up in long lines at their front doors, panicked to be first to purchase these very desirable "limited quantity" holiday gift items. The impending crowds expected at these stores had made the nightly news as well as the local papers.

The maverick minds from the agency decided that they would join the pack of early birds waiting in burgeoning lines at major stores that opened the earliest on that Black Friday. Once in the buildings, a gaggle of agency people would spread out, then don a special tee shirt that contained a bold message on both the front and the back of the garment. It read:

"Everything 50% off in this store."

The agency people would then saunter around the aisles of the targeted merchants, circulating throughout the floors of the buildings, and seek out locations where most shoppers seem to gather. Pretending to be buyers themselves, they took pleasure when pockets of consternation appeared at sales counters where clerks were confounded by clutches of people arguing with them (presumably about pricing) to the annoyance and despair of the emporium's staff.

The half-dozen of the largest department stores that were chosen for demonstrations by the "Tee Shirt brigade" during the opening hours of the Black Friday sale were slow in responding to this mysterious advertising virus, not quite certain that they had been invaded or what exactly was happening to their sales.

It turned out the "impact" made national news, and the advertising agency received a modicum of fame, albeit not necessarily the positive kind wished for by businesses attempting to attract customers. To be sure, the advertising agency did not list any businesses of the venue for which they pulled the stunt.

It did, however, give testimony to creative minds at work at one of Vancouver's more imaginative advertising media. Perhaps an enlightened department store executive might have perceived that such an agency could also be utilized to elegantly produce ads that could substantially increase its revenues.

Among the many aphorisms attributed to Benjamin Franklin, one particular observation seems to be more apropos and significant than his many others.

"In wine there is wisdom, in beer there is freedom, in water there is bacteria."

Leave it to scientists to check out his claim in an attempt to diminish this great man's primordial penchant to offer advice to mankind anywhere in the world.

In a number of carefully-controlled trials, the scientific community offered a statistic using a person who drank one liter of water every day for a year. At the end of that year, this person would have consumed (and absorbed) more than one kilo of *Escherichia coli* (E-coli), the bacteria typically found in water and feces. In other words, in an unkind manner, this person had consumed one kilo of poop.

Now compare that with avoiding that risk when drinking wine, beer, or any assorted hard liquor (rum, tequila, whiskey, etc.) because alcohol has to go through a purification process of boiling, filtering, and/or fermentation.

The conclusion drawn from this rationale leads one to realize that water = poop, wine = health.

Hence, it is better to drink wine and talk stupid, than to drink water and be full of shit.

Got that?

Just when we think our country might be making diplomatic headway with other nations, comes news of certain laws and customs that reveal erratic quirks in ethical judgment and behavior that render every appearance that they are nuts. For example:

- In Lebanon, men are legally allowed to have sex with animals – as long as they are female. Sex with male animals is a capital crime. *[Like that makes sense?]*

- In Bahrain, a male doctor may legally examine a woman's genitals, but is forbidden to look directly at them during the examination. He may only observe them from a reflection in a mirror. *[Do they look different reversed?]*

- Muslims are forbidden to look at the genitals of a corpse. The same goes for undertakers. The sex organs of the deceased must be covered at all times, either by wood or (get this) a brick. *[Figure that one out.]*

- In Indonesia, the penalty for masturbation is decapitation. *[It's safe to say this is much worse than "going blind."]*

- Guam has a law that expressly forbids virgins to marry. To solve this dilemma, the government hires men to travel the countryside to deflower those virgins anticipating marriage, an act for which the women must pay the *deflowerer. [Is this the best job in the world, or what?]*

- In Hong Kong, betrayed wives are legally allowed to kill their adulterous spouses – as long as they do it with their hands. A husband's illicit lover, however, can be dispatched in any manner desired. *[Ah! A two-fer, if the wife catches them in the throes of orgasm and strangles her husband first.]*

- Saleswomen in Liverpool, England, are allowed to go topless, but only if they work in tropical fish stores. *[Figure that one out!]*

- In Cali, Columbia, the first time a female has sex with her husband requires that his mother-in-law be present in the room to witness the act. *[And probably offer advice to both participants.]*

- The government of Santa Cruz, Bolivia, made it a crime for a man to have sex with a woman and her daughter at the same time. *[Apparently this must have been a big problem for the city fathers to enact, probably prompted by eliminating the future possibility that mother and daughter might be giving birth on the same day down the line fertilized by whomever inseminated them.]*

- In Maryland, condoms can only be sold in vending machines in establishments where alcoholic beverages are consumed on the premises. *[Is this a great country, or what? Well, not really as good as Guam.]*

- Science has unearthed the fact that humans and dolphins are the only species that have sex for pleasure. *[Now we know why Flipper is always smiling.]*

- Scientific research (government?) of ants reveals that they can lift 50 times their own weight, and always fall over on their right side when intoxicated. *[This research did not include evidence of hangovers – at least not yet.]*

- A potpourri of studies included the discoveries that turtles can breathe through their anuses, butterflies taste with the feet, a ostrich's eye is bigger than its brain *[we all know people like that],* and starfish don't have brains *[and we all know some people like that, too.]*

A BETTER MOUSETRAP – SORT OF

It's safe to say that rats and roaches will never find their ilk on the list of "endangered species" – anywhere in the world. Well, maybe rats will, that is, in certain parts of the globe. Like India, for example. Inventing a better mousetrap always improved society; inventing a better rat-trap brought a segment of India's poor rural population an unexpected bonanza

With a population of 1,100,000,000, that country has a reputation as a habitat for the poorest of the poor people living in a quasi-civilized society, so to speak. In this land where some 3,000 castes (social levels) exist, being born means having to live one's entire life in a stratum ranging from the financially elite to the financially desperate where rats are the commodity that furnishes the daily income as well as cuisine for one of this lowest of castes – the *"untouchables."*

In India, the *"untouchable"* designation is awarded the lowest residue of society that are condemned by birth to perform menial work just to survive. Uneducated, illiterate, living in abject poverty with no hope of rising to a higher caste level, this segment of society has never drawn the attention of India's government's castes even though the country claims to be a democracy. Every so often, voices from the wilderness of do-gooders rises to the thankless task of changing the strata of Indian society but drown in the response and dereliction of a government that has consistently eschewed change especially pursuing unpopular causes of the rich.

In India's southern Tamil Nadu state, the Irula community is home to such low caste *untouchables* where rat-catchers are hired to eliminate the untold flood of these rodents from consuming up to 25% of the annual crop of millions of farmers.

But then, mirabile dictu, at the turn of the century, a simple invention appeared to rescue some *untouchables,* whose livelihood and sustenance revolved around catching and eating field rats, whose prolific reputation for multiplying their numbers at least assured the rat-catchers that they would never have to worry where their next meal or rupee would come from. For every rat that was captured, dead or alive, the farmers' largesse to these *untouchables* was 5¢ each. The average number of rats caught per man per day in the states inundated with field rats was 25¢, hardly enough to sustain a family, but locking them in to a life of despair and desperation.

Since India is a vastly rural country growing grains and textiles, rats were its worst enemy, feasting on a wealth of edibles at the doorstep of their nests.

Understanding the method of catching field rats that burrow underground havens had relied for centuries on finding their lairs that had multiple entrances, plugging all but one of them, and then physically blowing smoke by mouth through a bottom hole of a clay smudge pot into the rat nest. It was a time-consuming task. At that point, either the rats would emerge or die from inhaling the smoke and then having to be dug out of the burrows. Many of them even escaped by hearing the footstep approach of their enemy. The danger to the rat-catcher was a high incidence of inhaling smoke himself or being burned by the hot earthenware pot attempting to extricate his prey and the hours it took to physically blow enough smoke into the orifice of the nests to expect results. Rat-catchers life span typically lasted 45 years.

The device that changed rat-catching used a smoke-producing device that incorporated a hand-operated air pump that forces a greater volume of smoke into burrows more quickly that using the centuries-old time-honored clay-pot version. It was fast and also eliminated smoke inhalation and skin burns to the operator. Suddenly, catches of 5 rats a day for 25¢ grew to 20, resulting in average incomes rising to one dollar a day, a figure that gave rise to the field workers' expectations of sending *untouchable* children to school. It was an unimaginable event to society's poorest of the poor, equal to inventing a pump that could bring water up from the earth, eliminating the need to haul it from the closest river.

There was a catch, however, to affording the price of the new Rat-trap. The cost of the device was $25 (versus the 50¢ cost of a clay pot), an amount few of the laborers could afford, most of whom had to put their children to work alongside them in the field just to make ends meet. The vast number of small farmers in the region posed a wealth of customers to the Irula rat-catchers. They preferred rat-catching to poisons that could hurt soil productivity, let alone pose a risk to animals and humans.

What made a dramatic change in the fortunes of the *untouchables* was the creation of microcredit banks, instituted by a sympathetic luminary businessman within the wealthy Indian elite community. He began by loaning small amounts of money, $25 to $100, to the poor that created motivation for them to start their own small businesses. To his amazement, less than 5% ever defaulted on paying back the loans that included nominal interest. Many even paid off their loans in advance, something totally unexpected by the banker. Soon his microcredit banks began expanding across other parts of India, spreading to other countries, and ultimately worldwide where poverty had trapped ambitious but distressed people for centuries.

It was one of these microcredit banks that allowed the Irula community rat-catchers to borrow $25 to purchase the device that suddenly brought new hope and money to their families. It didn't change the multi-layered caste system in India, but it opened a window for the *untouchables* to improve their lives, some creating businesses that morphed in size large enough to attract Wall Street investors.

The wonder of such a simple low-cost device had twin benefits: elimination of a pestilence while substantially increasing the wherewithal of people relegated by birth to live the wretched life dictated by a social system that has the temerity to describe itself as *democratic.*

WELCOME TO KVORKA!

It is with great pride and perseverance that I welcome you all today en route to our mutual goal of salvation. If you're wondering why we are meeting in Heaven's Cave, let me assure you that it is a reminder that at life's end, we will *descend* into heaven rather than get swept away into the hell of a universe laced with tornado's, famine, disease, pestilence, and ending up, god knows where, in some kind of black hole.

Now, you are all aware about "black holes", aren't you? If you need a refresher in them, I have brought along three decades of *National Geographic* with me. Just don't take them home with you. Return them to the niche you find them, keeping them out of reach of any dripping stalactites or still pools obscured by ambient light.

It is a testimony to your diversity of skills, education, race and temperament that brought you here today, although I would have liked to have seen more females among the faithful.

For those who are new to Kvorka, I was selected to be its prime progenitor in gathering a chosen few to enjoy the blissful contentment of whatever years we have remaining on the subsurface of this planet until summoned by our higher Being to find the path leading to our ultimate nirvana in the unexplored depths below. [In case you're wondering what Kvorka means, it is Latvian for "The lure of Salvation", something that everyone lusts for whether he knows it or not.]

When I say depths, I don't mean that the cavity that we occupy now hasn't been checked out. I, personally have pedometer readings in excess of twenty-three miles of walking and swimming passages that form the network of our holding-pattern home en route to the eternal reward of achieving heaven. Some of the areas that I spent months mapping out down here have designated pathways. Some have ropes, well, actually it's fish line, 20-pound fish line, to guide you through what you might think is a confusing maze. You will find knots on the fish line as you feel your way along the many trails that branch out from the main corridor, so to speak. All you have to remember is, if you feel a single knot, veer left. If you feel a double knot, go right. As of now we have a limited number of candles, so I suggest you explore in groups until replenishments arrive.

Your rewards will be discovering alcoves and recesses of astounding beauty, and areas where you can meditate in silence for as long as you like. Just keep in mind not to stray too far from the fish line. Eventually we will complete total exploration of the maze of caverns without fear of becoming lost along the way. The whistle necklaces you were given on entering today are your lifeline in the event you wander beyond the known perimeters of our Kvorka heavenly home.

THE "FUNNIES"

Movie star and singer, Julie Andrews commemorated her 69th birthday at a special appearance at New York's *Radio City Music Hall* for the Benefit of the AARP.

She sang this ditty from the legendary "Sound of Music" film to the melody of "My Favorite Things." It brought down the house.

Maalox and nose drops and needles for knitting,

Walkers and handrails and new dental fittings,

Bundles of magazines tied up in string,

These are a few of my favorite things.

Cadillacs and cataracts, and hearing aids and glasses,

Polident and Fixodent and false teeth in glasses,

Pacemakers and golf carts and porches with swings,

These are a few of my favorite things.

When the pipes leak,

When the bones creak,

I simply remember my favorite things,

And then I don't feel so bad.

Hot tea and crumpets and corn pads for bunions,

No spicy hot food or food cooked with onions,

Bathrobes and heating pads and hot meals they bring,

These are a few of my favorite things.

Back pain, confused brains and no need for sinnin',

Thin bones and fractures and hair that is thinnin',

And we won't mention our short shrunken frames,

When the joints ache,

When the hips break,

When the eyes grow dim,

Then I remember the great life I've had,

And then I don't feel so bad.

One particular county in Texas is noted for its treating *Driving Under the Influence (DUI)* a local sport. According to a police blotter account, one of its highway police patrol cars was routinely parked outside a bar in Austin, Texas *(coincidentally)* at the time of *last call* to its patrons. The officer in the patrol car noticed a man leaving the bar so visibly inebriated that he could hardly walk.

The man stumbled around the parking lot for a few minutes while the officer quietly observed his behavior. After which seemed to be an eternity in which he tried his keys in five different vehicles, the guy managed to find his car and fall into it. He sat in it for a few minutes while a number of people exited the tavern and drove off.

Finally, the man in the stupor started his vehicle, switched the windshield wipers "on" and "off", even though it was a clear, dry night, then flicked his blinkers "on" and "off" a few times, honked his horn, and then switched on the car's lights.

Edging his auto forward a few inches, and then reversing it, he remained still in the driver's seat, as others departed the tavern and left the parking lot. When there were no more cars left outside the bar, the patrol officer watched while the stumble-bum started his vehicle, pull slowly out of the lot and proceed down the highway.

At this point, the police car lit up its flashers and promptly pulled the man over, and administered a breathalyzer test. To his amazement, it registered no evidence that the man had consumed alcohol at all. Dumbfounded by the results, the officer determined that the instrument was malfunctioning, and told the driver, "the breathalyzer must be broken", and to follow him to the police station.

"I doubt it," replied the redneck. "It was my turn tonight to be the designated decoy."

[Out of mercy for the victimized cop, his name was omitted from the story that reached a local beat reporter.]

When *Monty Python's Flying Circus* burst on English television screens on September 7, 1969, viewers weren't quite prepared to know what to make of the six zany college-educated characters in the program's plots of non-sequiturs that targeted the idiosyncrasies of British life. From Oxford came Terry Jones and Michael Palin. Cambridge grads added Eric Idle, John Cleese, and Graham Chapman. Terry Gilliam from Oxidental College was America's donation to the team of actors. A total of forty-five episodes ran for four seasons until 1974.

The most prominent of this gang of six was *John Cleese.* He stood out if only because of his tall gangly presence and ability to assume roles akin to a comic chameleon that brought rollicking laughter, especially when they were imported to America. As an avid observer of the inanity of how America developed since it shunned British oversight in 1776, John Cleese offered up his panacea for correcting such a disastrous decision. In a sixteen point plan to remedy the "Dumbing of America", the comedian listed these proposals:

"To the citizens of the United States of America: in light of your failure in recent years to nominate competent candidates for President of the USA and thus govern yourselves, we hereby give notice of the revocation of your independence, effective immediately.

Her Sovereign Majesty Queen Elizabeth II will resume monarchial duties over all states, commonwealths, and territories (except Kansas, which she does not fancy.)

Your new Prime Minister, Gordon Brown, will appoint a Governor for America without the need for further elections. Congress and the Senate will be disbanded. A questionnaire may be circulated next year to determine whether any of you noticed.

To aid in the transition to a British Crown Dependency, the following rules will be introduced with immediate effect. (You should look up "revocation" in the English Oxford Dictionary.)

1. Then look up aluminium, and check the pronunciation guide. You will be amazed at just how wrongly you have been pronouncing it.

2. The letter "U" will be reinstated in words such as 'colour', 'favour and neighbour.' Likewise you will learn to spell 'doughnut' without skipping half the letters, and the suffix '-ize' will be replaced by the suffix '-ise.' Generally you will be expected to raise your vocabulary to acceptable levels. (Look up 'vocabulary'.)

3. Using the same twenty-seven words interspersed with filler noises such as "like" and "you know" is an unacceptable and inefficient form of communication. There is no such thing as US English. We will let Microsoft know on your behalf. The Microsoft spell-checker will be adjusted to take account of the reinstated letter 'u' and the elimination of –ize.

4. July 4th will no longer be celebrated as a holiday.

5. You will learn to resolve personal issues without using guns, lawyers, or therapists. The fact that you need so many lawyers and therapists shows that you're not adult enough to be independent. Guns should only be handled by adults. If you're not adult enough to

sort things out without suing someone or speaking to a therapist, then you're not grown up enough to handle a gun.

6. Therefore, you will no longer be allowed to own or carry anything more dangerous than a vegetable peeler. A permit will be required if you wish to carry a vegetable peeler in public.

7. All intersections will be replaced with roundabouts, and you will start driving on the left with immediate effect. At the same time you will go metric with immediate effect and without benefit of conversion tables. Both roundabouts and metrification will help you understand the British sense of humour.

8. The Former USA will adopt UK prices on petrol (which you have been calling gasoline) – roughly $6/US gallon. Get used to it.

9. You will learn to make real chips. Those things you call French fries are not real chips, and those things you insist on calling potato chips are properly called crisps. Real chips are thick-cut, fried in animal fat, and dressed not with catsup but with vinegar.

10. The cold tasteless stuff you insist on calling beer is not actually beer at all. Henceforth, only proper British Bitter will be referred to as beer, and European beers of known and accepted provenance will be referred to as Lager. South African beer is also acceptable as they are pound for pound the greatest sporting Nation on earth and it can only be due to the beer. They are also part of British Commonwealth – see what it did for them. American brands will be referred to as Near-

frozen Gnat's Urine so it can be sold without risk of further confusion.

11. Hollywood would be required occasionally to cast English actors as good guys. Hollywood would also be required to cast English actors to play English characters. Watching Andie MacDowell attempt English dialogue in *Four Weddings and a Funeral* was an experience akin to having one's ears removed with a cheese grater.

12. You will cease playing American football. There is only one kind of proper football; you call it soccer. Those of you brave enough will, in time, be allowed to play rugby (which has some similarities to American football, but does not involve stopping for a rest every twenty seconds or wearing full kevlar body armor like a bunch of nancies.) Don't try rugby – the South Africans and the Kiwis will thrash you, like they regularly thrash us.

13. Further, you will stop playing baseball. It is not reasonable to host an event called World Series for a game that is not played outside America. Since only 2.1% of you are aware that there is a world beyond your borders, your error is understandable. You will learn cricket, and we will let you face the South Africans first to take the sting out of their deliveries.

14. You must tell us who killed J.F.K. It's been driving us mad.

15. An internal revenue agent (i.e., tax collector) from Her Majesty's government will be with you shortly to

ensure the acquisition of all monies due (backdated to 1776.)

16. Daily Tea Times begins promptly at 4pm with proper cups, saucers, and never mugs, with high-quality biscuits (cookies); plus strawberries (with cream) when in season."

God Save the Queen!

In the matter of Kilroy, as in *KILROY WAS HERE,* this American original graffiti first **appeared in the 1940's, illustrated by a simple** drawing of a head with an elongated nose peering over a fence with a message that *Kilroy Was Here.* Soon the cartoon was so ubiquitous that it showed up in the most remote and weird locations around the world.

The American Transit Association in 1946 was so bothered by discovering the origins of *Kilroy* that it offered to award a trolley to the person who could prove that he was the real Kilroy.

It dispensed the message through the Association's nationwide radio program, "Speak to America."

Of the forty men who stepped forward to make the claim, only James Kilroy from Halifax, Massachusetts had evidence of his identity. He was a 46-year-old shipyard worker during WW II, an inspector of rivets at the Fore River Shipyard in Quincy. His job was to count the individual rivets on construction projects and report them to company officials who paid the riveters piecemeal for each one they anchored in place. To establish an accurate account of his inspection, this James Kilroy would count a block of rivets and put a check mark in semi-waxed yellow chalk, so they wouldn't be counted twice. When Kilroy went off duty, workers would come along and erase his marks.

Later on, an off-shift inspector would come through and count the rivets a second time, resulting in double pay for the riveters.

One day, Kilroy's foreman called him into his office and complained about the higher wages being paid the riveters, and asked him to investigate. Only then did Kilroy realize what had been going on.

In tight spaces he had to crawl to check rivets, he ruled out dragging along a can of yellow paint, and resorted to using his waxy chalk. He did, however, also leave a message in king-size letters that KILROY WAS HERE. Later on he added the drawing of the chap with the long nose peering over the fence that became part of the Kilroy message. Once he did that, the other riveters stopped trying to wipe away his marks.

Ordinarily these rivet chalk marks would have been covered up by paint, but with the war on, ships were leaving the Quincy yard so fast, there wasn't time to paint them.

As a result, Kilroy's inspection trademark was seen by thousands of servicemen who boarded the troop ships the yard produced. His message apparently rang a bell with the servicemen, because they picked it up and spread it all over Europe and the South Pacific. Before the war's end, "Kilroy" had been here, there, and everywhere on the long haul to Berlin and Tokyo.

To the unfortunate troops outbound in those ships, however, he was a complete mystery. All they knew for sure was that some jerk named Kilroy had "been there first." As a joke, U.S. servicemen began placing the graffiti wherever they landed, claiming that it had already arrived by the time they got there.

Kilroy became the super GI who had always "already been" wherever the GI's went. It became a challenge to place the logo in the most unlikely places imaginable. (It is said to be on top of Mt. Everest, the Statue of Liberty, the underside of the Arch de Triumph, and even scratched in the dust of the moon.)

As the war went, the legend grew. Underwater demolition teams routinely sneaked ashore on Japanese-held islands in the Pacific to map the terrain for the coming invasions of U.S. troops (and thus, presumably, be the first GI's there.) On one occasion, however, they reported seeing enemy troops painting over the Kilroy logo. In 1945, an outhouse was built for the exclusive use of Roosevelt, Churchill, and Stalin at the Potsdam conference. The first person inside was Stalin. When he emerged he asked his aide (in Russian), "Who is Kilroy?"

To prove his authenticity in 1946, James Kilroy brought along officials from the shipyard and some of the riveters. He won the trolley car that he gave to his nine children as a Christmas gift, and set it up as a playhouse in the Kilroy front yard in Halifax, Massachusetts.

So now you know!

Very often, some of the most unintentional humor comes to us from government forms requisite to obtain financial assistance for those who fill in the blanks of documents explaining their domestic situations. Detroit, in particular, stands out as providing a plethora of examples of such hilarity.

The source of the following citations comes from applications filled out by women written on Child Support Agency Forms listing "Father's Details." To be blunt, the Agency wants to know "Who's your daddy?" These are genuine excerpts from a select number of forms:

"Regarding the identity of the father of my twins, Makeesha was fathered by McLearndon McKinley. I am unsure about the identit of the father of Marlinda, but I believe that she was conceived on the same night."

"I am unsure as to the identity of the father of my child as I was being sick out a window when taken unexpectedly from behind. I can provide you with a list of names of men that I think were at that party if this helps."

"I do not know the name of the father of my little girl. She was conceived at a party at 3600 East Grand Boulevard where I had sex with a man I met that night. I do remember that the sex was so good I fainted. If you do manage to track down the father, can you please send me his phone number? Thanks."

"I do not know the name of the father of my daughter. . . He drives a BMW that now has a hole made by my stiletto in one of his door panels. Perhaps you can contact BMW service stations in this area to see if it had been replaced."

"I have never had sex with a man. I am still a Virginian. I am awaiting a letter from the Pope confirming that my son's conception was ejaculated and that he is the Savior risen again."

"I cannot tell you the name of Alleshia dad as he informs me that to do so would blow his cover and that would have cataclysmic implications for the economy. I am torn between doing right by you and right by the country. Please advice."

"I do not know who the father of my child was as they all look the same to me."

"Tyrone Hairston is the father of child A. If you do catch up with him, can you ask him what he did with my AC/DC CD's? Child B who was also born at the same time . . . Well I don't have a clue."

"From the dates it seems as my daughter was conceived at Disney World; maybe it really is the Magic Kingdom."

"So much about that night is a blur. The only thing I remember for sure is Delia Smith did a program about eggs earlier in the evening. If I had stayed in and watched more TV than going to the party at 8956 Miller Ave, mine might have remained unfertilized."

"I am unsure as to the identity of the father of my baby, after all, like when you eat a can of beans you can't be sure which one made you fart."

CUES TO KEEP EVERYONE OFF BALANCE

At lunch time, park your car along the roadside; wear sunglasses, and point a hair dryer at passing cars to see if they slow down.

Page yourself over the office intercom. Don't disguise your voice.

Every time anybody asks you to do something, ask the "Do you want fries with that."

Put your wastebasket on your desk, and label it "In."

In the memo line on your checks, write "For smuggling diamonds."

End all your sentences with "In accordance with prophecy."

Don't use any punctuation.

As often as possible, skip, rather than walk.

Always order a "Diet water" when eating out, and with a serious look on your face.

When ordering food through a drive-thru window, always say the food is "to go."

When attending an opera, sing along with the performers.

When attending poetry recitals, always ask why the poems don't rhyme.

Complain to restaurant managers that their toilet paper is scratchy.

Drape your work area with mosquito netting, and play tropical music all day.

When invited to a party, give five day's notice that you can't attend because you're not in the mood.

Ask your co-workers to address you by your wrestling name: "Rock Bottom."

When money is ejected from an ATM, yell "I won! I won!"

When leaving a zoo, run toward the parking lot yelling, "Run for your lives. They're loose!"

Over dinner one evening, tell your children that the "Economy is so bad, we're going to have to let one of you go."

Always mix a little bit of insanity with everything you say or do.

Don't ever let anyone ever get your number.

Express sadness to anyone winning something.

Ask people how they got "that stain" on the back of their coat, shirt, or dress.

When hearing that someone got a new car, remind them of the bad report it received recently in "Consumer's Report."

Tell tattooed people that recent evidence reveals that tattoos cause cancer.

Always shake hands with your left hand.

Never button the middle button of a dress shirt.

Eat soup with a fork.

Salute every door before you open it.

Never fail to criticize someone's haircut as "uneven."

Include pocket change with any tip given restaurant help.

Use the "thumbs up" sign when recognizing fellow employees.

Always back into parking places.

Keep a fistful of coupons handy when paying for anything.

Carry a tabloid newspaper with you when going to church.

Blow kisses to cars that you pass.

When meeting well-dressed people, wrinkle your nose and ask them if they tramped in dog dirt.

Always direct your sneezes into someone else's face.

HISTORY YOU MISSED

By 1960, Adam Hats, a national chain store, had a thriving business selling a variety of hats for every occasion. The majority of its sales were to businessmen and casual design head covers for just about any outdoor event. So ingrained was the fashion for males to wear hats wherever they went, that most owned more than a half-dozen, styled to reflect the attire they were wearing when stepping out. They ranged from conservative to snappy, with or without feathers in the decorative ribbon that adorned the base of the hat.

Wearing a hat had much of its mystique held over from military service that demanded head cover any time a soldier was exposed to weather conditions. Boot camp protocol demanded wearing some kind of hat depending on what kind of event was being attended. Violations of missing head cover could result in citations that could affect advancement in military careers. Coming out of the military, the tradition of wearing some kind of cap seemed *de rigueur* to avoid feeling naked on top of the head.

Photographs taken of bread lines during the depression years of the 1030's showed long lines of men waiting for handouts – all wearing hats. As down and out as these men were, waiting patiently for the meager sustenance being doled out, their heads were covered with a generic hat that all looked alike.

IBM went so far as to mandate every male employee, especially its sales staff, to wear a certain style of hat, maintaining that "people trust people who wear hats."

But then, a fateful day in January, 1961, arrived that would change the hat-wearing of American men. It was the inauguration day of President-elect John F. Kennedy, who stood at the ceremonial rostrum to take the oath of office. The wind was blowing fiercely, and John Kennedy's hair was wafting wildly because – *he was hat-less*. It was a moment in history that changed men's fashion overnight. It became a watershed event for Adam Hats across the country. Within the next three years the company was out of business. A peculiar anomaly then occurred: seeing a man wear a hat seemed out of sync with contemporary attitudes and fashion. And it all could be traced to the youthful John F. Kennedy who ignored trends. After all, he promised the country "change", and this was his first great triumph.

Another political event that spawned a new word in the English lexicon happened during the 1841 election campaign of William Henry Harrison, the Whig (Republican) choice. In an attempt to describe the aging Harrison (he was only 67 at the time), the Whigs decided to launch its presidential choice as a homespun man of the people after a Democratic newspaper suggested that "Harrison would be happy spending the rest of his life in a log cabin with a jug of whiskey."

The Whigs jumped on the "Log Cabin" idea spread by the Democrats, and began publishing "Log Cabin" newspapers that chronicled the carnivalization of its party. To enhance the "down home" feature of Harrison, a Philadelphia distiller, *E. C. Booz,* started selling whiskey in bottles shaped like log cabins, giving birth to the word *booze* that has been synonymous with liquor ever since.

Clark Gable, voted "King of Hollywood" in the 1930's, starred in a film with Claudette Colbert titled "It Happened One Night." The movie was a romantic comedy, and its only attraction was the pairing of Gable and Colbert, two box office favorites at the time.

But something dramatic occurred in the film that immediately changed the way male viewers of the flick dressed themselves.

In a bedroom scene with Colbert, a waist high close-up of Gable showed him unbuttoning and removing his shirt to reveal just his brawny chest – *and no undershirt!*

Overnight, the sale of undershirts plunged nationally. Every man wanted to be perceived as sexy as Clark Gable. That fashion trend lasted for years until deodorants became popular for men, showing models wearing the tank-top variety of underwear. By then Gable was dead and the movie that started it all was long forgotten.

GAMES PEOPLE PLAY

United Parcel Service (UPS) has become the largest private transportation company delivering packages and mail around the globe. Using only huge aircraft, second only to the military's special planes that move super-sized munitions, UPS can brag that it has never sustained any crashes in its long history of postal movement of commercial mail.

Company management attributes this to a constant mechanical monitoring system of its aircraft between its highly-educated pilots and ground crew efficiency second to none in the industry. That a college-educated and highly experienced group of seasoned flyers have such a rapport with a talented organized group of mechanics on the ground boasting high school diplomas indicates the unique marriage that UPS management has over its competition.

In reviewing pilot and mechanic trouble reports exchanged over the years reveals the imaginative, and often humorous, side of how the two crews' efforts dovetail so well.

When UPS pilots detect potential deficiencies with their aircraft, they fill out a "Problem" report and submit them to the ground crew mechanics for "Solutions." The very descriptions of some of these communications offer a window into the world of why the airline employees have such a sophisticated respect for one another.

Here are some actual maintenance complaints submitted by UPS' pilots (marked with a "P"), and the solutions recorded (by an "S") by maintenance engineers:

P: Left inside main tire almost needs replacement.
S: *Almost replaced left inside main tire.*

P: Test flight OK, except auto-land very rough.
S: Auto-land not installed on this aircraft.

P: Something loose in cockpit.
S: *Something tightened in cockpit.*

P: Dead bugs on windshield.
S: Live bugs on back order.

P: Auto-pilot in altitude-hold mode produces a 200 feet per minute descent.
S: Cannot reproduce problem on ground.

P: Evidence of leak on right main landing gear.
S: Evidence removed.

P: DMV volume unbelievably loud.
S: DMV volume set for more believable level.

P: Friction locks cause throttle levers to stick.
S: That's what friction locks are for.

P: IFF inoperative in OFF mode.
S: IFF always inoperative in OFF mode.

P: Suspected crack in windshield.
S: Suspect you're right.

P: Number 3 engine missing.
S: Engine found on right wing after search.

P: Aircraft handles funny.
S: Aircraft warned to straighten up, fly right, and be serious.

P: Target radar hums.
S: Reprogrammed target radar with lyrics.

P: Mouse in cockpit.
S: Cat installed.

And this one is choice!

P: Noise coming from instrument panel. Sounds like a midget pounding on something with a hammer.
S: Took hammer away from midget.

DISPARATE DISPATCHES

ANNALS OF LAW

Court reporters around the country are privy to record the exact words said by anyone involved in a trial – the prosecution lawyers, the defense lawyers, the judge, and witnesses testifying on behalf of both sides involved in the machinations to be resolved by the courtroom procedure.

There are moments when unexpected questions to witnesses by the lawyers precipitate responses that compel anything from shock to guffaws from those in the courtroom.

A recent book, "Disorder in American Courts," reveals some testimony of the actual questions and answers recorded by some of these court reporters that tested the physical reactions of those attending the trials to remain calm while these exchanges were actually taking place. Here are some choice examples that provoked just such behavior described above:

Attorney: "Are you sexually active?"
Witness: "No, I just lie there."

Attorney: "What gear were you in at the moment of impact?"
Witness: "Gucci sweats and Reeboks."

Attorney: "This myasthenia gravis does it affect your memory?"
Witness: "Yes."

Attorney: "And in what way does it affect your memory?"
Witness: "I forget."

Attorney: "And specifically, you forget? Can you give us an example of what you forgot?"

Attorney: "What was the first thing your husband said to you that morning?"
Witness: "He said, 'Where am I, Cathy'?"

Attorney: "And why did that upset you?"
Witness: "My name is Susan."

Attorney: "Do you know if your daughter has ever been involved in voodoo?"
Witness: "We both do."

Attorney: "Voodoo?"
Witness: "We do."

Attorney: "You do?"
Witness: "Yes, voodoo."

Attorney: "Now doctor, isn't it true that when a person dies in his sleep, he doesn't know it until the next morning?"
Witness: "Did you actually pass the bar exam?"

Attorney: "The youngest son, the twenty-year-old, how old is he?"
Witness: "Uh. He's twenty."

Attorney: "Were you present when your picture was taken?"
Witness: "Are you shittin' me?"

Attorney: "So the date of the conception (of the baby) was August 8th?"
Witness: "Yes."

Attorney: "And what were you doing at that time?"
Witness: "I was getting laid!"

Attorney: "She had three children, right?"
Witness: "Yes."

Attorney: "How many were boys?"
Witness: "None."

Attorney: "Were there any girls?"
Witness: "Are you shittin' me? Your honor, I think I need a different attorney. Can I get a new attorney?"

Attorney: "How was your first marriage? Terminated?"
Witness: "By death."

Attorney: "And by whose death was it terminated?"
Witness: "Now whose death do you suppose terminated it?"

Attorney: "Can you describe the individual?"
Witness: "He was about medium height and had a beard."

Attorney: "Was this a male or female?"
Witness: "Guess."

Attorney: "Is your appearance here this morning pursuant to a deposition notice which I sent to your attorney?"
Witness: "No. This is how I dress when I go to work."

Attorney: "Doctor, how many of your autopsies have you performed on dead people?"
Witness: "All my autopsies are performed on dead people. Would you like to re-phrase that?"

Attorney: "All your responses must be oral, OK? What school did you go to?"
Witness: "Oral."

Attorney: "Do you recall the time that you examined the body?"
Witness: "The autopsy started around 8pm."

Attorney: "And Mr. Denton was dead at the time?"
Witness: "No. He was sitting on the table wondering why I was doing an autopsy on him!"

Attorney: "Are you qualified to give urine sample?"
Witness: "Huh . . . Are you qualified to ask that question?"

Attorney: "Doctor, before you performed the autopsy, did you check for a pulse?"
Witness: "No."

Attorney: "Did you check for blood pressure?"
Witness: "No."

Attorney: "Did you check for breathing?"
Witness: "No."

Attorney: "So, then is it possible the patient was alive when you began the autopsy?"
Witness: "No."

Attorney: "Then how can you be so sure, Doctor?"
Witness: "Because his brain was sitting on my desk in a jar."

Attorney: "I see, but could the patient have still been alive, nevertheless?"
Witness: "Yes, it is possible that he could have been alive and practicing law."

THE PERFECT SQUELCH

Amid a large number of people at a fairly large conference in England, American Secretary of State Colin Powell was asked by the Archbishop of Canterbury if America's plans for Iraq was just another example of "empire building" by President George W. Bush. Powell explained, saying, "Over the years, the United States has sent many of its fine men and women into great peril to fight for freedom beyond our borders. The only amount of land we have asked for in return is enough to bury those that did not return.

It became very quiet in the room.

At a gathering of international engineers in France, attended by French and American representatives as well as other countries, a break in the conference offered an opportunity for one of the French engineers to wonder out loud, "Have you hear the latest dumb stunt Bush has done? He has sent an aircraft carrier to Indonesia to help the tsunami victims. What does he intend to do? Bomb them?"

A Boeing engineer stood up and quietly replied, "Our carriers have three hospitals on board that can treat several hundred people. They are nuclear-powered and can supply emergency electric power to shore facilities. They have three cafeterias with a capacity to feed 3,000 people three meals a day. They can produce several thousand gallons of fresh water each day, and they carry half-dozen helicopters for use in transporting victims and injured to and from their flight deck. We have eleven such ships. How many does France have?"

Once again, dead silence again in the room.

A United States Navy Admiral was attending a naval conference that included Admirals from the U.S., England, Canadian, Australian, and French navies. At a cocktail reception, he found himself standing with a large group of officers that included personnel from most of those countries. Everyone was chatting away in English as they sipped their drinks, but a French admiral suddenly complained that, whereas Europeans learn many languages, Americans learn only English. He then asked, "Why is it that we have to speak English in these conferences rather than speaking French?"

Without hesitating, the American admiral replied, "Maybe it's because the Brits, Canadians, Australians, and Americans arranged it so you wouldn't have to speak German."

You could have heard a pin drop.

PALLIATIVES

Leave it to grandmothers to find alternative cures for ailments that just happen to be regular household items. Check out these revelations for using the mundane for purposes that proved to have uses other than what they are known and sold for.

Got a headache? Drinking two glasses of Gatorade will cure it faster than an over-the-counter analgesic.

Burn yourself? For minor burns, rub some Colgate toothpaste on the area. It makes an excellent salve for burns.

Nose stuffed up? Chewing on a couple of Altoid peppermints will clear it up rather than buying those high-priced inhalers with their mysterious chemicals.

Has the flu left you with achy muscles? Mix a tablespoon of horseradish with a cup of olive oil, let it sit for half an hour, then apply it as a massage for aching muscles.

Sore throat got you down? Mix ¼ cup of vinegar with an equal amount of honey, take one tablespoon of the mixture six times a day. (The vinegar kills the bacteria.)

Urinary problem starting to act up? Dissolve two Alka-Seltzers in a glass of water at the onset of symptoms. It will begin eliminating (excuse the pun) urinary tract infections almost immediately. Curiously, the product was never advertised for this common ailment.

Got a skin blemish? Put a dab of honey on it, cover with a Band-Aid, and overnight the honey will kill the bacteria, keeps the skin sterile, and speeds healing.

Got that nasty-looking toe fungus? Soak your feet in Listerine mouthwash. The antiseptic quality of Listerine makes your feet look healthy again.

Got a broken blister? Dab the same Listerine on it. Again, the antiseptic ingredients in the mouthwash will disinfect it.

Loose screws in eyeglasses? To keep from loosening, apply a small drop of Maybelline Clear Nail Polish to the threads before tightening them.

Got menacing bees, yellow jackets, wasps, or hornets in your home? Spraying them with Formula 409 will makes an excellent bug killer.

Bothered by a pesky splinter? Pour a drop of Elmer's Glue on the suspect area, let dry, and then just peel it off. The splinter sticks to the dried glue.

Got those nasty fruit flies (gnats) buzzing around your fresh fruit? Pour a few ounces of CIDER VINEGAR in a glass, add two drops of DAWN or other dishwashing detergent, and your gnats will disappear.

Dog been out in the rain? Does the animal have that doggy odor? Wipe the animal down with BOUNCE or any other clothes dryer sheet to make your pet smell springtime fresh.

Arthritis pain kicking up? Mix two cups of QUAKER OATS with one cup of water, microwave for a minute, cool slightly, and then apply to your hands for soothing relief from arthritis pain.

GOSPEL OR GOSSIP

Flying Air Force One (the President's plane) and Air Force Two (the Vice-President's plane) were accolades bestowed on very few seasoned pilots. Although pledged never to speak about their experiences with White House staff aboard, the crews that flew these aircrafts often exchanged comments among themselves over a beer or any social event that brought them together.

These flights, designated *SPECIAL AIR MISSIONS,* had the added interest of comments from the Secret Service agents in attendance to the President and Vice-President, people whose duties extended beyond accompaniment of flights around the world, but also in the daily lives of these political kingpins.

Some excerpts that were leaked to relatives of these pilots over the years render a private portrait profile that most Americans would never know or have privy to unless revealed in books written long after leaving the service of the White House.

Here are few fascinating stories that they told:

"I flew four Presidential support missions in the C-141 out of Dover Air Force Base in Delaware. Two for President Johnson and two for President Nixon.

Johnson was a first-class jerk, and on the two occasions I flew for him, if the Secret Service and their liaison in the Pentagon hadn't intervened, we would have had to stay on the airplane for hours while he (Johnson) was off somewhere. Nixon never required that, and the four stops we made with him, he was cordial to the Secret Service and to me and my crew.

We had a neighbor when lived in D.C. who was part of the Secret Service presidential detail for many years. His stories of Kennedy and Johnson were the same as I heard from the guys who flew the President's plane.

Yes, Kennedy did have Marilyn Monroe flown in for secret 'dates', and LBJ was a typical 'good ole boy' womanizer. [Editor's note: this was confirmed in a four-volume definitive biography written by Pulitzer Prize winning author, Robert Caro.] Nixon, Bush 41, and Carter never cheated on their wives. Clinton cheated, but couldn't match Kennedy or Johnson in style or variety.

The information below is accurate. The elder Bush and the current Bush make it a point to thank and take care of their crews who fly them around. When the President flies, there are several planes that also go; one carries the armored limo, another, the security detail, plus a press aircraft. Both Bush's made it a point to stay home on holidays, so the Air Force and security people could have a day with their families.

Hillary Clinton was arrogant and orally abusive to her security detail. She forbade her daughter, Chelsea, from exchanging pleasantries with them. Sometimes Chelsea, miffed at her mother's obvious conceit and mean-spiritedness, ignored her demands and exchanged pleasantries regardless, but never in her mother's presence. Chelsea was a really nice, kindhearted, and a lovely young lady. The consensus opinion was that Chelsea loved her mom, but did not like her. Hillary Clinton was continuously rude and abrasive to those who were charged to protect her life. Her security detail dutifully did their job, as professionals should, but they all loathed her and wanted to be on a different detail.

Hillary Clinton was despised by the Secret Service as a whole. Former President Bill Clinton was much more amiable than his wife. Often the Secret Service would cringe at the verbal attacks Hillary would use against her husband. They were embarrassed for his sake by the manner and frequency in which she verbally insulted him, sometimes in the presence of the Secret Service, sometimes behind closed doors. Even behind closed doors, Hillary would scream and holler so loudly that everyone could hear what she was saying. Many felt sorry for President Clinton and most wondered why he tolerated it instead of just divorcing his 'attack dog' wife. It was crystal clear that the Clintons neither liked nor respected each other, and this was true long before the Monica Lewinsky scandal. Theirs was genuinely a 'marriage of convenience.'

Chelsea was much closer to her father than her mother, even after the Lewinsky scandal, which hurt her gravely. Bill Clinton did in fact have charisma, and would occasionally smile and shake hands with his security detail. Still, he always displayed an obvious air of superiority towards them.

His security detail uniformly believed him to be disingenuous, false, and that he nothing without a motive that in some way would enhance his image and political career. He was polite, but not kind. They did not particularly like him and nobody trusted him.

Al Gore was the male version of Hillary Clinton. They were friendlier toward each other than either of them was toward former President Clinton. They were not intimate, so please don't read that in. They were very close in a political way. Tipper Gore was generally nice and pleasant. She initially likes Hillary, but soon after the election she had her 'pegged' and no longer liked her or associated with her except for events that were politically obligatory.

Al Gore was far more left wing than Bill Clinton. Al Gore resented Bill Clinton and thought he was too 'centrist.' He despised all Republicans. His hatred was bitter and this was long before he announced for the Presidency. This hatred was something that he and Hillary had in common. They often said as much, even in the presence of the security detail. Neither of them trusted Bill Clinton and, the Secret Service opined, neither of them even liked him. Bill Clinton did have some good qualities, whereas Gore and Hillary had none, in the view of their security details.

Al Gore, like Hillary, was very rude and arrogant toward his security detail. He was extremely unappreciative and would not hesitate to scold them in the presence of their peers for minor details over which they had no control. Al Gore also looked down on them, as they finally observed and learned with certainty on one occasion. Al got angry at his offspring and pointed at his security detail and said, "Do you want to grow up and be like them?" Word of this insult by the former Vice-President quickly spread and he became as disliked by the Secret Service as Hillary. Most of them prayed that Al Gore would not be elected President, and they really did have private celebrations in a few of their homes after President Bush won. This was not necessarily to celebrate President Bush's election, but to celebrate Al Gore's defeat.

Everyone in the Secret Service wants to be on First Lady Laura Bush's detail. Without exception, they concede that she is, perhaps, the nicest and most kind person they have ever had the privilege of serving. Where Hillary patently refused to allow her picture to be taken with her security detail, Laura Bush doesn't even have to be asked; she offers. She just doesn't shake their hand and say 'thank you.' Very often, she will give members of her detail a kindhearted hug to express her appreciation. There is nothing false about her, this is her genuine nature. Her security detail considers her a 'breath of fresh air.' They joke that comparing Laura Bush to Hillary Clinton is like comparing 'Mother Teresa' to 'the Wicked Witch of the North.'

Likewise, the Secret Service considers President Bush to be a gem of a man to work for. He always treats them with genuine respect and he always trusts and listens to their expert advice. They really like the Crawford, Texas detail. Every time the President goes to Crawford, he has a Bar-Be-Que for his security detail and he helps serve their meals. He sits with them, eats with them, and talks with them. He knows each of them by their first name and calls them by their first name as a show of affection. He always asks about their family, the names of which he always remembers. They believe that he is deeply and genuinely appreciative of their service. They could not like, love, or respect anyone more than President

Bush. Most of them did not know they would feel this way, until they had an opportunity to work for him and learn that his manner was genuine and consistent. It has never changed since he began his Presidency. He always treats them with the utmost respect, kindness, and compassion."

REMEMBERING WHEN

[Warning: Readers under the age of 40, please disregard. You wouldn't understand.]

To watch television, spread the rabbit ears as far apart as you could get them. Then pull up a chair and watch "Good Night, David," and "Good Night, Chet."

Mothers used to use the same cutting board to cut chicken, chop eggs, and spread mayo with the same knife, and not even use bleach on them. And nobody got food poisoning.

Moms used to defrost hamburger on the counter, and I used to eat some of it raw (remember "Cannibal sandwiches?" School sandwiches were wrapped in wax paper, not in ice-pack coolers. But nobody got e-coli.

Kids would rather go swimming in a lake, rather than a pristine pool (how boring!)

A cell phone would have meant a phone in a jail, and a pager would be something in a school's PA system.

We all took GYM, not PE. We risked physical injury wearing high-top Keds (only worn in gym) instead of having cross-training athletic shoes with air cushion soles and built-in light reflectors. I can't recall any injuries, but they must have happened because they tell us how much safer we are now.

Flunking gym just didn't happen, even for stupid kids. I guess PE must be much harder than gym.

Speaking of school, we all said prayers and sang the national anthem. And staying in school for detention after school caught all sorts of negative attention.

We must have had horribly damaged psyches. What an archaic school system we had then. Remember school nurses? Ours wore a hat and everything.

It's hard to remember how bored we were without computers, play stations, Nintendo, X-Box or 270 Digital TV Cable stations.

And yeah! Where was the Benadryl and sterilization kit when we got that bee sting? We could have been killed.

We played "King of the Hill" on piles of gravel left on vacant construction sites, and when we got hurt, mom used the 48-cent bottle of Mercurochrome (kids like it better because it didn't sting like Iodine did), and then we got our butt spanked.

Now it's a trip to the Emergency Room, followed by a 10-day dose of a bottle of $49 antibiotics, and then mom calling an attorney to sue the contractor for leaving a particularly vicious pile of gravel where it was such a threat to kids.

To top it off, not a single person I knew had been told he came from a dysfunctional family. How could we ever have known that?

We needed to get into group therapy and anger management classes? We were so duped by so many societal ills that we didn't even notice the whole country wasn't taking Prozac.

The wonder of it is *how did we ever survive.*

OUT OF THE MAINSTREAM

Stand-up comic George Carlin, 1934-2008, had a tradition of offering annual advice to his fans that had national appeal unless, of course, the subject of his comments just happened to be you.

For the year 2008, Carlin advised:

NEW RULE:
No more gift registries. You know, it used to be just for weddings. Now it's for babies and new homes and graduations from rehab. Picking out the stuff you want and having other people buy it for you isn't gift giving, it's the white peoples' version of looting.

NEW RULE:
Stop giving me that pop-up ad for classmates.com! There's a reason you don't talk to people for 25 years. Because you don't particularly like them! Besides I already know what the captain of the football team is doing these days. Mowing my lawn.

NEW RULE:
Don't eat anything that's served to you out of a window unless you're a seagull. People are acting all shocked that a human finger was found in a bowl of Wendy's chili. Hey! It costs less than a dollar. What did you expect it to contain . . . lobster?

NEW RULE:
Stop saying that teenage boys who have sex with their hot, blonde teachers are permanently damaged. I have a better description for these kids: *Lucky Bastards.*

NEW RULE:

If you need to shave and still collect baseball cards, you're a dope. If you're a kid, the cards are keepsakes of your idols. If you're a grown man, they're pictures of men.

NEW RULE:

Ladies, leave your eyebrows alone. Here's how much men care about your eyebrows: do you have two of them? Good, we're done.

NEW RULE:

There's no such thing as flavored water. There's a whole aisle of this crap at the supermarket. Water, but without that watery taste. Sorry, but flavored water is called a soft drink. You want flavored water? Pour some scotch over ice and let it melt. Now *there's* your flavored water.

NEW RULE:

Stop screwing with old people. TARGET is introducing a re-designed pill bottle that's square with a bigger label. And the top is now the bottom. And by the time grandpa figures out how to open it, his ass will be in the morgue. Congratulations TARGET, you just solved the Social Security crisis.

NEW RULE:

The more complicated the STARBUCKS order, the bigger the asshole. If you walk into a STARBUCKS and order a 'decaf Grande, half- soy, half-low fat, iced vanilla, double-shot, gingerbread cappuccino, extra-dry, light ice, with one Sweet 'n' Low, and one NutraSweet, "Ooooh, you're a huge asshole."

NEW RULE:

I'm not the cashier! By the time I look up from sliding my card, entering my PIN, pressing 'Enter', verifying the amount, deciding, 'No, I don't want cash back', and pressing 'Enter' again, the kid who's supposed to be ringing me up is standing there eating my Almond Joy!

NEW RULE:

Just because your tattoo has Chinese characters in it doesn't make you Spiritual. It's right above the crack of your ass. And it translates to 'beef with broccoli'. 'The last time you did anything spiritual, you were praying to God you weren't pregnant. You're not spiritual, you're just high.'

NEW RULE:

Competitive eating isn't a sport. It's one of the seven deadly sins. ESPN recently televised the U.S. Open of Competitive Eating., because watching those athletes at the poker table was just too damned exciting. What's next? Competitive farting? Oh wait, they're already doing that . . . it's called the 'Howard Stern Show'.

NEW RULE:

When I ask how old your toddler is, I don't need to hear '27 months'. 'He's two' will do just fine. He's not a cheese. And I didn't really care in the first place.

NEW RULE:

If you ever hope to be a credible adult and want a job that pays better than minimum wage, then for God's sake don't pierce or tattoo every available piece of flesh. If so, plan your future around saying, 'Do you want fries with that?'

Scientists at a Danish chemical plant have discovered a heretofore useless waste product that can be converted into plastics, soap, moisturizer, fertilizer, de-icer for roads and airplanes, and any number of things that will help the world in reducing its reliance on oil. It has been heralded as a "dream product" by groups dedicated to the greening of the globe.

This chemical, of which 90,000 tons is produced daily worldwide, is a gift to mankind from (don't hold your nose!) pigs. It is an ingredient that flows readily into pigpens in the form of urine. That's right. Pig pee, hog piss, the fluid that can be captured from pens as soon as it flows from the pig and directly into a filter system that removes the color, odor, and particulate matter in this golden fluid.

And, by the way, it also keeps pigpens clean and disease-free from the sludge formed by mixing with pig feces.

It seems that pig urine has the benefit of being a bulking agent in the production of the above-named riches, and much cheaper to extract than oil, the ingredient whose properties have been used for decades for manufacturing plastic for thousands of everyday applications.

The first plant of its kind was built by Agroplast some twenty miles from Copenhagen. Plans to take advantage of America's vast pig farm residue are in the works for Iowa and North Carolina, home to some of the vast pork industry and the largest depository of this animal's sludge.

One visionary from Agroplast conceived the erection of high-rise pig pens in the future that would enhance the production process of pig pee on a massive scale.

Some concerned scientists have risen the potential hazard that disposing of such products, say in a landfill that could happen if the bio-products made from pig pee could end up being buried in earthen depositories. The downside of this potential is that the chemical, urine, would degrade into releasing greenhouse gas methane. Worse, there is no waste management companies in existence equipped to sort out regular plastics from bioplastics.

One of Agroplast's engineers predicted the possibilities that "pig cities" could arise, what with the price of farmland and gas at a premium, and skyscrapers would house pigs in a self-contained processing plant that could convert their waste onsite into plastic and fertilizer.

ONCE UPON A TIME . . .

The late comedian Rodney Dangerfield's spiel always started with the phrase, "I don't get no respect . . ." and then proceeds with a cascade of situations illustrating his demeaning existence in life. Here are some of his famous woes:

"I'm so unlucky, if the last woman on earth was cut in half, I'd get the half that talked."

"My wife only has sex with me for a purpose. Last night she used me to time an egg."

"It's tough to stay married. My wife kisses the dog on the lips, yet she won't drink from my glass."

"Last night my wife met me at the front door. She was wearing a sexy negligee. The only trouble was, she was coming home."

"A girl phoned me and said 'Come on over. There's nobody home. I went over . . . nobody was home."

"A hooker once told me she had a headache."

"If it weren't for pickpockets, I'd have no sex life at all."

"My wife is such a bad cook, if we leave dental floss in the kitchen, the roaches hang themselves."

"The other day I came home and a guy was jogging . . . naked. I asked him why. He said because you came home early."

"I know I'm not sexy. When I put my underwear on, I can hear the Fruit-Of-The-Loom guys giggling."

"My wife likes to talk on the phone during sex. She called me from Chicago last night."

"My family was so poor that if I hadn't been born a boy, I wouldn't have had anything to play with."

PAPAL FUN AND GAMES

Catholicity certainly had its problems in the late 800 AD beginning with Pope Formosus (891-896), especially after he died, and was succeeded by Pope Boniface VI who managed to leave this world two weeks after he was elevated to the Papacy, and nine months after Formosus' body had been ceremoniously interred.

Boniface's successor, Stephen VII (896-897) started his papal reign with an axe to grind. He discounted the validity of how some of his predecessors had been elevated to high positions within the Catholic Church; a subterfuge that he felt was his duty to correct. In particular, he maintained that Pope Stephen VI was illegitimate because of the political machinations that got him elected Pope to begin with. At this point, Stephen VII declared Stephen VI a non-Pope, *and Stephen VII assumed the title of Pope Stephen VI.*

[Editor's note: It's confusing, but try to stay with the story.]

Part and parcel of the "new" Stephen VI's acrimony included persecution of those clerics that the original Pope Stephen VI had appointed during his tenure as a rising star in the church's hierarchy. In particular was a bishop who ultimately succeeded him and became Pope Formosus, an action that the "new" Stephen considered sacrilegious. What he decided to do was to put Formosus on trial nine months *after he had died*, and two weeks after his successor, Boniface VI had, too.

Announcing a Cadaver Synod, he declared a posthumous ecclesiastical trial for Pope Formosus to be held in Rome at the Basilica of S. John Lateran in January 897. After exhuming Formosus' body, Stephen had it dressed in full papal regalia, propped the body up in a courtroom throne, and proceeded to question the corpse as a chief prosecutor, accusing the dead Pope of miscellaneous and assorted religious crimes, and then declaring him guilty on all counts (of course.)

According to Liutprand of Cremora, the 10th century historian, Stephen VI asked Formosus' corpse why he "usurped the universal Roman see in such a spirit of ambition" after the death of Pope John VIII, echoing John VIII's own assertion that Formosus had tried to seize the papal throne while he was alive. Two other accusations were made against the mordant body sitting motionless before Stephen: that he had committed perjury, and had attempted to exercise the power of a bishop while still a layman.

For the penalty of being found guilty, Stephen had Formosus' body stripped of papal garments, cut off the three fingers of his right hand used for benedictions, and declared all of his appointments, acts, and ordinations (including that of the original Pope Stephen VI) null and void. The angry pope had Formosus buried in a plot reserved for foreigners, only to be dug up later and thrown into the Tiber River.

The historian Liutprand records Stephen asking the corpse, "When you were Bishop of Porto, why did you usurp the universal Roman see in such a spirit of ambition?"

The events that followed this macabre spectacle in Rome saw public opinion turn against Stephen, especially when Formosus' body washed up on the banks of the Tiber. It was said to perform miracles. A public uprising led to Stephen being deposed and imprisoned. While confined he was strangled to death sometime in July or August of 897.

What followed this Cadaver Synod is a sequence that almost equals the crazy events that led up to it.

In November, 987, Pope Theodore II (897) convened a synod that annulled the Cadaver Synod, returned Formosus to his previous status, and had him reburied in St. Peter's Basilica in pontifical investments. In 898, John IX (898-900) convened two synods in Rome and Ravenna that also nullified the Cadaver Synod and destroyed records of it while prohibiting any future trials of a dead person. Then, Pope Sergius III (904-911), who had been a bishop and a participant in the Cadaver Synod, overturned the rulings of Theodore II and John IX, reaffirming Formosus's conviction, and had a praiseworthy epitaph inscribed on Stephen VI's tomb. [Later church authorities corrected the VI and VII to the proper popes of that era.]

This exercise was known in Latin as *Synodus Horrenda* and remembered as one of the most bizarre episodes of the medieval papacy. The Cadaver Synod is generally referred to as the years between 872-965, a period of instability and upheaval in the Catholic Church that saw 24 Popes come and go, with these brief reigns being the result of political machinations of local Roman factions. Unfortunately, few sources exist that can historically define that era.

DEATH BY A THOUSAND SLICES

When it comes to designing the cruelest form of torture and death, history has revealed that none can top the Chinese method of slicing and dicing living persons who have committed offenses ranging from treason, murder, killing paternal grandparents to cheating on taxes. The method of dispatching the condemned was called *lingchi*, meaning slow slicing, and the length of the gruesome torture was anticipated to last three days.

The intention of *lingchi* was threefold: as a form of public humiliation, as a slow and lingering death, and as a punishment after death.

This uniquely oriental ruthlessness dates from 900 AD to 1905 AD when it was officially banned by Chinese officials. This dictum, of course, did not mean that it was abandoned by other human beings later on who begged to differ from the official termination of this most hideous manner of dispatching people into the hereafter.

Medieval accounts of rendering a person dead for whatever crimes or offenses he might (or might not have) committed was a common practice of *drawing and quartering* the physical body of the condemned. This consisted of dragging the bound-up live body through the streets or roadways until it was disemboweled, and then dismembering it in front of an audience gathered to observe the celebration of sending the victim (hopefully) into a shameful future in the hereafter. Depending on the gravity of the crime committed by the condemned, he might have undergone tarring and feathering prior to being dragged on the ground.

The *lingchi* method has never been eclipsed for being the acme of sadistic treatment of the human body. Of the dozens of accounts over a millenium that describe the process, it begins with the live subject bound to a cross, and then slowly having small slices of flesh cut from the body by the executioner (*Fondler*), i.e., eyebrows, ears, nose, tongue, lips, breasts, fingers, toes, and sometimes stabs in the eyes, all while the slicee is aware of the continuing mutilation of his body. By selecting bits and pieces of the human form early on that do not cause extreme blood loss, the death of the person can be prolonged, hopefully up to three days, the anticipated length of the ritual. Should the moribund subject die prematurely, then larger chunks of flesh would be whacked off, such as hands, elbows, knees, arms, legs, feet, hips, torso, and then internal organs. The head would be saved for the finale of organ separations, acknowledging that no human being had survived decapitation. The purpose of the total degradation of the body was intended as a post-death humiliation for it to arrive in pieces in eternity for its final disposition.

The slicing and dicing was expected to render some 3,600 pieces of human flesh that was then put on parade and displayed for public viewing.

The process of *lingchi* was not without some minor semblance of mercy rendered the *sacrifice du jour.* If his relatives had wealth, they could afford a bribe to the executioner to permit some opium to be stuffed into his mouth to allay any cognizance of his being sliced and diced by the Fondler, the hand with the sharpened sword. Most written accounts described by witnesses over the centuries indicated that few of the condemned lived even two days, let alone the anticipated three for which the execution festivities were designed.

The last execution by the *lingchi* methodology was on April 10, 1905. It had to do with a Mongol guard who had killed his master. Originally condemned to be burned alive, the Chinese emperor deemed that manner of death to be too cruel, and ordered the guard to undergo the less savage death by a thousand pieces - the assumption here being a slow death is less painful than immolation of a body. Two weeks after the Mongolian guard met his slicer; the process of *lingchi* was abolished.

CONFESSION

Far-flung news reporter Duard Fahrquard was forced to resign from the Tribune News Network yesterday following intensive investigations that revealed his fudging the truth in some of his stories for the past decade. In a confession he produced for the agency's top editors were some tales that had escaped the keen eyes of the committee that originally brought Mr. Fahrquard's bogus articles to the attention of Network examiners.

Network News owner Malcolm Merde deemed it essential that the viewers and readers of his communication network be aware of important stories where Mr. Fahrquard bent the truth or simply produced a far out fairy tale. Here is a cross section of some of them that brought the attention of his investigators.

MUNICH WINE AUCTION – 2008. The tasting of a *1921 Chateau Ausone* magnum was not held at the famous Hofbrauhaus. It was at a sidewalk café several blocks away from the famous beerhaus. The leading tasting authorities from Zimbabwe and East Timor were late to the wine sampling of the vintage Ausone and had to settle for whatever Beaujolais was left. In fact, the *Ausone* vineyard produced no magnums of wine that year. The product served to the tasting authorities had heretofore been bottled leftover wines from last year's tasting in Vienna, Ohio. The actual grade given this sampling (and this is the truth) was B+++ by a majority of the judges from Bangladesh. They asked to be invited to next year's tippling sample of rare wines scheduled at the Canary Island's airport lounge.

KUDZU: THE MIRACLE PLANT: This 2002 gardening article and interview with Pat Kudzu in North Carolina actually took place in a lovely suite at a Days Inn motel in Newark, New Jersey. Her story claiming to be the heir to the Kudzu family seemed a little specious to me, but the benefits to goat farmers of this edible delicacy turned out to be true. My claim that kudzu is hard to grow, however, was false. The timing of the Secretary of Agriculture calling kudzu a "weed" instead of a windfall product for making homemade jelly was unfortunate, and I apologize for misleading my readers.

BUS STATION BROTHEL: Truth to tell, this 1998 story of reckless sex in a men's room in a Paducah bus station was supposed to have taken place in Crawford, Texas. I got the story second hand from a government worker who spent holidays nearby and was working on a book about the high incidence of male prostitutes in government. When we got together at his motel room, he told me that actually the story was about female floozies that worked for a Washington D.C. madam, and he was privy to a stack of her clients' phone numbers and names that paid big money to be massaged by her employees. He said one of the names on her list was the guy that owned a cable network news station, and that I probably knew who he was. Couldn't remember his name except that it rhymed with "shit." My story never got into print until an anonymous source gave it to our competition. Sorry about that.

THE JESUS CHRIST INTERVIEW: This once-in-a-lifetime talk with one of the greatest religious scions in the world changed my life. He read my mind to the extent that he answered questions before I had a chance to utter them. His baritone voice made his message even more compelling than the words he used to convey them. That my interview with him happened in Jesus' (that's what he wanted me to call him) home town of Acapulco was edited out of my story, as was his changing his last name from Rodriguez to Christ when he assumed the role of pastor at the *Christ Church of Acapulco.* I truly apologize for the confusion and all the letters that the Network received accusing it of blasphemy.

THE AVOCADO SEED MIRACLE: Dr. Simeon Bolivar's claim that avocado seeds swallowed whole or inserted as a suppository cured dozens of maladies for his patients in the Amazon Valley did seem rather outlandish when a bartender I trusted in Brooklyn first confided it to me. My reports quoting Dr. Bolivar from his office in Brazil actually happened over the phone. I really couldn't understand his Portuguese very well, but the bartender, listening in on the speakerphone, translated them for me. I truly did not know that Bolivar was a health nut and an advocate of alternative medicine, and he was a PhD, not an M.D. Perhaps if I had known that Dr. Bolivar's grandfather had advocated ground-up peach pits as a cancer treatment (marketed as *Laetrile*) decades earlier, I would have had second thoughts about writing that story.

KIDNAPPING IN KARSOZA: The mother of five who was kidnapped in Karsoza and threatened with rape of her children by a band of horny men did not originate in the Middle East. The source of the story came from a cousin of mine who is a member of a polygamist Mormon sect in Utah. The band of men was actually her husbands who were involved in their own lottery to see which one could take her 13-year-old as a wife. I thought the theme of the story had extreme public interest, but I apologize for saying they were Muslim rather than Mormons. It just didn't seem that disconnected to me, you know, substituting one religion for another. Like, what's the difference?

"THROW ALL THE BUMS OUT!'

One of the handfuls of American commercial business geniuses of the 20th Century was Lee Iaococca who helped vault the Ford Motor Company to its acme with the introduction of the popular Ford Mustang in 1964, and then rescued Chrysler from the clutches of bankruptcy in the 1970's as its CEO. He was respected nationally as a scion *par excellence* by the American business community. At the turn of the century, he had seen so much of the success of the 20th century vanish due to the dereliction of government and effete elected officials that he expressed his frustration in an April 2008 book *Realjock.*

Always known for his straight-shooting language, here are some excerpts that vent his frustration circulated by email.

"Am I the only guy who's fed up with what's happening? Where the hell is our outrage? We should be screaming bloody murder. We've got a gang of clueless bozos steering our ship of state right over a cliff, we've got corporate gangsters stealing us blind, and we can't even clean up after a hurricane much less a hybrid car. But instead of getting mad, everyone sits around and nods their head when the politicians say, 'Stay the course.' Stay the course? You've got to be kidding. This is America, not the damned 'Titanic.' I'll give you a sound bite: 'Throw all the bums out!'

You might think I'm getting senile, that I've gone off my rocker, and maybe I have. But someone has to speak up. I hardly recognize this country anymore. The most famous business leaders are not the innovators but the guys in handcuffs. While we're fiddling in Iraq, the Middle East is burning and nobody knows what to do. And the press is waving 'pom-poms' instead of asking hard questions. That's not the promise of the 'America' my parents and yours traveled across the ocean for. I've had enough. How about you?

I'll go a step further. You can't call yourself a patriot if you're not outraged. This is a fight I'm ready and willing to have. The biggest 'C' is Crisis!

Leaders are made, not born. Leadership is forged in times of crisis. It's easy to sit there with your feet up on the desk and talk theory. Or send someone else's kids off to war when you haven't seen a battlefield yourself. It's another thing to lead when your world comes tumbling down.

On September 11, 2001, we needed a strong leader more than any time in our history. We needed a steady hand to guide us out of the ashes. A hell of a mess.

So here's where we stand. We're immersed in a blood war with no plan for winning and no plan for leaving. We're running the biggest deficit in the history of the country. We're losing the manufacturing edge to Asia, while our once-great companies are getting slaughtered by health care costs. Gas prices are skyrocketing, and nobody in power had a cogent energy policy. Our schools are in trouble. Our borders are like sieves. The middle class is being squeezed every which way. These are times that cry out for leadership.

But when you look around, you've got to ask, 'Where have all the leaders gone?' Where are the curious, creative communicators? Where are the people of character, courage, conviction, omnipotence, and common sense? I may be a sucker for alliteration, but I think you get the point.

Name me a leader who has a better idea for homeland security than making us take off our shoes in airports and throw away our shampoo? We've spent billions of dollars building a huge new bureaucracy, and all we know how to do is to react to things that have already happened.

Name me one leader who emerged from the crisis of Hurricane Katrina. Congress has yet to spend a day evaluating the response to the hurricane, or demanding accountability for the decisions that were made in the crucial hours after the storm.

Everyone's hunkering down, fingers crossed, hoping it doesn't happen again. Deal with it. Make a plan. Figure out what you're going to do the next time.

Name me an industrial leader who is thinking creatively about how we can restore our competitive edge in manufacturing. Who would have believed that there could ever be a time when 'The Big Three' referred to Japanese car companies? How did this happen, and more important, what are we going to do about it?

Name me a government leader who can articulate a plan for paying down the debit, or solving the energy crisis, or managing the health care problem. The silence is deafening. But these are the crises that are eating away at our country and milking the middle class dry.

I have news for the gang in Congress. We didn't elect you to sit on your asses and do nothing and remain silent while our economy is being hijacked and our greatness is being replaced with mediocrity. What is everybody so afraid of? That some bonehead on Fox News will call them a name? Give me a break. Why don't you guys show some spine for a change?

Had enough? Hey, I'm not trying to be the voice of gloom and doom here. I'm trying to light a fire. I'm speaking out because I have hope I believe in America. In my lifetime I've had the privilege of living through some of America's greatest moments. I've also experienced some of our worst crises: the 'Great Depression', 'World War II', the 'Korean War', the 'Kennedy Assassination', the 'Vietnam War', the 1970's oil crisis, and the struggles of recent years culminating with 9/11. If I've learned one thing, it's this: You don't get anywhere by standing on the sidelines waiting for somebody else to take action. Whether it's building a better car or building a better future for our children, we all have a role to play. That's the challenge I'm raising in this book. It's a call to 'Action' for people who, like me, believe in America. It's not too late, but it's getting pretty close. So let's shake off the crap and go to work. Let's tell 'em we've all had enough.'

Make a 'real contribution' by sending this to everyone you know and care about. Our future is at stake! My big question is – Why are they still in office? What this administration has been concentrating on is how to assist Big Business virtually steal the manufacturing sector and the middle class. Gas was $1.42 a gallon when Bush took office. I paid $3.53 a gallon this morning. How many $BILLION A QUARTER are the fuel companies making? How do they manage to maintain such enormous profit margins? Just one example of greed.

So, again I ask, WHY ARE THEY STILL IN OFFICE?"

RECONSTRUCTION

With Dr. James Watson and Francis Crick's monumental discovery of DNA (**d**eoxy**n**ucleaic **a**cid) in 1953, the double helix that would later be refined into defining identities of every living or dead life on earth, the whole concept of forensic classification took a quantum leap forward.

No field of science benefited more (or better) than law enforcement with the inauguration of *Criminal Science Investigation,* CSI, whose sophisticated laboratory staffs developed ways and means of solving previously intractable problems and mysteries that plagued investigators from time immemorial relative to the commitment of crime.

Singular among its benefits was the ability to take a physical sample of just about any substance on earth the size of a speck of sand and render a history of its origin, chemically as well as location found anywhere in the world. Applications of the results of DNA exploded when scientists began to announce significant advances monthly from countries whose names most people never knew existed - like Upper Mendoza, one of Finland's 176,000 islands in the Baltic Sea.

The singular achievement coming out of this community had to do with the analysis of the ingredients that produce urine and feces in all living species. Examining a sample of the waste product of rats literally revealed every single thing that the rat ingested to produce a bowel movement or urinary discharge.

CHILIHEADS

Those devotees of that singular American gruel called chili have taken challenges to perfect their own recipe so seriously that chili cook-offs have become commonplace across the country. Held in malls, clubs, parks, fields, and even large driveways, these contests to reward the best concoctions are held yearlong and celebrated in every state of the Union.

The author prides himself in being one of these champions in several chili cook-offs sponsored by local churches, American Legions, as well as an extended family who consider their own "Bowls of Red" to be *haute cuisine*, albeit made with or without beans.

The origin of chili dates back to the cattle drives of the mid-1800's where chuck wagons followed cowboys along their trails to feed these rough and tumble cowboys with a gruel that was cheap, tasty, and easily made. Originally called *margut,* it was a stew made from the worst cuts of meat left over after the prime sections of a cow had been consumed by the hungry men, cooked slowly and seasoned with whatever aromatic weeds or plants that grew nearby to add a modicum of flavor. Stray animals that ventured too close to the chuck wagon often found themselves part of the meal prepared for the hired help, and would render the chili variegated flavors from time to time. But, truth to tell, beans were not introduced to the soup until the 20th century, and then only after a howl of protests arose from the purists who eventually lost out to a chorus of anarchists that demanded such an additive.

In the age of the Internet, an early story was emailed to just about everybody about a chili cook-off taken place in Houston. A Rodeo had come to town, and a chili contest was held in the parking lot of the Astrodome. Certain comments were made by an east coast visitor who was pressed into service as a judge in the event when a third judge pleaded sickness for his absence.

The visitor's name was "Frank". This is an account of his tasting memoir that fateful day.

"Recently, I was honored to be selected as a judge at a chili cook-off. The original person had called in sick at the last moment, and I just happened to be standing at the judges' table asking directions to where the Budweiser truck was when the call came in.

I was assured by the other two judges (who turned out to be native Texans) that the chili wouldn't be all that spicy, and a further inducement was added that I could have all the free beer I wanted during the tasting. So, I accepted.

CHILI #1: Mike's Maniac Mobster Monster Chili

Judge #1: "A little too heavy on the tomato. Amusing kick."

Judge #2: "Nice, smooth, tomato flavor. Very Mild."

Judge #3 (me): "Holy shit! What the hell is this stuff? Took me two beers to put the flames out. I hope that's the worst one."

CHILI #2: Arthur's Afterburner Chili

Judge #1: "Smoky, with a hint of pork. Slight jalapena tang."

Judge #2: "Exciting BBQ flavor needs more pepper to be taken seriously."

Judge #3: "Keep this out of the reach of children. I'm not sure what I'm supposed to taste besides pain. I had to wave off two people who wanted to give me the Heimlich Maneuver. They had to rush in more beer when they saw the look on my face."

CHILI #3: Fred's Famous Burn Down the Barn Chili

Judge #1: "Excellent firehouse chili. Great kick! Needs more beans."

Judge #2: "A bean-less chili, a bit salty, good use of peppers."

Judge #3: "Call the EPA. I've located a uranium spill. My nose feels like I've been snorting Drano. Everyone knows the routine by now. Get me more beer before I ignite. Barmaid pounded me on the back. Now my backbone is in the front part of my chest. Plus, I'm getting shit-faced from all the beer."

CHILI #4: Bubba's Black Magic

Judge #1: "Black bean chili with almost no spice. Disappointing."

Judge #2: "Hint of lime in the black beans. Good side dish for fish or other mild foods."

Judge#3: "I felt something scraping across my tongue, but was unable to taste it. Is it possible to burn out taste buds? Sally, the barmaid, was standing behind me with fresh refills. That 300 lb. bitch is starting to look HOT – just like this nuclear waste I'm eating. Is chili an aphrodisiac?"

CHILI 35: Linda's Legal Lip Remover

Judge #1: "Meaty, strong chili. Cayenne peppers freshly ground, adding considerable kick. Very impressive."

Judge #2: "Chili using shredded beef; could use more tomato. Must admit, the cayenne peppers make a strong statement."

Judge #3: "My ears are ringing, sweat is pouring off my forehead, and I can no longer focus my eyes. I farted, and four people behind me needed paramedics. The contestant seemed offended when I told her that her chili had given me brain damage. Sally saved my tongue from bleeding by pouring beer directly on it from the pitcher. I wonder if I am burning my lips off. It really pisses me off that the other judges asked me to stop screaming. Screw those rednecks!"

CHILI #6: Vera's Very Vegetarian Variety

Judge #1: "Thin, yet bold vegetarian variety chili. Good balance of spices and peppers."

Judge #2: "The best yet. Aggressive use of peppers, onions, and garlic. Superb."

Judge #3: "My intestines are now a straight pipe filled with gaseous flames. I shit myself when I farted, and I'm worried it will eat through the chair. No one seems inclined to stand behind me anymore except that slut, Sally. She must be kinkier than I thought. Can't feel my lips anymore. I need to wipe my ass with a snow cone."

CHILI #7: Susan's Screaming Sensation Chili

Judge#1: "A mediocre chili with too much reliance on canned peppers."

Judge #2: "Ho hum. Tastes as if the chef literally threw in a can of chili peppers at the last moment. I should take note that I am worried about Judge #3. He appears to be in a bit of distress as he is cursing uncontrollably."

Judge #3: "You could put a grenade in my mouth, pull the pin, and I wouldn't feel a thing. I've lost sight in one eye, and the world sounds like it is made of rushing water. My shirt is covered with chili, which slides unnoticed out of my mouth. My pants are full of lava – like shit to match my shirt. At least during the autopsy, they'll know what killed me. I've decided to stop breathing, it's too painful. Screw it! I'm not getting any oxygen anyway. If I need air, I'll just suck it in through the 4-inch hole in my stomach."

CHILI #8: Tommy's Toe-Nail Curling Chili

Judge #1: "The perfect ending. This is a nice blend chili. Not too bold, but spicy enough to declare its existence."

Judge #2: "This final entry is a good balance chili. Neither mild nor hot. Sorry to see that most of it was lost when Judge #3 passed out, fell over, and pulled the chili pot down on top of himself. Not sure if he's going to make it. Poor bugger, I wonder how he'd have reacted to a really hot chili."

WHAT WILL THEY THINK OF NEXT!

Scientists at a Danish chemical plant have discovered a heretofore useless waste product that can be converted into plastics, soap, moisturizer, fertilizer, de-icer for roads and airplanes, and any number of things that will help the world in reducing its reliance on oil. It has been heralded as a "dream product" by groups dedicated to the greening of the globe.

This chemical, of which 90,000 tons is produced daily worldwide, is a gift to mankind from (don't hold your nose!) *pigs*. It is an ingredient that flows readily into pigpens in the form of urine. That's right. Pig pee, hog piss, the fluid that can be captured from pens as soon as it flows from the pig and directly into a filter system that removes the color, odor, and particulate matter in this golden fluid.

And, by the way, it also keeps pigpens clean and disease-free from the sludge formed by mixing with pig feces.

It seems that pig urine has the benefit of being a bulking agent in the production of the above-named riches, and much cheaper to extract than oil, the ingredient whose properties have been used for decades for manufacturing plastic for thousands of every day applications.

The first plant of its kind was built by Agroplast some twenty miles from Copenhagen. Plans to take advantage of America's vast pig farm residue are in the works for Iowa and North Carolina, home to some of the vast pork industry and the largest depository of this animal's sludge.

One visionary from Agroplast conceived the erection of high-rise pig pens in the future that would enhance the production process of pig pee on a massive scale.

Some concerned scientists have risen the potential hazard that disposing of such products, say in a landfill that could happen if the bio-products made from pig pee could end up being buried in earthen depositories. The downside of this potential is that the chemical, urine, would degrade into releasing greenhouse gas methane. Worse, there is no waste management companies in existence equipped to sort out regular plastics from bioplastics.

One of Agroplast's engineers predicted the possibilities that "pig cities" could arise, what with the price of farmland and gas at a premium, and skyscrapers would house pigs in a self-contained processing plant that could convert their waste onsite into plastic and fertilizer.

Stay tuned.

SALIENT TRIVIA

SALIENT FACTS OF LITTLE IMPORTANCE

More money is printed every day for the game Monopoly than is printed by the U.S. Treasury.

Men can read smaller print than women can. However, women can hear better than men.

When Coca-Cola was introduced, its color was green.

It is impossible to lick your elbow.

Alaska has the highest percentage of people who walk to work.

Don't think for a second that "Pizza" is a Johnny-come-lately popular choice of the masses. According to National Geographic, Pizza was first mentioned in a manuscript from the southern Italian town of Gaeta in 997 AD. This food icon was the center of contention between two Italian towns as to the ingredients to properly prepare this tasty pie.

The percentage of Africa that is wilderness is 28%. In North America, the percentage of wilderness is 38%.

The average cost to raise a medium-sized dog to the age of eleven is $16,400.

In any given hour in the United States, the average number of people airborne is 61,000.

Science has determined that intelligent people have the most zinc and copper in their hair.

The only mobile National Monuments in the United States are San Francisco's cable cars.

In a deck of cards, the four kings represent great historical figures: for Spades, it is King David; for Hearts, it is Charlemagne; for Clubs, it is Alexander the Great; for Diamonds, it is Julius Caesar.

Statues in parks of military figures on horses have certain significance depending on how many of the horse's hoofs are on the ground. With all four on the ground, the figure died of natural causes. With one front leg lifted, the figure died in a particular battle. With two front legs lifted, the figure died later from wounds in a particular battle. With three legs lifted, the figure died on his horse.

Half of all Americans live within fifty miles of their birthplace.

The most favorite name requested for a boat is "Obsession."

Bulletproof vests, fire escapes, windshield wipers and laser printers all have common inventors: they were *women.*

The only food that doesn't spoil is honey.

Pub frequenters in ancient England were served their favorite beverages in ceramic cups that had whistles molded into their handles. When a refill was needed, all one had to do was use the whistle for service. Thus was born the phrase 'Wet Your Whistle' to summon service at the bar.

Certain behavior of people living in 2008 (and beyond) is significant when they:

Accidentally enter their PIN number on a microwave.

Haven't played Solitaire with real cards in years.

Have a list of 15 phone numbers to reach a family of three.

Email the person who works at the desk next to them.

The only reason for not staying in touch with friends and family is their lack of email addresses.

Using a cell phone from the driveway to see if anyone can help you carry the groceries into the house.

Leaving the house without your cell phone is reason to panic, and you turn around and go back to get it (keeping in mind that the first 20, 30 or 40 years of your life they didn't exist.)

Get up in the morning and go on-line before getting a cup of coffee.

ODE TO THE DIMPLED WHITE BALL

In my hand I hold a ball
white and dimpled, rather small.
Oh how bland it does appear,

this harmless-looking little sphere.
By its size I could not guess
the awesome strength it does possess.
But since I fell beneath its spell
I've wandered through the fires of hell.
My life has not been quite the same
since I chose to play this stupid game.
It rules my mind for hours on end,
a fortune it has made me spend.
It has made me swear and yell and cry
I hate myself and want to die.
It promises a thing called par
if I can hit straight and far.
To master such a tiny ball
should not be very hard at all.
But my desires the ball refuses
and does exactly as it chooses.
It hooks and slices, dribbles and dies
and even disappears before my eyes.
Often it will take a whim
to hit a tree or take a swim.
With miles of grass on which to land
it finds a tiny patch of sand
then has me offering up my soul
if only it would find the hole.
It's made me whimper like a pup
and swear that I will give it up
and take a drink to ease my sorrow,
but the ball knows . . . I'll be back tomorrow.

LITTLE KNOWN FACTS

Since recorded history began, around 3200 B.C.,
with the invention of writing in the Middle East, there

has been some 200 human generations (calculating one generation being 25 years) that have elapsed from then until the year 2000 A.D.

Forty-five hundred generations separate the time span from the earliest *Homo Sapiens* to the earliest evidence of human cave artists, living between 37,000 and 11,000 years ago, discovered in southern France and northern Spain. And another 1500 generations passed from these early cave artists and us today.

It was during this time span that generations of man learned to walk upright, mastered speech and the use of tools, reached puberty, reproduced and died.

Sport fans that have a fetish to own items that are integral to playing popular professional games, (i.e., footballs, baseballs, hockey pucks, basketballs, soccer balls, etc.) will be disappointed to learn that any baseball that they purchase, thinking it is the same kind used by the big leagues, isn't.

Baseballs used by the major leagues undergo a physical transformation before being allowed to be used in games in the United States: *they all are given a special rubdown mud bath prior to being used in competition.* Not just any old mud, but a special feldspar rich clay from a secret swamp location in New Jersey known only to its discoverer, a former player and baseball coach, R. A. "Lena" Blackburne. Extracted from two top secret holes by Blackburne, and processed to filter out debris, the brown mud is given a special additive that allows the pitcher to get a better grip on the ball.

Introduced to baseball in 1938, the product, *Lena Blackburne Baseball Rubbing Mud,* has been helping pitchers control their throws, and reduced the chances of an untimely wild pitch. Overnight this special tactile mud became a big-league staple, with the Baseball Hall of Fame acknowledging the sticky paste in 1968.

The Blackburne Company collects its swamp mud with six harvests a year. After "aging" it for six weeks, it is parceled in two three-pound vats that are sent to each team. Batboy duties on the teams include a vigorous rubbing massage of all baseballs to be used in a game shortly before the umpire yells, "Play ball!"

Unknown to baseball fans is whether Ernest Thayer, the author of the poem *Casey at the Bat* in 1888, was prescient of this future special rubbing compound when mentioning it in his fictional saga describing the "Joy in Mudville."

MEN FOR ALL AGES

Nelson Mandela and Bishop Desmond Tutu, both from Africa, are luminaries that have emerged in a world where political and religious conflicts have wrought death, suffering, and starvation on the masses.

These two men of immense wisdom were both victims of extreme racism and political attempts to break their spirit, but to no avail. They stood steadfast in their inborn sense of justice, mercy, and forgiveness - God-like qualities bestowed on certain men with the capacity to inspire others.

PALLBEARERS

On a July day in 1971, the following group of honorary pallbearers assembled at Flushing Cemetery in New York to mourn the passing of a Great American Original.

Governor Nelson Rockefeller, Mayor John Lindsay, Bing Crosby, Ella Fitzgerald, Guy Lombardo, Duke Ellington, Dizzy Gillespie, Pearl Bailey, Count Basie, Harry James, Frank Sinatra, Ed Sullivan, Earl Wilson, Alan King, Johnny Carson, David Frost, Merv Griffin, Dick Cavett and Bobby Hackett.

That Great American Original was Louis "Satchmo" Armstrong.

STUDS

There are many images that the mind connects with the city of Chicago, but none more compelling of the man whose life was spent writing and recording the lives and images of the city's people through interviews who were induced by him to bare their souls with unexpected stories that poured forth when asked his famous follow-up question, "And then what happened?"

His name was Louis "Studs" Terkel (1912-2008), historian, actor, broadcaster and attorney. Born in New York City, his father, Samuel Terkel, moved the family to Chicago when the boy was eight, making a living by operating a rooming house, renting out rooms to a mélange of people of various backgrounds.

After getting his 1934 law degree from the University of Chicago, the young Terkel told his friends that instead of practicing law, he'd rather be a concierge in a hotel that was a collecting point for an assortment of human characters. His interest was so intense of being part of this mainstream of people; he joined a theatre group that ultimately led to his foray into other communication jobs he pursued along the way.

How he got the moniker "Studs" happened when a theater director had to distinguish him from another actor named Louis. Since Terkel was reading an acting part of "Studs Lonigan" at the time, a rough-and-ready-for-anything character from the novelist James Farrell. It was a serendipitous nickname that stuck. That Louis "Studs" Terkel was physically a short man void of any visible muscular physique, his new adopted first name often gave reactions of bemusement from those he interviewed.

During the Depression of the 1930's, Terkel joined the *Works Progress Administration Federal Writers' Project* doing work in radio that ranged from acting, voicing soap opera productions, announcing news and sports, recorded music shows, advertisements, and writing radio scripts. In 1952 he began a radio program, *The Studs Terkel Program,* airing on Chicago's WFMT. His one-hour daily program of interviews ran for forty-five years until 1997. His specialty was listening to stories from a wide spectrum of American people that included Okies, homeless street people, down-and-out, prison inmates, immigrants, the wealthy, and celebrities that would drop by.

Terkel's 1974 book, *"Working"* was subtitled *"People Talk About What They Do All Day and How They Feel About What They Do."* As an author of blockbuster oral histories of the Depression, World War II, Terkel criss-crossed the country tape recording chats with an amalgam of diverse people. He was interested in their dreams, why they chewed gum, what they thought about racism, their fears, dirty floors, and even The Beatles.

He had a knack of putting people at ease, oftentimes interrupting them when they mentioned something of substance that he thought listeners would like to hear. And if he thought the person was holding back on a fascinating story, he'd then utter his signature question, ". . . And then what happened?" which would invariably lead to the meat of the tale, bursting a dam of fascinating minutiae withheld by his subject believing it to be of no interest to anybody.

151

Once setting his subjects at ease, Studs Terkel would wangle his way into their confidence by encouraging their memories about everyday truths and predictions, adopting an avuncular style that produced a flood of admissions from famous jazz vocalists, insecure housewives, Ku Klux Klan leaders, Marlene Dietrich, Bob Dylan, Dr. Martin Luther King, Jr., Bertrand Russell, parking lot attendant, a lesbian grandmother, a piano tuner, and a barber. He was a master listener with an easy rapport with just about everyone.

Transcribing the interviews into books, he received a lion's share of major awards and honorary degrees as the books always ended up on the best-sellers list. Terkel was the recipient of laudatory praise as the most extraordinary social observer this country ever produced.

CBS newsman Charles (On the Road) Kuralt maintained, "When Studs Terkel listens, everybody talks."

Terkel's fascination with chit chat began as a youth, talking to blue-collar workers who stayed at his father's rooming house, got drunk on Saturday night, and would talk to the kid for hours on end. He liked to speak to people he thought interesting. Never hiding his liberal politics, he sought to reach across the lines of political thought, race, class, education and geography, sampling diverse people opinions from society patricians and the *hoi polloi* struggling to survive economic hardships.

In 1949, already accepted as a Chicago institution, Terkel expanded into television with "Stud's Place", and informal unscripted show of banter and jazz, set in a bar scene akin to the later TV show "Cheers." It developed a devoted audience on radio and TV, running from 1949 to 1953 when it abruptly closed when Senator Joseph McCarthy's crusade for communists lurking in show business managed to name Terkel among his roster of black-listed writers. Accusations against him ranged from having a liberal bias, supporting causes like rent control, desegregation, abolishment of the poll tax, and laws that discriminated against the poor.

Terkell spent the 1950's and '60's continuing his broadcasts, acting in theaters, and penning his own scripts. In 1967 he developed his keen sense for interviewing, beginning a career of blending journalism, history, sociology and literature. For the next 35 years, Studs Terkel took the verbal temperature and comments of America's common folk, wanting his readers to feel what it was like to be a laid-off factory worker during the Depression, a soldier facing his first enemy fire, a black businessman, poor Latino – and even Miss America.

Terkel's longtime editor, Andre Schiffrin confessed that people would tell the writer truths that they had lied to themselves for their whole lives. They had so much respect for him, knew they weren't being used by him, or use them to make a point. They realized that he really wanted to hear what they had to say. And he *respected* them.

Studs Terkel maintained, "We don't remember anything. There's no yesterday in this country. I want to re-create those yesterdays."

The Chicago writer was famous for his red and white checkered shirt and red socks. Later in life he would entertain visitors to his home with monologues composed of a variety of allusions. Long rants against President Bush would be mingled with Shakesperian quotes, thoughts about Henry Kissinger, and suddenly details of the 1920 Teapot Dome scandal.

Louis Studs Terkel planned for his death years before he passed away in 2008. He requested readings from Mark Twain, George Bernard Shaw, music from Schubert and Mississippi bluesman Big Bill Broonzy. His ashes were to be scattered in a Chicago square where he used to pitch his leftist views on a soapbox.

And, he wanted his epitaph to read, "Curiosity did not kill this cat!"

POTPOURRI

Few scientists will disagree that the discovery of DNA (DioxiNucleaic Acid) and its double helix by Francis Crick and James Watson in 1953 was the most spectacular event of the 20th Century. The wonders that have subsequently been born in science from that event have ranged from saving lives of the wrongfully criminally convicted to forensically determining relationships, and as of 2008, how the earth was originally peopled since man had the wunderlust to scatter to all parts of the world.

Previously accepted theories of how people reached North America have been blown away thanks to more sophisticated methods of DNA testing that can assemble a chemical path of bits and pieces of human remains that clearly debunk previous theories of where and when man arrived in North and South America.

The curious ingredient that has been the most productive element in deciphering the movement of man's trail has come from, of all things, the calcified remains of what he left behind: his poop. DNA analysis of discovered excrement by archeologists in site excavations as remote as deeply buried sites in caves have produced the most accurate evidence of where different races and tribes came from and when they came.

By assembling and comparing similar DNA samples derived from human *scat* from all parts of the world, a picture has congealed evidence that North and South America were settled by seafaring tribes that traveled the length and breadth of the continent's Pacific coastline in boats instead of the heretofore accepted theory that humans arrived in different parts of the continent by traveling over northern land masses that had provided passage during shifts of weather conditions (ice ages) and proximity of peninsular islands to the Asian continent.

And all of this knowledge was derived from the poop left behind by those wandering souls searching for a better life. Truth to tell, it does not render a very prosaic history of how man populated the more remote parts of the world.

RATTED OUT

Rats have accounted for spreading plague around the world for thousands of years. Actually, they have been the hosts to a vermin that feasts on them that have caused outbreaks of massive deaths in the 14th century when a quarter of the earth's population were wiped out by "the black death" spread by rats carried to foreign cities and ports by ships plying their trade.

Few pests are more despised than the common rat, a rodent that has become the target of massive attempts at eradication. Until scientists discovered an unusual talent that all rats embody, a highly developed sense of smell, did entrepreneurs realize how easily these critters could be trained to help mankind sniff out diseases and dangerous chemicals from objects designed to cause human casualties.

From samples of human tissue, blood and sputum, rats can identify diseases such as cancer, tuberculosis, diabetes, and other such ailments, often before any medical diagnosis is made by healthcare professionals.

In countries that have been laced by land mines, rats can detect their distinctive chemicals and locate them for disposal without triggering an explosion because of their light body weight in ferreting out the deadly weapons left on battlefields in the wake of wars.

Rats are being trained to locate victims of earthquakes, their small size allowing them to enter the cracks and crannies of debris that prevent access of other rescue animals to find life (or death) among the ruins.

The ease of breeding rats and the inexpensive maintenance of producing them is a bonus to companies who have discovered the benefits they can render mankind.

Perhaps knowing this will make people cringe less when they are suddenly faced with a pest whose evolution rivals that of humans.

UNKNOWNS

Why are there so many religions on earth?

Why are some people born with both male and female sex organs?

How can something smell so wonderful and taste so terrible?

How can some foods taste so wonderful and smell so terrible?

Why are 10% of people born left-handed?

Why do some people have six fingers and six toes?

Why are some people born albinos?

What makes people steal?

What makes people living in tropical weather aggressive?

Why do some people believe in God, don't believe in God, or aren't sure if there is a God?

Does the choice of food one eats influence one's behavior?

How do savages know right from wrong?

Is it right to bring children into the world without the means to feed or educate them?

How come only humans can laugh?

WHAT'S IN A NAME?

A certain segment of class-conscious home owners are obsessed with having an address that denotes their affinity to reside in an area of the affluent, the upper crust, or the patrician society of the famous. American towns such as Podunk, Peoria, or Shantytown would be anathema as a potential residence to them regardless of the regal mansions they could buy or build there. Pompous pride prevails overall when choosing a home site that will be revealed to their peers on envelopes, business cards, letterheads, and on legal papers visible to anybody viewing printed references to them and their abode(s.)

Except in England.

The English countryside with quaint names of towns and oddball street designations that are centuries old are immune to change because of history, tradition, and the pride of the English people to acknowledge any connotation relative to the images of their names suggestive of body parts, sexuality, or low-life language.

Take the village of Penistown, for example. Locals refer to it as *"Penniston,"* and ignore any outsider chuckling at their evasion of the normal evocative pronunciation of their town.

Then there is *Crapstone,* a one-store village in Devon whose residents have suffered for decades from people who can't contain their laughter pronouncing it.

The English have dozens of towns with names that evoke humor (or should it be humour) such as *Ugley, East Breast, North Piddle*, and *Spanker Lane.*

One can only imagine what kind of a response locals get when, applying for a job when their applications reveal they live in *Crotch Crescent, Wetwang, Slutshole Lane, Thong*, and *Pratts Bottom* (pratt being a local euphemism for a *jerk*.)

A District Council in East Sussex tried to address the problem of changing the names of roads with lewd-sounding words like *Gasworks Road, Quare Street, Hoare Road, Typple Avenue, Tumbledown Dick Road,* and *Butt Hole Road*, but were met with the problem that these names had been used for centuries and did not reflect the contemporary connotation to which they evolved.

A doctor who moved from a village called *Horrabridge* to *Crapstone* was resigned to the sniggering that both of these towns evoked from outsiders. The East Sussex District Council did manage to negate the naming of any future streets and roads in their community from having any suggestive relationship to off-color words, acts, or socially offensive expressions.

One particular incident that galvanized the Council to adopt their ban on embarrassing street names was a gag photo a tourist took of a guy who had dropped his pants to moon the viewer in front of the street sign *Butt Hole Road.*

Unmentioned here were names of communities so obscene and foul that, as unprintable as they are now, were not rude or salacious centuries ago before double-entendre in language changed their perception.

39 THINGS YOU SHOULD HAVE LEARNED BY NOW

1. Never, under any circumstances, take a sleeping pill and a laxative on the same night.

2. Don't worry about what people think; they don't do it very often.

3. Going to church doesn't make you a Christian anymore than standing in a garage makes you a car.

4. Artificial intelligence is no match for natural stupidity.

5. If you must choose between two evils, pick the one you've never tried before.

6. My idea of housework is to sweep the room with a glance.

7. Not one shred of evidence supports the notion that life is serious.

8. It's easier to get forgiveness than permission.

9. For every action, there is an equal and opposite government program.

10. If you look like your passport picture, you probably need the trip.

11. Bills travel through the mail at twice the speed of checks.

12. A conscience is what hurts when all of your other parts feel so good.

13. Eat well, stay fit, die anyway.

14. Men are from earth. Women are from earth. Deal with it.

15. No man has ever been shot doing the dishes.

16. A balanced diet is a biscuit in each hand.

17. Middle age is when broadness of the mind and narrowness of the waist change places.

18. Opportunities always look bigger going than coming.

19. Junk is something you've kept for years and throw away three weeks before you need it.

20. There is always one more imbecile than you counted on.

21. Experience is a wonderful thing. It enables you to recognize a mistake when you make it again.

22. By the time you can make ends meet, they move the ends.

23. Thou shall not weigh more than thy fridge.

24. Someone who thinks logically provides a nice contrast to the real world.

25. It's not the jean that makes your ass look fat.

26. If you had to identify, in one word, the reason why the human race has not achieved, and never will achieve, its full potential, that word would be "meetings."

27. There is a very fine line between "hobby" and "mental illness."

28. People who want to share their religious views with you almost never want to share yours with them.

29. You should not confuse your career with your life.

30. Nobody cares if you can't dance well. Just get up and dance.

31. Never lick a steak knife.

32. The most destructive force in the universe is gossip.

33. You will never find anybody who can give you a clear and compelling reason why we put our clocks back.

34. You should never say anything to a woman that even remotely suggests that you think she's pregnant unless you can see a baby emerging from her at the moment.

35. There comes a time when you should stop expecting other people to make a big deal of your birthday. That time is age eleven.

36. The one thing that unites all human beings, regardless of age, gender, religion, economic status, or ethnic background, is that, deep down inside, we all believe we are above-average drivers.

37. A person, who is nice to you, but rude to the waiter, is not a nice person.

38. Your friends love you anyway.

39. Never be afraid to try something new. Remember that a lone amateur built the ark. A large group of professionals built the Titanic!

DISTRACTIONS

Just when you think you've heard or read about the most apocryphal story or tale beyond belief, a 2011 newspaper article out of Florida recounts a police docudrama involving a pert young female, driving her Thunderbird, that crashed into a pickup truck at 45mph while driving the long, strait, and scenic stretch of highway connecting Florida en route to Key West.

It seems the young lady was distracted while driving, and grooming a southern part of her bikini often referred to in polite circles as a *hoohah*. What captured her attention was shaving unwanted pubic hair in anticipation of a tryst with a waiting paramour when she arrived. The paraphernalia she was using in such a delicate area demanded her full attention to detail. Not that she didn't have her focus of attention on the road – she had her ex-husband (that's right) in the passenger seat taking over the task of steering the T-Bird. Somehow, I guess, her ex might have taken his eyes off the road to watch her vaginal ablutions proceeding when, yes – all of a sudden- the crunching sound of metal on metal distracted the couples' attention to the rear-ending of the sport vehicle kissing the rear-end of a pickup truck.

Before Florida's Highway Patrol arrived, the quick thinking ex-husband changed places with the young-lady-in-waiting to mitigate whatever charges might be forthcoming.

Police noticed that the man behind the wheel had bruises from an air bag that had deployed following the crash. What seemed strange to them was the observation that only the passenger side of the car's air bags had deployed, and the driver's side hadn't.

It didn't take the officers long to deduce that something here was awry – that things were not the way they seemed, and the physical conditions of the T-Bird's two occupants indicated some kind of body ritual probably caused the accident.

The Highway Patrolman accident report listed the activity in almost sanitary terms (as best they could.)

When investigating Megan Barnes, the person assigned the blame in the collision (and her former husband as an accessory after the fact), a past history of her young life included:

- She had no valid driver's license.
- The day before she had been convicted of a DUI and driving with a suspended driver's license.
- Her car had been seized and had no insurance or registration.
- She was also presently on probation.
- Her behavior was described as "a flippin' lunatic", albeit well-groomed.

Author's note: I could only wish that the television "COPS" drama had included this episode in its Saturday night features, a special treat for the show's multitude of viewers.

Oh well, hope springs eternal.

BUREAUCRACY AT ITS BEST

Bureaucracy is dumb anywhere, but a recent example donated by a New Orleans lawyer, helping a client to obtain a FHA loan and using a parcel of land there as collateral, resulted in the epitome of bureaucratic wrangling.

In requesting the loan, the FHA responded that it would be granted as long as the borrower submitted satisfactory Title to the parcel of land being used as collateral for the loan.

In New Orleans, residents are often faced with the task of tracing home titles that go back hundreds of years. And with a community rich with history going back some two hundred years, homes have been passed along through generations of families, making the search required by the FHA loan officer a formidable task indeed.

The lawyer, however, was steadfast in doing his best to trace the title back to 1803, a date that took him three months to determine actual evidence of a title to the property being offered as collateral for the loan.

After sending the information to the FHA, he received the following reply:

"Upon review of your letter adjoining your client's application, we note that the request is supported by an Abstract of Title. While we compliment the able manner in which you have prepared and presented the application, we must point out that you have only cleared title to the proposed collateral property back to 1803. Before final approval can be accorded, it will be necessary to clear the title back to its origin."

Annoyed by the government's response to his efforts to even trace the title back to 1803, the attorney sent the following letter to the FHA agent handling the loan application:

"Your letter regarding title in Case No. 189156 has been received. I note that you wish to have title extended further than the 194 years covered by the present application. I was unaware that any educated person in this country, particularly those working in the property area, would not know that Louisiana was purchased, by the U.S., from France in 1803, the year of origin identified in our application.

For the edification of uninformed FHA bureaucrats, the title to the land prior to U. S. ownership was obtained from France, which had acquired it by Right of Conquest from Spain.

The land came into the possession of Spain by Right of Discovery made in the year 1492 by a sea captain named Christopher Columbus, who had been granted the privilege of seeking a new route to India by the Spanish monarch, Isabella.

The good queen, Isabella, being a pious woman and almost as careful about titles as the FHA, took the precaution of securing the blessing of the Pope before she sold her jewels to finance Columbus' expedition.

Now the Pope, as I'm sure you may know, is the emissary of Jesus Christ, the Son of God, and God, it is commonly accepted, created this world.

Therefore, I believe it is safe to presume that God also made that part of the world called Louisiana. God, therefore, would be the owner of origin.

I hope you find God's original claim to be satisfactory. Now, may we have our damn loan?"

The loan was approved.

ORIENTATIONS

Only until the last half of the 20th Century did the world come to grips that there was more than one sexual orientation: heterosexuality. Anything other than that was considered a mental deficiency, many of which were considered incurable albeit myriad attempts to render such people "normal" included treatments that included inhuman palliatives known today as torture or even witchcraft.

Aiding and abetting the medical community and witch doctors were world religions that condemned people who didn't conform to the only acceptable sexual orientation that religions would tolerate: heterosexuality.

Among the human deficiencies that surfaced early was *homosexuality* even though history had indicated that this malady was thousands of years old and didn't pose a contagious threat to mankind. It was also a human condition that didn't respond to whatever curatives were tried by societies around the world to "normalize" those stricken with this disease. It simply became one of those infirmities whose cure was left to future generations to solve.

In the last half of the 20th Century more physical conditions began to gain prominence in the medical community akin to homosexuality, words and descriptions that included gay, lesbianism, bi-sexuality, trans-gendered, trans-sexual, asexual, and other mental conditions yet unnamed (or discovered.)

It was confounding that so many of these other sexual deviations had gained in numbers never before encountered by organizations that surfaced to poll different types of people. The polls didn't bother to include any reference to the numbers they calculated to indicate the probability of their being "diseased" or somehow medically deficient.

In 1973, the American Society of Psychiatry made the astounding admission that none of the above-named mental deficiencies had been deficiencies after all. Suddenly, this admission of multiple sexual orientations confounded mankind around the world, especially when mass demonstrations by these very same former-mental patients began protest marches, began boycotts, hired lobbyists, and, *sare bleu*, even ran for political office.

Polls were now regularly taken to find the numbers of such odd-ball orientations that were slowly increasing in numbers. It took decades to divine that younger and younger people began indicating that their sexual orientation included one (or some) of the above-named former maladies.

It was just a matter of time until a few churches began to consider that some of their fellow parishioners came from this sexual minority, and that changes would have to be made to retain their flocks. This transition spawned a movement that polarized many religions whose creeds were adamantly opposed to the acceptance of alternate sexuality from what mainstream had embraced for thousands of years.

Splinter groups from major creeds began to form over the question of whether to accept alternative sexual orientations among their followers. A crack in the door of sexual determination had become a full-blown *cause celebre*, especially when more and more prominent people either declared themselves sympathetic to this minority, or even admitted being part of it.

As the more educated countries of the world began to accept and assimilate the notion of multiple sexual orientations, the less educated retreated to a fortress of solidarity based on a religion(s) inability to accept any changes in its original concept and rationale to even exist. It was tantamount to admit that change was an outward admission of guilt, a situation intolerable to those grown accustomed to infallibility.

As the 21st Century emerged from decades of turmoil that changed sexual orientation from being radically singular to acceptance that reality revealed it to be plural was a benchmark in history. Only the hope that education of the masses would eventually convince the world that humanity includes everyone, despite genetic differences, would there finally be a consensus of unity void of the divisive element of sustained ignorance.

PENDING RELEASE FROM HELL

As my release date from Hell approaches (I am in my seventh living decade of punishment for deeds I did, *or did not do,* in past lives), it behooves me to speak out to all those fellow unfortunates who had no choice of being born while their parents were denizens of this state-of-being uncommonly described in religious circles around the globe as "HELL."

Even though occupants of Hell dreamed up their concept of what constitutes *Hell* thousands of years ago (perhaps millions of years ago since human beings as we know ourselves are supposed to have emerged in present form on this planet called *Earth* some fifty million years ago), the social nature of these people realized early on that there they could accomplish more if they functioned as a group rather than singly trying to scrounge out a life by oneself.

Of course, trying to keep a group together requires some unity of purpose, i.e., searching for food, shelter, clothing (if necessary), and finding the ways and means of fending off the daily rigors posed by being in Hell. It didn't take long for the condemned to figure out there had to be some kind of rules-of-the-road to keep these people from wiping out those in their group that they didn't like.

Some groups found it intolerable to accept the rules and regulations of others, and splintered off into tight-knit societies with their own version of mandates and behavior, many of which clashed with each other's basic premise for creating such an offbeat group. What differentiated many of these splinter groups from each other were the creeds required by them for membership in their specific society. Over the millenniums they became known as religions, embracing some of the most bizarre concepts ever introduced to human thought. By forbidding those interested in joining their religions from examining the history or background of how they came to be, and as difficult as it is to understand the rationale of it, these groups began to flourish, many to the point of forming armies bound and determined to convert skeptics, by force, if necessary, to join their organizations, even to the point of exterminating them if they didn't. At this point, wars broke out between and among the ever-increasing numbers of new religions that appeared in all areas of the globe.

By the 21st Century, religions numbered in the tens of thousands, with no end in sight. Concomitant with this flood of new religions was an almost universal tenet by them in embracing an indefinable state-of-being of something called *"Heaven"* and *"Hell,"* terms used to describe the afterlife of those who passed on via death. Some of the most dreaded consequences imaginable were used to define what they thought *Hell* was like was offset by the more exhilarating rewards awaited those headed for *Heaven.*

The logic behind the existence of Heaven/Hell, however, had nothing tangible to sustain proof positive of either to people who had doubts about anything that couldn't be seen, tasted, smelled, or touched. This was dismissed by religion hierarchies who told their followers, "You have to have faith!"

The sheer volume and variety of tenets that some religions required their followers to believe exceeded the bounds of logic in most cases, but self-appointed clerics used their personal charm, clerical apparel, and vociferous elocution to attract those with little or no education, let alone interest, in researching the basic foundation of the religion they chose to embrace.

Inconceivable as it seems, these basic religious mandates were dismissed as irrelevant by those who chose to join a congregation more for the social and political acceptance and activities than for the historical reality of how the religion came into being.

Curiously absent by most people was any interest as to why there were so many religions in the world. Having inherited a parent's creed seemed to override any indication to investigate why they made that their choice, which was probably the same way it was passed down to the parents.

What this author found incredible was the research that was so easily in evidence for those whose descriptions of Hell consisted of other-worldly scenarios, born of imaginations only sustained by comparable events on Earth that they were familiar with.

In that sense, it's hard to argue that Hell is nothing less than a chronic state of dire discomfort (using human physiological terms), or worse.

A cursory example of such discomforts would easily include:

Marrying the "wicked witch from the west."
Being allergic to ice cream, booze, and pizza.
Having to work at a job you hate, let alone having to work.

Needing to buy toilet paper the rest of your life.

Being nice to a neighbor you despise.

Driving a lemon.

Susceptible to outbursts of flu, nausea, rashes, or debilitating disease.

Skin color not of your choice.

Born with a sexual orientation not of your choice, anathema to others, and not being able to do anything about it.

Spending time in jail for act(s) you didn't commit.

Never having enough to eat.

Living in an area and fearing for your life every day.

Chronically unable to hold down a job.

Born with congenital deformities.

After ruminating on these discomforts of life, weighing what they have done to create misery and despair in trying to survive, say, like, in what Hell is described by religions, it wouldn't be difficult to arrive at the epiphany that you're in Hell and don't even know it. The only release from this state of being is, guess what?

OFF THE WALL

We all know those cute little computer symbols called 'emoticons' where

:) means a smile
:(means a frown

Sometimes these are represented by:

:~) smile
:~(frown

Well, let me introduce you to "ASSICONS"

(_!_) A REGULAR ASS
(__!__) A FAT ASS
(!) A TIGHT ASS
(_*_) A SORE ASS
{_!_} A SWISHY ASS
(_o_) AN ASS THAT'S BEEN AROUND
(_x_) KISS MY ASS
(_X_) LEAVE MY ASS ALONE
(_zzz_) A TIRED ASS
(_e=mc²_) A SMART ASS
(_$_) MONEY COMING OUT OF HIS ASS
(_?_) DUMB ASS

If you just read this, consider yourself **MOONED!**

THINGS TO TELL YOUR GRANDCHILDREN

Just to show you what a difference life was like 100 years ago in America, consider these statistics:

In 1908, the average life expectancy was 47 years.

Only 14% of homes had a bathtub.

Only 8% of homes had a telephone.

There were only 8,000 cars, and only 144 miles of paved roads.

The speed limit in most cities was 8 mph.

The tallest structure in the world was the Eiffel Tower.

The average wage was 22¢ an hour.

The average worker made between $200 and $400 a year.

More than 95% of births occurred at home.

90% of all doctors had no college education. Instead, they attended so-called medical schools, many of which were condemned in the press and the government considered them substandard.

Sugar cost 4¢ a pound.

Eggs were 14¢ a dozen.

Coffee was 15¢ a pound.

Most women only washed their hair once a month, using Borax or egg yolks for shampoo.

Canada passed a law prohibiting poor people from entering its country.

The five leading causes of death were:
1. Pneumonia and influenza
2. Tuberculosis
3. Diarrhea
4. Heart disease
5. Stroke

The American flag had 45 stars.

The population of Las Vegas, Nevada was 30.

Two out of ten adults could not read or write.

Only 6% of all Americans graduated from high school.

Marijuana, heroine, and morphine were available over-the-counter at drug stores. (Pharmacists maintained that heroine clears the complexion, gives buoyancy to the mind, regulates the stomach and bowels, and is, in fact, a perfect guardian of health.)

There were about 230 murders in the entire country.

CHIVAREES EXPOSED

An early North American tradition was a mock-serenade celebrated on newly-wed nights by friends, family, and well-wishers bound and determined to interrupt any attempt at consummation of the married couple in their anxiety to, well, couple. The party was typically held on the newly-weds' lawn at dusk where this army of well-wishers would announce their presence by banging on pots and pans, raising a sonorous clatter of shouts and advice, throwing various things at windows to get the attention of the bride and groom before they celebrated the pleasures of the marriage bed.

Tradition then demanded that the couple invite everybody inside the house for a soiree with the understanding that the crowd would all leave at a pre-arranged time, and let the socially-exhausted pair to fall into each other's arms and attempt to make the best of lovemaking in that impaired physical state.

Minnesota was a particularly fond state of continuing these chivarees much to the dismal anticipation of the bride more than to the groom. Somewhere along the way, another variation crept into the routine of celebration that frustrated brides no end. The buddies of the groom dreamed up a kidnapping exercise of seizing him moments after departing the church and spiriting him away to a pre-arranged undisclosed location for a fortnight of activities akin to a post-bachelor party for an agenda left up to the imagination of the kidnappers.

Try as they may, many brides' attempt to interrupt this damnable social custom went down in flames. Truth to tell, most grooms looked forward to their two-week honeymoon away from their intended. It was a last foray of fun and games before life would suddenly become serious, and buddies would be replaced by a single person, a woman, and all past cherished activities would become just a memory. It was the end of childhood, adolescence, and a sobering introduction hallmark of life to come.

It was this author's searching the history of his parent's marriage that occasioned a curious account of their *chivaree,* an event that his mother went to extreme measures to defeat.

Living in Rochester, Minnesota, she made secret arrangements to drive 100 miles into Wisconsin to be married at a country church at six o'clock in the morning, fending off any opportunity of anybody pulling off this variation of a *chivaree* after her nuptials.

Alas, her well-made plans failed when her Bridesmaid revealed her deception to her husband who just happened to be the groom's Best Man.

Guess what?

RECYCLED BEVERAGE

In May, 2009, the Hubble Telescope was visited by seven astronauts to service and update the telescope in its heavenly search of the Universe for at least another half-dozen years.

Having finished their task and awaiting return to earth, a celebration was held on board the space shuttle. It consisted of three of the astronauts holding up plastic bags of a substance they were toasting and drinking, a photo of it appearing in newspapers across the country. The news feature was about the clear-looking fluid in their plastic containers. The contents were revealed to be a combination of recycled moisture from the astronauts' own bodies, including sweat and - urine.

The photo ignited massive news articles about everyday recycling, revealing facts about people unknowingly ingesting reprocessed water that had once been man and animal waste from sewers, storm drains, and factory impurities dumped into streams, waterways, and lakes and oceans. Included in the sources of recycled water were public swimming pools and hot tubs, which, including peoples' urine, introduced the shocking words – fecal residue. A universal "yuck" factor brought comments from readers that inspired more humor than horror.

A sample:

Drink up ... gags...I can see how it is possible to obtain water from our waste products, but if you gave me a drink baggie labeled "reclaimed urine", my brain would imagine a horrible taste and I would simply not want to drink this "water" unless I was on a desert island and dying of thirst. Then, maybe ...

If it was good enough for Mahatma Gandhi, then I suppose it's good enough for the rest of us.

...I would drink purified urine, though I'm sure I would feel more comfortable not knowing from whence it came from one of only a few people. "Hey Bob, your pee tastes great today." ...feels a little uncomfortable.

"Pass the pee, baby."

This is probably the one thing that would make me hesitate if ever offered a chance to travel in space! As noted above, it's a concept I just cringe thinking about...

How are they filtering for infectious diseases? I really don't want to drink someone else's Chlamydia or E.coli.

That will really make me want to seek employment in the Astronaut Corps.

Change the name from ISS: International Space Station to PISS: People Inventing Space Soda.

I really don't think it was necessary for that headline ("Astronauts Enjoy Recycled Urine"). They have to do what they need in space, but we don't have to know all the gory details.

People being grossed out by the astronauts drinking urine are silly. Anyone who gets their water from a river or lake must know they are drinking the urine of every human living upstream. It is being naturally recycled mostly, but it is not completely clean. That is why your city water department uses lots of chlorine to sanitize it enough before you use it. And, of course, fish and animals in and around those waterways, urinate (and more) into that water too. The system on the station provides higher quality and better tasting water than the average city water system.

Astronauts are of a certain breed, so I am not surprised that they are eager to check out the pee machine. It's not so gross to me considering the fact that I frequently eat at fast food restaurants. My only concern would be that the reclaimed water should be from my own urine. I wouldn't want to gasp at the taste of real pee in discovering the machine had malfunctioned.

Not a big deal at all. A sports energy drink or a like company will come along with "Lemonly Yellow," "Rip Roaring Red," "Green Goddess," "Grapey Grape," or "Blizzard Blue," etc. Add a little salt, sugar, and coloring in a fancy plastic 12 ounce bottle with a $2 price tag and the people will stand in line at the 7-11 or Piggley Wiggley to buy them. Helps the economy, employment and takes care of the recycled urine, so it's all good.

This is news? Hell, where I work they call it iced tea in the cafeteria.

Anyone for a bottle of Peeroni?

What's the next goal? Turning feces into meatloaf?

This is no biggy. We use feces as fertilizer. Jello is made from gelatin in ground up bones. Food manufacturing plants provide canned foods with plenty of roach feces, rat parts, etc., that we consumers would be surprised to find out....Oh, one more thought, when you sleep at night most people have swallowed bugs with their open mouths. Bugs with urine and feces in them ... big whoop, right? Won't kill us.

Makes a lot more sense than foolish earthlings paying $1.50+ for a landfill clogging, oil-depleting plastic bottle of city tap or river water that is merely filtered and wrapped in a fru fru label that is made appealing by slick marketing geeks.

Sounds great! ... I suppose I would just add some lemon-flavored Crystal light and drink up.

Budweiser has had a patent on the reverse process for decades.

Another monument to billions spent on space travel
1. Tang
2. Cheese-flavored dog food
3. A bag of moon rocks
4. Men and women with 'The Right Stuff" drinking urine

Several beer companies have been putting unfiltered piss water in their products for years. I'm not sure what the big deal is.

If I have to drink someone's recycled urine, I would like it to be from a heavy smoker, since I am a recent former smoker, cherry-flavored please.

I don't see why not. We are all drinking recycled whale urine out of the tap.

People around the world don't hesitate to frolic in swimming pools loaded with everybody's urine, or marinate in hot tubs that are bacteria ponds of sweat, urine, and fecal derivatives. Ahh, the pleasures of being ignorant of the forces of nature attacking us every day. Have a nice day!

GODAMMIT REDUX

In the first half of the 20th century, the most reviled word one could utter in casual conversation was the *godammit* word. Nobody had yet to use the *fuck* word as an adjective, verb, or noun in describing anything in denigrating terms or glorifying the merits of something.

The shame of abandoning *godammit* has been long lost to the "f" word that reached its acme in political notoriety when the Vice-President of the United States (and President of the Senate) used the active verb aspect of it to a Senator, on the sanctimonious floor of the U. S. Senate, no less, during the George W. Bush administration.

Ho hum. It didn't raise the shackles of indignation that one would expect of a nation that had already adopted the "f" word where some people could not complete any sentence or thought without repeated uses of it.

A popular email of several dozen examples of using the "f" word flooded computers via emails in countries where English was the dominant language. The "f" word had also reached the Supreme Court in a claim that using the word in a song should not be legitimized or construed as poetry as the defendant(s) had so characterized it. Well, the "f" word won.

The author feels that *godammit,* or its alternate choice *goddamn,* should not take a back seat to the "f" word, let alone fade into the oblivion of emphatic expletives. It does have historic value, however. Humorist James Thurber's memoir of Harold Ross, the founder of *The*

New Yorker magazine *(The Years With Ross)* recounted Ross' prolific use of *godammit* in conversations with his writers (sorry, Ross referred to them as "editors.") He would use the *godammit* word interchangeably for scolding (admonishing staff writers for excessive use of "commas"), or as an accolade honoring them at a retirement party (God bless you, *godammit"*)

Some popular period examples of its use were commonplace in this author's home and workplace where his father was unable to say anything that did not include the use of this questionable obscenity.

"Godammit, get your feet off the godamn couch." (Variation: "Get your goddamn feet off the couch.")

"This soup is too godamn hot!" (Variation: "This godamn soup is too cold.")

"Godamn, it's got to be 100° outside."

"Godammit, woman, what did you do with my goddamn cigarets?"

"It's the godamn truth."

"Tell him he's a godamn liar."

"Does anyone know where I put the godamn keys?"

"He knows his godamn shit."

"It's your godamn mother-in-law."

"I paid that godamn bill!"

"That's a godamn shame."

"I love that godamn woman."

"I hate that godamn sonofabitch."

As one can see, the flexibility of using *godammit* lends its choice more to civilized conversation than the "f" word that could be revolting even if used (and quoted, no less) on the floor of the United States Senate.

So, the next time you feel the need to emphasize a thought, think of *godammit* as a replacement or supplement to make your point.

And that's the *godamm* truth, *godammit.*

AWARDS THAT WENT AWRY

Nobel prizes have been awarded annually for any number of multiple achievements in human endeavor since Alfred Nobel, the Swedish inventor of *dynamite,* decided to divert attention away from the destructive aspects his explosive invention that had negative connotations of maiming or killing mankind to focusing attention to "those who have conferred to the greatest benefit of mankind."

He decided that an annual series of awards, Nobel Prizes, would be given out in the fields of Physics, Chemistry, Literature, Physiology, Medicine and Peace. The program was funded by the $millions he had accumulated over the years from his exotic invention.

Despite the reputation of how dynamite had unleashed a whole new dimension of destroying things, Alfred Nobel was a *pacifist.*

Oftentimes, multiple awards for a singular field were given to more than one person in a single year contingent on the importance deemed worthy by the Nobel Prize Foundation operating out of Stockholm, Sweden, the country of Mr. Nobel's birth in 1833. Years could pass before such a prestigious award was presented, an insurance of sort to allow time to elapse to measure the effectiveness and warranty of why the Prize was given out to the deserving recipient judged by the prize foundation committee members.

The awards were first given out in 1901, five years after Nobel died, by a Foundation established by the inventor.

In1949, the Nobel Prize for Medicine was shared by two physicians. Walter Rudolph Hess (1881-1973), a Swiss doctor was named a Laureate "for his discovery of the functional organization of the interbrain as a coordinator of the activities of the internal organs."

The other laureate was a Portuguese neurologist, Antonio Caetano De Abreu Freire Egas Moniz, (1874-1955), for his "discovery of the therapeutic value of leucotomy in certain psychoses." Egas Moniz, as he was popularly known at the time, is generally credited with inventing the prefrontal lobotomy for mental illnesses, especially a treatment for severe schizophrenia for which there were no viable cures or treatments until Egas Moniz began a process in 1935 that involved invasive surgery to the brain that brought dramatic results immediately. At first the procedure was widely heralded as a surgery that oftentimes corrected wild behavioral symptoms beyond the treatment scope of any medication or physical palliative available in the early years of the 20th century.

Essentially the prefrontal lobotomy involved entering skull of the patient and severing the connection between the prefrontal lobes of the brain and the thalamus, two areas of the brain that were considered to control certain types of human behavior. Assessing the operation took years for the medical community to realize the failure of the psychosurgery, eventually deeming it as a barbaric episode in psychiatric history, but only after the Nobel laureates were awarded Watts and Moniz.

In time, a large study demonstrated a significant reduction in "alertness" and "fear" in patients with social phobia as well as improvement in their quality of life.

A famous case involving the sister of President John F. Kennedy, Rosemary Kennedy, whose parents, Joseph and Rose Kennedy, agreed for their daughter to undergo the operation were forever guilt-ridden for that decision. Their daughter's life became a nightmare overnight and she was committed to institutional care for the rest of her life at a Wisconsin facility, mentally incapacitated thereafter at the age of 23 to perform the most minimal tasks and activity of human behavior. Rosemary died in 2005 at the age of 87.

The most vehement of complaints from those whose relatives have undergone prefrontal lobotomies include the patients' apathetic behavior, docility, lacking in social graces, and decision making abilities of even the simplest kind.

It was for this discovery that the Nobel Prize Foundation in 1949 prematurely awarded Doctors Watt and Egas Moniz its prize for Medicine, a stain of monumental magnitude on the wisdom of those who chose to honor a surgical procedure that was not one for "the greatest benefit of mankind."

A typical response from a mother in 1948, whose daughter had undergone a lobotomy, reported, "She is my daughter but yet a different person. She is with me in body but her soul is in some way lost." The patients were no longer distressed by their mental conflicts, but also seemed to have little capacity for any emotional experiences – pleasurable or otherwise. They were described by the nurses and doctors, over and over, as dull, apathetic, listless, without drive or initiative, flat, lethargic, placid and unconcerned, childlike, docile, needing pushing, passive, lacking in spontaneity, without aim or purpose, preoccupied and dependant.

This is one Nobel Prize that the committee that chose the 1949 award for Medicine wishes they had waited a little longer to investigate its merits before deciding to award its financially robust laureate to the men for the most inhuman act in medical history.

HOW TO CREATE AND EAT A SALAD

Good afternoon class. Let me introduce myself to our new students who have hungrily (excuse the pun) enrolled in Templeton University's online class of *Nutritional Supplements for Living,* a mandatory four-credit course toward receiving your doctorate here at the University.

I'm Professor Lydia Templeton, the oldest of the founder's thirteen daughters, who was born, of all things, on our family's kitchen table. After much bleaching, of course, my destiny in pursuing a career in edibles was heavily influenced by also growing up in our kitchen and utilizing that very table to create recipes that provide maximum nutrition at modest cost for those unfamiliar with consuming food.

Today's program will concentrate on preparing and eating salads, a side dish or a main ingredient, depending on a person's reaction to the taste and flavor of what's actually in the salad. In choosing the items for the salad it is necessary to determine just how the salad is going to be consumed – whether by fingers (if you are Persian, or anywhere in the middle-East) or by a utensil appropriate for transferring the victuals (also referred to as "grub, vittles, eats, or chow") from the plate to the palate.

Today we are going to concentrate on making a chicken salad. Since chicken has a wide popularity around the globe, and is usually inexpensive to purchase, preparation of this main protein-rich ingredient will focus on de-boning chicken wings, the least costly part of this feathered bird.

Cooking chicken wings can be easily be prepared by boiling them, deep-frying them, baking them in an oven in a baking pan (using ¼ inch of water, sprinkling them with seasoned salt, at 350° for 45 minutes) or purchasing pre-cooked frozen ones (if you are financially well-off.)

At this point I should mention that it would be helpful to have taken our University's course on *Everything You Ever Wanted to Know about Chicken* that specializes in the most efficient method of removing the complex meat from the network of chicken wing bones. Be prepared to spend extra time to extract every sliver of meat from the bones because you know the old expression, "The closer the bone, the sweeter the meat", an expression my first husband had at bedtime, and which I never quite understood, to tell you the truth.

With this task done, you can now begin to design your salad. Set aside those ingredients you want to use to form the perimeter, main core, and top of your creation. Sometimes people like to use some kind of a leafy base vegetable to line the plate, dish, or container. Arugula, endive (pronounced *on deev*), romaine, and leaf lettuce are the most popular. Spinach, bean sprouts, nasturtium leaves, and fresh dandelion fronds (taken before the weed blooms) are other options to consider that can add their own zest to your creative salad.

At this point you have to make a major decision: to sprinkle the base with your shredded chicken meat throughout the construction of your masterpiece (so to speak), use it throughout the center core of it, or use it as a crown over the top. This decision is crucial especially if you intend to "croutonize" it, because croutons have a way of destroying the esthetic touches you employ to display your artistic talent.

Before I go any further, I should have mentioned earlier that the dressing (if any) you anticipate using determines how you stratify the fruits, vegetables, or nuts that form center or base core of your salad. Nothing is more important in the success of a salad than the choice of a top dressing utilized to enhance the ingredients on which it is laced.

Lemon juice, oil and vinegar, vinaigrette, bleu cheese, ranch, French, and dozens of other commercial salad dressings can pose a difficult problem to the edible appeal of any salad. As mentioned earlier, the *Everything You Ever Wanted to Know about Chicken* course goes into detail about these details. An alternate source for choosing the best dressing for your masterpiece can be searched on *Google*, which probably has several hundred thousand websites available for suggestions.

Having produced your one-of-a-kind masterpiece salad, you now have to make a more difficult choice as to who are going to consume it, and with what, if any, utensils to provide for the eaters. This decision has to be made by the eating habits of the nationalities and cultures of a variety of styles indigenous to the people for whom the salad was prepared. Contrary to popular thinking that people only sit on chairs, cushions, or some kind of elevated support device, most of the six billion humans who live on earth consume their food sitting on the ground, crossed-legged, splay-legged, lounging on their side, in the Lotus position, or other configuration that their social habits derived from centuries, if not eons, ago.

And, most of them eat with their hands. It is also common for people sitting side by side to dip into the plate or serving of a neighbor to sample his/her victual as a demonstration of politeness and camaraderie. Forget about any transfer of disease or bacteria that is easily spread by such meal manners, the best advice is "When in Rome, do as the Romans do."

Needless to say, those who eat with their fingers don't relish any salad dressing that could stain or make a mess of the robes worn for the meal.

Class, remember, as wonderful as salads can be as a comestible, it also has its hazards depending on where and with whom they are consumed.

A note of caution dining in foreign cities or countries: an appointment with your primary physician "for a general checkup" is advised.

WHO FIRED THAT ROUND?

Anybody who has ever been in a crowded elevator, and suddenly realized that someone had *farted,* usually tries to hold his breath until his designated floor has been reached, possibly bursting out from the crowd to catch a fresh breath.

Of course, by then, the fumes of the stench might have permeated the clothes of the entrapped, saturating the fabric, and accompanying the victims to wherever they're going. People who have been exposed to an anonymous farter in an elevator are notoriously shy about revealing their experience even if seeing some flared nostrils from co-workers passing by.

What most persons subjected to a powerful intestinal aerosol don't realize is the stench factor of what was released, audible or silenced by rectal muscles. It was the mystery of what combination of bacteria in the intestines produced the hydrogen sulfide smell (rotten eggs) that constituted the various aromas in passing gas that fascinated two Cornell University student computer engineering whizzes. As their senior project, they decided to construct a machine that could differentiate all the individual molecular components that caused farts to produce the various stinks and their potency in delivery by fellow humans.

First on the list was their fraternity house where there was an abundance of flatulent volunteers albeit ignorant of the two senior's project.

Beginning with a breath analyzer, they learned how the device worked and assembled a fart detector from a sensitive hydrogen sulfide monitor, a thermometer, and a microphone. Writing a computer program that would rate emissions from a slight perturbance in the air near the stench detector, it was set to measure three levels of fart quality: sound, stench, and temperature. The latter was judged important because the hotter the fart, the quicker it spread. The fart machine would then emit a voice that measured the fart on a scale of one (mild) to nine (powerful.) A rating of "nine" would automatically initiate a fan to disperse the smell. Any perceived sonic transmission from the fart would also be recorded for playback later on, if needed.

After a few months construction time, the two students field-tested it in and around different areas of Cornell University. Needless to say, their fraternity house was a major factor early in their fine-tuning the stench machine.

The boys received an "A" from their professor, and accolades from their fellow students because the mission of their invention provided a nicer atmosphere for those working around them.

To demonstrate the effectiveness of the stench machine to the curious, just the audible sound of a phony fart combined with heavy breathing around it would produce results because human exhalations contain sufficient hydrogen sulfide to trigger its sensors.

There were practical applications for using the stench machine commercially, especially in hospitals to measure bacteria counts, dentists for detecting malodorous smells, and especially for dairy farmers where the potency of fumes from cattle manure could identify the health of their livestock by measuring the strength and noxiousness of their farts, let alone the potential for explosions in their barns from the methane quantity of their highly explosive contents that could be triggered by the simple act of lighting a cigarette from a careless barnyard employee or anybody in close proximity to these structures.

Such an explosion occurred in the past when an employee of a utility company, summoned to investigate problems on a milk farm, either ignored or failed to see posted multiple "NO SMOKING" warning signs on and in barns forbidding such activity. His lighting a cigarette followed by an enormous blast caused parts of the barn roof and pieces of his body to be found three miles from the site of the farm.

The recorded history of human flatulence is mentioned back in the days of Socrates and Aristotle with brief mention of it in scribes' writing without any sense of humor incorporated in their choice of words. It was simply a foul smell occasionally emitted from body orifices sometimes announced audibly and easily recognized as a preliminary aerosol signal of unpleasant air to come.

The sounds generated by flatulence became a favorite humor recording in the mid-19th century that featured a farting (crepitation) contest between an elderly British Lord Windesmere and Australian Max Boomer. The level and length of their farts were awarded points by the judges who somehow dismissed any powerful unpleasant aerosol effects that were generated by the contestants as part of winning points in the game.

The garments that they wore for the exhibition, though, did influence the judges inasmuch as they were designed to accentuate the sound, length, description, and volume of the anal emissions of the two men performing for the title (not mentioned during the recording, though.)

Lord Windesmere wore a royal purple brief without buttock covering that he referred to as his "Zephyr Hole." Max Boomer simply dropped his pants to display a more-than-ample-ass to emit the variable sounds to win this enviable contest.

The announcer who breathlessly described the activities included the food that both men consumed to prepare for this epic encounter. Lord Windesmere's choice was beans grown at his own estate north of London. Max Boomer's diet of only cabbage (cooked or raw) and lots of it gave him the best advantage especially in the sonorous category that had the highest rating points awarded the high and low frequencies of each man's farts.

The farts themselves had given names with points awarded for the time of effort as well as sonic effects included in the production of them. A Tripple-Flutter-Blast garnered the most points, and more if followed up by a few Squealers as a finish.

Both men were well-informed that any flatulent effort that produced feces ended the contest, and a win was awarded to the remaining contestant. Amazingly, the enormous amounts of air both men ingested prior to emitting anal sounds, and their manipulating their gluteus maximus cheeks for audible advantage had to be mindboggling to the audience as well as the judges.

And as to who won the contest? Well, you just have to hear the tape or record to get the results. Enjoy!

CHOOSING NEXT-OF-KIN SALE

Spermatorifics LTD, the company that refined the human choice of selecting the best for your future children, is having a sale, the first ever in its history.

What is unique in this sale is the revolutionary opportunity to select no less than a combination of three (3) sperm from our banks of celebrities from any of our donations from the arts and sciences from all parts of the world, all races, all nationalities, all gender orientations, and even the choice of multiple births should the adult, parent, paramour, or whomever is making the purchase of this trio of sperm choices.

The very fact that science can combine sperms to take advantage of the assets that brought fame and fortune to these men was incomprehensible not too long ago. Our catalogue of the famous includes Nobel Laureates of every one of its classifications in addition to hundreds from *Mensa,* the intellectual society accepted as the world's cream-of-the-crop (no pun intended.)

Our advisory staff is available to help our customers as to selection of donor name combination to ward off any disappointments of producing, say, female offspring from a predominantly male skill, i.e., professional basketball player, boxer, or spelunker.

ENCORE

Over the centuries, musical composers have always been perplexed as to how their efforts to produce a *magnum opus* would be received by audiences throughout the civilized world. Most of them knew that concert-goers can be fickle when introduced to new music, and often do not embrace compositions initially, but over time, the familiarity of hearing a different symphony orchestra's rendition of a budding masterpiece can change the public's mind as to its magnitude in acceptance as a classic.

Complicating this acceptance of a composer's effort includes the possibility that orchestras and soloists performing such music could simply lack the technical ability to execute the notes as written by the men and women whose inspiration generated the original piece in the first place.

An example of this would be Pieter Tchaikovsky's violin concerto that received less than rave reviews when first performed simply because there were no violin virtuosos at the time that could render the notes in the tempo and sonic demands deemed proper by the composer. In fact, twenty years passed before such a person arrived on the scene that could perform this magnificent concerto as written. It was then deemed the masterpiece that Tchaikovsky dreamed it would be.

Some of Beethoven's work suffered the same indignities when first presented to audiences, but in time came to be accepted as the work of that genius.

Then there are instances when an original piece of music when performed for the first time brings an unexpected response from those gathered in a concert hall to judge an evening featuring "new music."

Russians, Muscovites in particular, have always self-appointed themselves as the world's elite critics when it comes to opining the status of listening to composers' introductory music, be it symphonies, concertos, or shorter supplementary variety of selections used to break up sitting through a program of lengthy scores of music familiar to appeasing crowds.

One such evening stands out in the history of introducing new music to a Muscovite audience of concertgoers in 1938, primed to pass judgment on the performance of an American composer/conductor and his orchestra that was passing through the country on a world tour. Music they played on the evening's early program received a somewhat muted response from those prime critics sitting in judgment.

As a finale to the concert, the conductor had scheduled a small twelve-minute composition from the American composer Samuel Barber. It was his *"Adagio For Strings"*, a somber work displaying gradations of soft strings rising and falling in crescendos and near silent hushes that resonated in the concert hall. The people sat there stone-faced throughout the performance.

When the conductor turned to bow to his critics at the end of it, he saw their expressions and immediately translated them into dissatisfaction. He quickly turned to depart the stage when he heard some clapping emanate from a small segment of his concertgoers. Then, some more clapping. Suddenly the whole audience was a thunderous roar of clapping, people standing up and smiling. They continued this response that shocked the conductor and his orchestra members who responded by standing up to acknowledge the applause.

In an extraordinary move, the people demanded that the conductor give an encore performance of the *Adagio*. The concert hall was dead silent all through the short masterpiece. At the end, the conductor again bowed to the audience and left the stage slowly in a funereal fashion that reflected the music's impact along with his orchestra members.

Half of the Muscovites got up silently and wandered out of the hall. The rest sat in their seats as if inert, unable to move from the spell that the composition they just heard had inflicted on them. Some even sat quietly still after the orchestra members had left the stage.

Adagio For Strings was an instant sensation throughout the world. The dirge-like music often heard as background accompaniment to announcements of deaths, usually military, or sad events of tragedy throughout the globe, has become the premier music of choice to accompany announcements of them in newscasts and motion pictures.

ANOMALIES

Anomaly: deviation from the common rule; irregularity; abnormality; something out of keeping with accepted notions of fitness or order . . .

Such is the definition as found in Webster's New International Dictionary, Second Edition.

Image examples:

George Washington crossing the Delaware with his crew on Christmas Eve to surprise the British on a boat with an outboard motor.

Nero playing a saxophone.

Ty Cobb in a baseball uniform with a number on his shirt.

Jimmie Doolittle flying an F86 jet.

Julia Child shown putting a package of margarine into her shopping cart.

Well, you get the idea. These amusing examples, however, do not suggest things that bring to mind history of another kind – disturbing history of actuality incomprehensible to behold until the four decades from 1960 to the year 2000.

The only sexual orientation accepted by most of the world was *heterosexual* up to 1960. By the year 2000, another five were determined by science and technology to be genuine and real, and not recognized or accepted by a world in budding intellectual turmoil (*homosexual, trans-sexual, trans-gendered, bi-sexual, asexual.*) These five were treated as anomalies, out of the ordinary, and most of them were considered and indeed prosecuted as criminal behavior.

By the 1950's, England prosecuted anyone whose outward sign of homosexuality brought the attention of the police. In a particular case that brought notoriety and shame to the British was the persecution of a brilliant young mathematician during World War II by the name of Alan Turing (1912-1954.) He was the 27-year-old wizard cryptologist who broke the Nazi code of Germany's Enigma machine, used by its military to send encrypted messages all over the world orders for conducting warfare on land, sea, and air. Turing was credited with saving thousands of lives of Allied soldiers whose deaths were averted by his inventing a mechanical device named the *Bomba* that unscrambled intricate messages that revealed the enemy's plans in advance of their being activated. In many cases the encryptions were deciphered almost simultaneously with their being transmitted by the Germans who never realized that their Enigma machine had been compromised by a genius group of scientific cryptologists hidden away in Bletchley Park, some fifty miles north of London.

Throughout the war, the Nazis imperious attitude never dreamed that there were superior intellects on the enemy side capable of unraveling their complex Enigma machine, a fatal error of the first magnitude for a country whose many inventions were beyond the pale.

The difficulty facing the Allied generals were devices on how to disguise knowledge obtained beforehand on strategy used by the enemy that betrayed the Nazi Enigma code had been hacked, the code word at the time designated *Ultra*.

In 1952 Turing was ousted as being gay, and arrested for homosexual acts, deemed "gross indecency" and criminal in the United Kingdom at the time. He was given a choice of incarceration or ingesting estrogen to suffer chemical castration. He chose castration. The 42-year-old, whose fame had been a classified secret, lived for two years after his condemnation, became demoralized by the physical changes to his body that estrogen produced, and committed suicide by eating an apple laced with cyanide.

Alan Turing has been credited as the founder of what is known as the modern day computer, and recognized as one of the world's top one-hundred scientists who changed the world in the 20th century. That he succeeded in the era that he did gives new meaning to being an *anomaly*.

By 2009, 30,000 of the world's pre-eminent scientists and luminaries called for England to apologize for its shameful action, even going so far as to demand that Queen Elizabeth II bestow posthumous Knighthood on Alan Turing for his brilliant work that changed the course of history for England, let alone the rest of the world.

On September 11, 2009, England Prime Minister Gordon Brown did just that, declaring,

Turing was a quite brilliant mathematician, most famous for his work on breaking the German Enigma codes. It is no exaggeration to say that, without his outstanding contribution, the history of World War II could well have been very different. He truly was one of those individuals we can point to whose unique contribution helped to turn the tide of war. The debt of gratitude he is owed is even more horrifying, therefore, that he was treated so inhumanely. In 1952, he was convicted of 'gross indecency' – in effect, tried for being gay. His sentence – and he was faced with the miserable choice of this or prison – was chemical castration by a series of injections of female hormones. He took his own life two years later.

Thousands of people have come together to demand justice for Alan Turing and recognition for the appalling way he was treated. While Turing was dealt with under the law of the time and we can't put the clock back, his treatment was of course utterly unfair, and I am pleased to have the chance to say how deeply sorry I and we all are for what happened to him.

At the end of the war, England destroyed all evidence of the secret work done at Bletchley Park even refusing to acknowledge that it ever existed. This act of destruction has never been justified by historians considering what an intellectual, let alone physical achievement of the first magnitude it represented that changed world history.

Did you know that the Japanese navy built three aircraft carriers toward the end of World War II under strict high secrecy that were 400' in length, longer than a football field and capable of circumnavigating the world one-and-a-half times without refueling or surfacing – because *they were submarines* capable of reaching the United States from either east or west coasts?

Each of these submarines, called *Seirans*, could launch three aircraft from waterproof hangars, housing folded-wing attack airplanes on the decks of the subs when surfaced. The wings of the *Seiran* folded back, the horizontal stabilizers folded down, and the top of the vertical stabilizer folded over so the overall folded profile of the aircraft was within the diameter of its propeller. They had a wingspan of forty feet and a length of thirty-eight feet. A crew of four could prepare and get all three planes airborne in forty-five minutes launched on 120' deck tracks from a catapult that enabled them to be quickly airborne from the giant submarine.

These I-400 class submarines also featured four anti-aircraft guns, a large deck gun, and eight torpedo tubes.

The mission of these special airplanes was to surprise, attack, and sink Allied ships far out at sea, especially aircraft carriers, the menace that the enemy recognized as its worst nightmare. The pilots chosen for such missions had to realize that there was no provision to land back on these special submarines, and that their flights were, in fact, suicide missions. Those that volunteered for such flights were awarded a *tokko,* a short sword, symbolic of the ultimate sacrifice.

Commander-in-Chief of the Combined Fleet, Admiral Isoroko Yamamoto, had devised these combat submarines to attack New York City, Washington D.C. and other cities, but in particular to destroy the Panama Canal from the Atlantic side of the continent, a surprise attack on the Allies being a critical target to prevent U. S. warships from using a short cut to accessing the Pacific ocean.

What short-circuited Yamamoto's grand plan was knowledge of an imminent attack on Pacific islands controlled by the Imperial Army close to home that diverted all military ships and aircraft to defend that theater of battle.

The very fact that these I-400 class submarines were still in their completion phase at the Japanese naval yards at *Maizuru* quickly changed the complexion of the war.

Only after Japan's surrender on September 3, 1945, on the deck of the USS Missouri, did the United States discover the existence of these super submarines, and that they had actually been launched into service before they could be captured by the U.S. military. Needless to say, the shock of this discovery to intelligence officials was so profound that word of such monstrous enemy weapons became a top secret for decades after the war ended.

At the end of the war, the U. S. Navy recovered and boarded 24 Japanese submarines, including three I-400 class ones. They took them to Sasebo Bay to study them. While there, the Soviets sent a message that they were sending a team of inspectors to examine them. To keep the technology out of the hands of the Soviets, *Operation Road's End* was instituted. The Navy took most of the Japanese subs to a point some 40 miles off the coast of Nagasaki, were packed with C2 explosives and destroyed. Today they rest at some 200 meters depth of the Pacific off the coast of the Goto Islands.

The three I-400 class monster subs were sailed to Hawaii by naval seamen for further inspection. Upon completion of the inspection, they were scuttled in waters near Oahu by torpedoes from the *USS Trumpetfish* on June 4, 1946, apparently because Soviet scientists were again demanding access to them.

The wreckage of the I-401 was rediscovered by the *Pisces* deep-sea submarines of the *Hawaii Undersea Research Laboratory* in March, 2005 at a depth of 820 meters.

Word of the existence of the super submarines remained one of the best-kept secrets from World War II.

So now *you* know!

As if the Japanese had not only built the world's first aircraft carrier submarines in World War II, they had been busy years before manufacturing scores of mini-subs capable of silently sneaking into places where an enemy was vulnerable to a surprise attack sight unseen.

These sixty-foot long, six foot wide, mini-subs, powered by silent electric motors, carrying two-man crews on suicide missions, were affixed to the deck of a conventional submarine and could be launched underwater clandestinely at targets unaware of their presence for attack. Each one was capable of launching two powerful torpedoes, anyone of which could upend and sink ships as large as the USS Arizona sitting in Pearl Harbor on December 7, 1941.

As a matter of fact, 65 years later, a battery of expert naval scientists and underwater marine archivists discovered that just such an event occurred when it determined that the source of the Arizona's sinking was indeed from a Japanese mini-sub torpedo, one of five small subs sent on such a specific mission to Pearl Harbor, was successful in penetrating the harbor and weaving its way through a maze of underwater nets and devices to foil such an attack.

Unlike torpedoes launched from enemy aircraft that didn't have the explosive power to totally damage a U. S. battleship, the mini-sub weapon was deadly enough to sink any vessel with a single stealthy successful strike.

It was on the morning of December 7, 1941, an hour before the Japanese attack, that Fireman 2nd Class Will Lehner, on the USS Ward, a patrol ship stationed at Pearl Harbor noticed a rusty-colored object that passed directly underneath his ship right where he was standing. He remembered it being kind of moss-covered and wondered is it was "one of ours." An hour later, when the all-out attack by Japanese air planes bombed and strafed Pearl Harbor, Lehner's ship was the first American vessel to fire a shot in the war.

[Four of the five mini-subs dispatched to Pearl Harbor never made it there, and were lost in transit for unknown reasons.]

In a 2005 investigation into the sinking of the USS Arizona, underwater scans of the debris on the Harbor's bottom revealed three rusting sections of a Japanese mini-sub that had come apart from the explosion of its torpedo to the Arizona. From the technical expertise filmed by experts using sophisticated underwater devices, the sections were found, and determined that the torpedo tubes from the mini-sub were empty. They were able to re-construct a scenario that provided the proof that the Arizona was sunk from one of the deadly torpedoes launched from a Japanese mini-sub.

At WW II's end (September 3, 1945), dozens of mini-subs were found intact in Japan's shipping docks too late to have had an impact on the outcome of the war.

The physical remains of Adolf Hitler, after he committed suicide with his wife Eva Braun in May, 1945, (bullets to the head) in their Berlin bunker, was never revealed until 2009, according to the head archivist of Russia's Federal Security Service (FSB), the successor to the former Soviet Union's KGB.

General Vasily Kristoforov admitted that previous secret documents indicated that KGB chief Yuri Andropov, at the time, had the consent of the Communist Party leadership to order a top secret operation to destroy the remains of the bodies of Hitler, Eva Braun, along with the family of Joseph Goebbels (Hitler's propaganda chief.)

According to the documents that Kristoforov quoted, the fear that consumed the KGB and the Soviet Communist leadership was that Hitler's burial site could evolve into a place of worship for disciples of fascist ideas. This operation, code-named *The Archives,* was carried out by the KGB in Magdeburg, East Germany. The bodies had been secretly buried there February 21, 1946, on a section of land that housed a Soviet military facility.

On April 4, 1970, the KGB mission was twofold: opening the graves of the Nazi leaders and their families, and detailing their physical destruction. General Kristoforov told CNN News these remains were consumed in a bonfire outside the town of Shoenebeck, some seven miles from Magdeburg, ground into ashes, and then tossed into the Biederitz River.

The Soviet army was the first to reach Berlin in May, 1945, when it entered the Nazi capitol. The bodies of Hitler and Braun who had committed suicide by gunshot and cyanide, April 30, 1945, were discovered in the crater of a Soviet artillery shell outside Hitler's bunker. The bodies of Goebbels and his wife were found in the garden of the Reich Chancellery on May 2, 1945; their children were located the next day. In early June all the bodies were buried in a forest near the village of Rathenau, Germany, only to be unearthed and re-buried secretly eight months later in the Soviet Garrison at Magdeburg.

As long as the bodies were within the confines of the Garrison, they could be kept secret and barred from visitors. In 1970, however, the Soviets decided to relocate this military post and a decision was made to burn the remains of the Nazi leaders.

General Kristoforov remarked that all that is left of Hitler are fragments of his jawbone and skull. He said no other pieces of the German dictator remain elsewhere in the world. The General said Hitler's jaw is kept at the FSB archives and all other parts of Hitler's skull are housed at the State Archives.

The Russian FSB Central Archive has fended off any attempts by outside scientists to conduct DNA tests on these parts of the skull, maintaining there is nothing in existence to compare them with. They also emphasize that this has put to rest any inquiry of what happened to the bodies of these Nazi leaders.

It is a rare person who speaks and writes the English language that hasn't, at one time or another, misspelled these classic everyday words. Are you among them?

acceptable acquire accommodate accidentally amateur apparent argument atheist believe bellwether calendar category cemetery changeable collectible column committed conscience conscientious conscious consensus daiquiri definitely discipline drunkenness dumbbell embarrassment equipment exhilarate exceed existence experience fiery foreign gauge grateful guarantee harass height hierarchy humorous ignorance immediate independent indispensable inoculate intelligence its/it's jewelry judgment kernel leisure liaison library license lightning maintenance maneuver medieval memento millennium miniature miniscule mischievous misspell neighbor noticeable occasionally occurrence pastime perseverance personnel privacy playwright possession precede principal/principle privilege pronunciation publicly questionnaire receive/receipt recommend referred reference relevant restaurant rhyme rhythm schedule separate sergeant supersede they're/there/their threshold twelfth tyranny until vacuum weather weird

CONUNDRUM

Where in the world did all the 35,000+ known religions in the globe come from? Who created them? How were they started? Why were they started? How were they spread? What made certain creeds prevail through the ages while others gradually disappeared? One thing is well-known, however: their origins began with male human beings under the auspices, perchance delusion, that they were appointed spokesmen or agents, selected by a spiritual deity, *whose name(s) number in the thousands,* that took possession of them at one point in their life with a mission to proselytize the message of their newborn creed to as many people that they could attract, and convince them of its divine origin – *through him, of course.* This method of gaining disciples and spawning splinter-related creeds has continued unabated into the 21st Century.

Two developments in the history of *Homo sapiens* led to the formation and origins of what is recognized as a religious cult. The first was speech, the ability for man to communicate thoughts among his peers via a vocal language. The second was the discovery to convey such thoughts through a written language. Speech among primitive people preceded written language by eons. Historians agree that the oldest example of man's written language dates only from 3500 BC, with archeological evidence which points to its origin either in Samaria or ancient Egypt.

Credible evidence of religious behavior, however, dates from the Middle Paleolithic era some 300-50 thousand years ago – and possibly earlier. First historical evidence of thoughts of an afterlife were discovered pictorially at a variety of excavated grave sites that manifested scenes of the departed accompanied by objects and symbols of daily life that reflected belief in sustaining some kind of existence in a world after death. Tombs of Egyptian pharaohs unearthed were loaded with treasure troves of items including foodstuffs as part of the journey the departed would need in their life after death. Some of these depictions even included armies of sculptured life-sized soldiers to defend the dead from harm in the afterlife.

Oral history, depending on collective memories, was used to pass down the religious tenets and thoughts of one generation to another of a cult's mandatory beliefs, behavior, and standard living practices. Those who strayed from such behavior often risked reprimand, social rejection, imprisonment, and even death from deviations of cult fiats ruled by iron-fisted clerics.

Some of the more restrictive of these religions and extreme penalties for abandoning such cults exist even in this day and age.

Twelve of the most popular religions active today go back only to 2000 BC. In the descending order of antiquity along with some of their founder's name and date, they are:

Hinduism – 2000 BC
Judaism – Moses, 1500-1350 BC
Zoroastrianism – 628-587 BC
Buddha – 563-483 BC
Taoism – Lao Tse, 580-500 BC
Confucius – 551-479 BC
Christianity – Jesus, 1-33 AD

Shinto – 100 AD
Islam – Mohammad, 570-632 AD
Sikhism – Gura Nanak, 1469-1538 AD
Baha"r – Baha'u'llah, 1817-1882 AD

Keep in mind that BC refers to "Before Caesar" and AD refers to "After The Lord." Caesar was always addressed as "Lord", and he maintained publicly to his subjects that he was God.

Prehistoric man began as hunter-gatherers, existing on whatever animals and edible plants they could find to survive. The next stage of their lives led to farming with productivity, then to food surpluses that allowed communities to expand. Crop productivity led to the emergence of the first villages, chiefdoms, states, nations, and empires.

Organized religions emerged as a means of providing social and economic stability to large populations. They also

Served to justify control authority, collect taxes in return for providing social and security services to the state.

Emerged as a means of maintaining peace between unrelated individuals, who would otherwise be more prone to enmity. After all, the leading cause of death among hunter-gatherers who had serious disagreements with others was murder.

First religious texts mark the beginning of religions' existence as found in *The Pyramid Texts* from ancient Egypt dating to 2400-2300 BC. Writing could easily be stored in sacred texts in large amounts that would otherwise be forgotten. Writing therefore enabled religions to develop coherent and comprehensible doctrinal systems that remained independent of time and place.

That the majority of religions began from single charismatic males who professed to have a singular connection to a deity, some have even maintained they bear a gene which gives them a predisposition to interpret episodes as religious revelation. Religious doubters call it hallucinations resulting from a mental disturbance genetically inherited, or even the fruits of ingesting any of the 3,500 exotic plants grown around the world that induce mind-altering behavior when consumed, smoked, or chewed.

Early evidence of native tribes in North America and Australian Aborigines indicated common rituals where certain plants were nurtured, chewed, chopped up, and/or devoured that altered their behavior patterns from peaceful and submissive to raging anger. Jungle societies in South America's deep Amazon River that Brazil has permitted to retain their historical past of thousands of years ago still practice their ancient rituals of clinging to a faith worshiping physical objects as spirits. Masticating certain barks and leaves of bushes that contain psycho-altering drugs is also a common activity among these tribes to relax and relieve them of daily mental stresses.

It is not a stretch of the imagination to think that hunter-gatherers soon learned which plants, trees, and vines provided them with making the best of their ordeal attempting to survive on earth.

[Author's warning: This article is written knowing of the wrath that all religions refuse to endorse any research into how a specific creed originated, who was the male that created it, description of the spirit/deity claimed as origin, and how it measures up to scientific and philosophical scrutiny.]

STUFF

Take it or leave it!

We owe that familiar option to an English livery stable owner by the name of Thomas Hobson (1544-1641) from Cambridge, England.

Hobson was the owner of some forty horses that he rented out to customers needing his animals for any variety of reasons. To insure that his horses were rotated properly for the exercise they would receive, people needing his services were awarded with the next horse in line to be rented out. If a person wanted a specific horse, he would be denied such a wish, and giving the customer the option of taking the next animal in line was the only choice available. Or, the customer could go elsewhere.

[Obviously, Mr. Hobson's business was quite successful since most of his clientele swallowed their pride, and accepted "Hobson's Choice", or opted out to try their luck elsewhere.]

Hobson 's choice became a familiar phrase in the English language – usually indicating that in any transaction, trade, sale, or any *quid pro quo* involving a seller and a buyer, the chooser had no choice at all: take what was offered, or take a hike!

In the vernacular, we know it as *Take it or leave it!*

Just looking at a saxophone makes one wonder how did it come into existence and why would anyone invent something so visually complex to play.

The answer was a Belgian by the name of Adolph Sax, born in 1814, and as a youngster had a flair for making musical instruments in his father's work shop. At Brussels Conservatory, he studied the clarinet and the flute. In 1840, Sax decided to make an instrument that had a sound akin to the woodwind tone of a clarinet and the brass sound of a trumpet. His original intent was use of the instrument in a military band. [Author's note: Figure that one out.]

Completed in 1845, the *"sax*ophone*"* began to influence French composers, was used in small orchestras, and, of course, by military bands. The instrument came into its own in the 1920's thanks to the popularity of jazz music. The rest is history in American contemporary musical favorites and the musicians whose virtuosity on the saxophone is legendary.

Three of the fourteen saxophones invented by Adolph Sax became instantly popular; the Alto sax, the Soprano Sax, and the Bass Sax. They range in size from sixteen inches (the Soprano) to six-and-a-half feet (Contra Bass.)

The use of saxophones in classical music was not readily accepted, being eschewed by many composers as a foreign sound for which they had no ear (or no intention) to include in their choice of orchestral sounds, let alone solo melodies.

The first serious use of the saxophone in classical music was written by George Gershwin in 1924 in his composition *American in Paris* for the New York Philharmonic. It was an instant success and has become a popular selection performed by major orchestras worldwide since then.

BAR STORY MEMOIRS

A popular snack dish set out on coffee tables used to be cubed candy called *Bridge Mix.* It featured brown and white-covered morsels in the shape of card-table dice, sweets piled together on glass plates usually on a table close to family television sets.

They were almost addictive to resist, with people munching on them while watching their favorite TV programs, and also served as card table centerpieces for the card game of *bridge.*

In a conversation I had with a client who worked for the local telephone company, the subject of *Bridge Mix* came up, and she confessed that it was the favorite snack of her husband who always insisted that they keep an ample supply on hand. He'd come home from work, sink into their couch, and munch away at the dishful of the brown and white goodies.

As it happened in their household, the family sofa was close to their dining room table that often served as a favorite place for his wife to change their baby's diapers. She could watch her soap operas while listening in to the ongoing sagas that intrigued many people swept up in the plights and dramas that continued *ad infinitum* for years from such television soap stars.

One particular evening, she had moved the dish of Bridge Mix to the table while she was changing diapers. Her hubby noticed it, and would lean back over the couch and grab a handful of the candy resting on the edge of the table.

Fearful that the mix was too close to falling off the edge, his wife shifted it a bit, continuing to wipe and clean the baby's buttocks, and replacing the soiled diaper with a clean one. At one point she saw in horror that her spouse had reached back and seized a chunk of baby poop, and popped it in his mouth. Then he quickly gulped another one. Before she was able to shift the candy dish back to its usual place, she heard him say, "Honey, I think we've got some stale candy here. How about opening another bag?"

My client told me she never had the courage to tell her hubby what happened that fateful day, but she shifted the diaper changing to the far end of their dining room table. She also told me that I was the only person to whom she had ever revealed her *Bridge Mix* story while giggling helplessly throughout her recollections.

Thereafter I could never think of Bridge Mix without connecting it to baby poop.

After listening to funny bar stories from guys in their cups, others, also in the bag, feel compelled to tell a tale of their own. And some are treasures.

One that I'll never forget had to do with a young man who professed to have the dumbest uncle in Christendom. He was an unpleasant man who enjoyed a reputation of being the black sheep of the family.

He told a story of how his relative was knocking mammoth ice cycles from his roof one winter when a particularly huge one came crashing down on his face, taking out every last tooth he had in his mouth. Faced with having to get dentures, he complained to his nephew that they would cost him "thousands."

Knowing that his uncle was notoriously cheap, and not someone he particularly liked anyhow, he told his elder that he knew of a place where he could get them "free."

His uncle was all ears. "Where", the old man asked.

"At the county morgue," the nephew replied. "They have baskets and baskets of false teeth they take from bodies that come in to the coroner's office. Not knowing what to do with these valuable body parts, they just keep them in baskets, and make them available for free to anyone who wants them. You could go down there and try on a few to see which ones fit the best. Won't cost you a thing."

The uncle promptly showed up the next day at the local morgue and had an encounter with a stern-faced assistant coroner. After recounting his story of the ice cycle and giving evidence of his mouth *sans* teeth, he asked to check out the basket of free dentures that had been taken from corpses that had been processed at the site.

After patiently listening to this man's bizarre story, the morgue employee simply stared at the stranger, then told the uncle to "Get the fuck outta here."

This bar story brought a round of raucous guffaws from the barflys. The teller of the story said that his uncle never really got the joke, and maintained the man he spoke with at the morgue was just ignorant to him.

LONGEVITY ANYONE? HAVE A BANANA!

Ever think there is a *wonder food* easily available that is the closest to perfection that humans could possibly invent to enjoy a long life?

Well, there is. It's the banana. You know, the prime choice sustenance that our closest human relatives in the jungles of Africa and South America devour with obvious pleasure.

Containing three natural sugars (sucrose, fructose, and glucose), combined with fiber, bananas give us an instant jolt of sustained energy. It is an athlete's favorite food to keep fit and fend off a number of illnesses and conditions to maintain a healthful life.

- Depression: bananas fend off depression because they contain tryptophan, a type of protein that converts into serotonin, a chemical that relaxes one's mood and make you feel better. Prisons around the world are famous for feeding its inmates foods that are high in tryptophan (i.e., poultry) to offset any aggressiveness they have against fellow prisoners, let alone rigid rules and regulations that come with any long-term confinement, especially life sentences.

- PMS (Pre-menstrual syndrome): bananas are an excellent choice of vitamin B6 that regulates blood glucose levels that can affect mood changes.

- Anemia: high in iron, bananas can stimulate the production of hemoglobin in the blood, an aid that fends off anemia.

- Blood Pressure: bananas offer a perfect way to overcome blood pressure problems because this tropical fruit is loaded with potassium yet low in salt. The FDA has just gotten around permitting the banana industry to make official claims of the fruit's ability to reduce the risk of blood pressure and stroke.

- Brain Power: tests done on 200 students at an English school eating bananas at breakfast, mid-morning break, and lunch manifested alertness in the students in a bid to boost their brain power.

- Constipation: because bananas are high in fiber, they contribute to restore normal bowel action, permitting less use of laxatives to relieve this problem.

- Hangovers: quick relief of a hangover can be achieved by drinking a milkshake of bananas combined with honey. While the banana calms the stomach, the honey builds up the depleted blood sugar levels. The milk soothes and hydrates the body's system.

- Nerves: high in B vitamins, bananas help calm the nervous system.

- Ulcers: it is the soft texture and smoothness of bananas in dietary food in intestinal disorders that allows this only fruit to be eaten without distress in severe cases. Besides coating the stomach lining, it also reduces over- acidity that could irritate its lining.

- Heartburn: bananas have a natural antacid effect in the body, and offers soothing relief.

- Morning sickness: snacking on bananas between meals keep blood sugar levels up and avoid morning sickness.

- Mosquito bites: massaging the bite with the inside of a banana skin works amazingly successful at reducing swelling and irritation.

- Overweight and at work? Studies at the Institute of Psychology in Austria revealed that obesity in people with high-pressure jobs lead to their eating comfort foods like chocolate or chips. A review of 5,000 hospital patients discovered most of them to have high-pressure jobs that induced panic-induced food cravings, and recommended their snacking on high-carbohydrate foods to control blood-sugar levels every two hours. Bananas were among the prime choices to accomplish this control.

- Temperature Control: an exotic benefit of eating bananas for the pregnant female is the physical property of this tropical fruit that has the ability to insure that her baby is born with a cool temperature.

- Smoking: bananas are effective in helping those who try to give up smoking. The B6 and B12 vitamins contained in them as well as the potassium and magnesium found in them assist the body recover from the effects of nicotine withdrawal.

- Aphids on your plants? Drape banana skins over its branches, and in less that one or two days, no more aphids.

- Quick shoe shine? Rub your shoes with the inside of a banana skin, and voila, the shine returns.

ACTS OF KINDNESS

The greatest act of kindness this author ever witnessed began early in his life as a student at Pittsburgh's Central Catholic High School in the 1950's.

It involved a six foot, six inch, fellow student by the name of John Kennedy "Jack" Twyman. The year was 1951, and 17-year-old Jack was a junior at the high school. His height caught the interest of Joe Penzelic, the school's basketball coach, forever scanning the all-male student body for whatever players might enhance Central's vaunted reputation for producing outstanding basketball teams.

Twyman had a vague interest in the sport and agreed, at Penzelic's urging, to try out for the school's team. The young man's sudden growth of six inches over a year had made him somewhat clumsy adjusting to this radical physical height, manifested early on by large feet that dragged and stumbled when he ran. Throughout his junior year, however, his performance on the court showed considerable improvement with every game he played. As a senior the following year, Twyman's talent bloomed to the point that he was being scouted by a number of college coaches in the area and offered athletic scholarships by a handful of them. He chose the University of Cincinnati where his basketball prowess potential as an All American was duly noticed – *and achieved*, graduating in 1955.

During Jack's years at Cincinnati, there was another student, six foot, seven inch, 250 lb. Maurice Stokes, also from Pittsburgh, who attended St. Francis College, a small school in Loretto, Pennsylvania, some 80 miles east of Pittsburgh, and whose stellar statistics on the basketball court paralleled Twyman's at the University of Cincinnati.

In 1955, upon graduation from college, both Twyman and Stokes were drafted into the National Basketball Association (NBA) team of the then *Rochester/Cincinnati Royals*, later to be renamed the *Sacramento Kings.* Stokes was a first round pick; Twyman was selected in the second round.

Jack Twyman's years as a pro extended from 1955-1966 where he became the first professional basketball player to average more than 30 points a game (31.2 during the 1959-1960 seasons.)

Maurice Stokes was named NBA Rookie of the Year in his first season as a pro, grabbing no less than 38 rebounds in a single game that year. Twyman and Stokes were close teammates with the *Cincinnati Royals* (a name change in 1957 when the *Royals* moved from Rochester, New York.)

An event that happened during the last regular season game of the1958 NBA season changed both Twyman and Stokes lives. While driving for a layup, Maurice Stokes drew contact, fell to the floor chasing a rebound, and hit his head. He was knocked unconscious. Revived with smelling salts, he later returned to the game. Three days later, he became ill on a flight from Detroit after a playoff game with the *Detroit Pistons*, a game where he scored twelve points and fifteen rebounds. He became ill on the plane, telling a teammate, "I feel like I'm going to die." Stokes later had a seizure, fell into a coma, and was left permanently paralyzed. The medical diagnosis was *post traumatic encephalopathy*, a brain injury that damaged his motor control center.

Stokes three years as an NBA All-Pro professional basketball player were over. The medical bills for his condition piled up beyond any means for him to pay them. His friend, Jack Twyman entered his life and discovered that there was a solution to cover such expenses. In a grand gesture of humanitarianism, Twyman decided to assume the sheer volume of Stokes medical bills by *adopting* Maurice Stokes and remove that horrific burden from his paralyzed friend.

For the years that followed, he was supported by his lifelong buddy and teammate Jack Twyman. Maurice Stokes died of a heart attack twelve years later in 1970 when he was only thirty-six years old. His immense talent as a pro was manifested by his unique ability to play center, forward, or guard. He was second in the NBA in rebounds, and third in assists, a double-feat that only Wilt Chamberlain had matched in a full season.

And, oh, by the way, Maurice Stokes was a black man, a rarity in the NBA during the early 1950's. Adding to this magnificent act of kindness was the manifesting relationship of a white man with a black man in an era when African Americans were still considered second-class citizens.

Twyman organized an NBA fund-raising *Maurice Stokes Memorial Basketball Game* at Kutcher's Hotel and Country Club in Monticello, New York. It was also the first annual event to raise funds for Maurice Stokes, and after his death, for needy former players from the game's early years.

This story was made into a film, *Maurie*, in 1973. Stokes, at his special request, was buried on the campus of St. Francis University in Loretto, Pennsylvania. The Stokes Athletic Center on the grounds of the school is named in honor of him.

Twyman went on to become an NBA analyst for ABC along with sports announcer Chris Schenkel including the NBA finals. He was inducted into the *Naismith Memorial Basketball Hall of Fame* in 1983.

Maurice Stokes was inducted into the *NBA Hall of Fame* in 2004.

Jack Twyman's adoption of his friend, buddy, and fellow NBA player, Maurice Stokes, following his catastrophic on-court injury, is one of the greatest acts of kindness by one human being for another in the Twentieth Century.

That this personal act involved the interracial love and caring of a white man for a black man in the era of its incidence, was, in itself, a classic manifestation and lesson in humanity for the ages.

WIKILEAKS.ORG

December, 2006, a month that will live in infamy for crooked executives, governments, corporations, religions, flim-flamers, and dishonest persons around the globe, was the birthday of a website dedicated to *whistleblowers* to reveal criminal acts of which they had personal knowledge and often documents to prove their claims – and, it allowed them to reveal such acts with anonymity and untraceability of its contributors. *It was called Wikileaks.org.*

As if this website wasn't enough to calcify intestines of the guilty, laws were changed to award the *whistleblowers* a certain percentage of any monies that were recovered or owed in the arrest, capture, and/or convicted individuals that perpetrated the illegal schemes. This also included countries that shared or participated in the nefarious activities brought to light from evidence provided by the do-gooders.

There was an immediate flood of hits to Wikileaks that almost overwhelmed the website. Within a year of the December, 2006, launch, its database had morphed to more than 1.2 million documents. The result led to a rash of front-page newspaper articles and political reforms.

The curious thing about why such whistleblowers exposed the illegal acts of which many of them were employed by the organizations that they snitched on, ranged from promotions denied them by superiors, layoffs, petty arguments with fellow workers, jilted romantic problems with workplace paramours, and the prospect of financial gains from whatever was recovered by law officials. Monetary awards came late to whistleblowers after officials realized what a bonanza of information was spawned by such generous *quid-pro-quo's.*

It is difficult to imagine whether the imminency of impoverishment or long-term jail time occupied the thoughts of those ultimately accused of high crimes and perdition.

A stellar example of whistle-blowing of the first magnitude began following a single Swiss bank's balking in 2008 at the United States claim that accused UBS, Switzerland's largest mega-bank, with financial tentacles throughout the world, being deeply involved in a multi-lending industry scheme by U.S. largest lending institutions that almost brought a total collapse of the economy of the United States.

A move by the U.S. Internal Revenue Agency (IRS) in 2009 against certain banks in Switzerland that helped and assisted concealing millions of dollars from Americans ultra-rich tax dodgers finally got the attention of that country's financial institutions. Long impervious to any threats and maneuvers from foreign countries to obtain confidential financial records of citizens who sought refuge for hiding money and other valuables, Swiss banks took a legendary in-your-face attitude to deny copious demands for revelations and access to such records, making them vulnerable from the protection of an industry that provided the lion's share of this small European country's total economy.

When the IRS in concert with the legal clout of the U.S. Justice Department prepared to sue UBS on evidence that the Swiss bank had lied to authorities and concealed fraudulent foreign accounts, the secrecy started a monumental earthquake in the fortifications that had held off coughing up tens of thousands of requested names of suspected American companies and wealthy citizens using the Swiss national subterfuge to elude paying taxes on ill-gotten money.

[Once UBS turned over selected names (albeit it grudgingly slow) requested by the IRS, the U.S. Justice Department announced a program that would allow the guilty to come forward, pay the taxes and penalties on concealed funds and earned income from them, and avert prison time. It was truly a soul-searching time for the guilty who had no knowledge if their name was included in the roster turned over to the IRS by UBS. Needless to say, it had to be aneurysm time for the foolhardy.]

An act of catastrophic proportions to the Swiss banking industry followed when an executive of one of the country's major lending institutions, *Julius Baer,* didn't get the promotion or pay raise that he felt he was entitled to, especially in light of the bank's expecting him to continue the scams that he ultimately revealed. His name was Rudolph Elmer, who ran the Caribbean operations of the Swiss bank, and decided to blow the whistle on his employer of eight years after being fired in 2002. He left, taking various incriminating paperwork about the bank and its assistance to nations' citizens in their zeal to avoid the tax burdens on their secret deposits.

He moved to Mauritius in the Indian Ocean, and began to parcel out to global tax authorities what he said were the secrets of his former employer. His story made the front pages of U.S. newspapers on January 20, 2010.

Here is a list of famous *whistleblowers* and leaks that brought dramatic changes from their revelations:

JOE DARBY: a member of the United States Military Police who in 2004 first alerted the U.S. Military command of prisoner abuse in the Abu Ghraib prison, in Abu Ghraib, Iraq.

SIBEL EDMONDS: former FBI translator and naturalized citizen of Turkish descent who was fired by the FBI in 2002 for attempting to report cover-ups of security issues, potential espionage, and incompetence. She was gagged by the State Secrets Privilege in her efforts to go to court on these issues, even being turned down by the Supreme Court to hear her case without comment. She is the founder of the National Security Whistleblowers Coalition (NSWC) lobbying Congress to help whistleblowers with legal and other forms of assistance.

DANIEL ELLSBERG: former State Department analyst who leaked the Pentagon Papers in 1971, a secret account of the Vietnam War and its pretexts to *The New York Times*, which revealed endemic practices of deception by previous administrations, and contributed to erosion of public support for the war.

W. MARK FELT: (aka Deep Throat), a secret informant (until 2005) who in 1972 leaked information about President Richard Nixon's involvement in Watergate. The scandal ultimately involved prison terms for White House Chief of Staff H.R. Haldeman and presidential advisor

John Erlichman, and resignation of the presidency by Richard Nixon.

BUNNATINE "Bunny" H. GREENHOUSE: former chief civilian contracting officer for the United States Army Corps of Engineers who exposed illegality in the no-bid contracts for reconstruction in Iraq by a Halliburton subsidy.

CATHY HARRIS: a former United States Customs Service employee who exposed rampant racial profiling against black travelers while working at Atlanta's Hartsfield International Airport. In a tell-all book, *Flying While Black: A Whistleblower's Story*, she personally observed numerous incidents of Black travelers being stopped, frisked, body-cavity searched, detailed for hours at local hospitals, forced to take laxatives, bowel-monitored, and subjected to private and public racist humiliation. The book also detailed allegations of mismanagement, waste, fraud, violations of laws, rules and regulations, corruption, nepotism, favoritism, workplace violence, racial and sexual harassment, sexism, intimidation, on and off the job stalking, and (as if that wasn't enough!) other illegal acts that occur daily to federal employees, especially female, at the U.S. Customs and other federal agencies.

MARK HODLER: International Olympic Committee, an IOC member, who, in December, 1958, blew the whistle on the Winter Olympic bid scandal for the 2002 Salt Lake City games.

HARRY MARKOPOLOS: early whistleblower of suspected securities fraud by Bernard Madoff, tipping off the

Securities and Exchange Commission (SEC) repeatedly beginning in 1999.

FRANK SERPICO: a former New York City police officer who reported several of his fellow officers for bribery and related charges. He is the first officer to testify against police corruption.

JOSEPH WILSON: former U.S. Ambassador, whose July 6, 2003, editorial in *The New York Times* exposed pretexts for the 2003 U. S. invasion of Iraq.

JEFFREY WIGAND: exposed the Big Tobacco Scandal, revealing that executives of the cigarette companies knew that cigarettes were addictive, and approved the addition of carcinogenic ingredients to the cigarettes.

"I WAS FIRED"

"Lucille and I have never been able to enjoy our summer cottage while I was involved with the department. I think it's time I did her justice to enjoy it in her golden years."

"What's this I hear about downsizing our unit?"

"Something about shortages, honey. You know that cruise we took last July? Well, somehow it got charged to the wrong section supervisor."

"I can explain everything. That money in the freezer is counterfeit, and *Testing* asked me to subject it to temperature extremes for long-term currency viability."

"It was nothing, really. While I was at lunch, some of the guys put a porn site on my computer and sent me phony salacious emails from girls who used to work here."

"They said that my Post Office address and lack of a phone number didn't meet their security standards."

"Something about an afternoon bonus program I qualified for at the Pink Pussycat Motel that ended up in the sales manager's mail."

RADIO CODES

Law enforcement agencies and many security companies have employed short cuts to radio transmissions for years to minimize air time to convey messages of importance between and among those monitoring the same radio wavelength as to the disposition and situation at hand during investigations or assignments.

Across the country there are people who have an extreme fascination to listen in on such transmissions. News organizations, journalists, free-lance writers, thieves and petty criminals, as well as news junkies are tuned to the frequencies that broadcast these message short cuts (Channel 1: 453.250, the main frequency, and Channel 2: 453.350, the secondary frequency.)

In the public interest of those wondering what exactly are the code numbers of the most frequently used radio short cut utterances mean in English – enjoy!

10-1 Radio transmission received poorly.
10-2 Radio transmission received well.
10-4 Acknowledgement.
10-5 Relay.
10-6 Busy.
10-7 Out of service.
10-8 In service.
10-9 Repeat.
10-10 Out of service but subject to call
10-11 Dispatching too rapidly
10-12 Visitor(s) present.
10-13 Advise weather and road conditions.
10-14 Escort.

10-15 Prisoner in custody.

10-17 Pickup papers at (location.)

10-18 Complete present assignment ASAP.

10-19 Go to or come to (location.)

10-20 What is your location?

10-21 Call (name) by telephone.

10-22 Disregard previous instructions or take no further action.

10-26 Motorist assist.

10-28 Check for vehicle registration.

10-29 Check for stolen information.

10-30 Does not conform to rules and regulations.

10-32 Is a breathalyzer operator available?

10-33 Emergency radio traffic.

10-36 What is the correct time?

10-37 Whom am I talking to, or who is the operator on duty?

10-38 Change your radio frequency to (channel)

10-39 Your message has been delivered.

10-42 I need a complete driver's license record or wanted status on (name and identification.)

10-43 What is the driver's license status on (name and identifiers)?

10-44 Check for criminal record or wanted status on (name and identifiers).

10-45 Coffee break at (location).

10-49 Personal business.

10-50 Negative.

10-56 Request wrecker at (location).

10-57 Request ambulance at (location).

10-58 Request fire department at (location).

10-59 Request supervisor at (location).

10-63 Radio net priority at (unit).

10-64 Radio net is now free.

10-67 Out of unit for service or unit cleanup at (location).

10-68 Emergency run with red light and siren.

10-75 Traffic stop (tag number and location).

10-76 Fire department en route to (location).

10-77 Ambulance en route to (location).

10-78 Meal break at (location).

10-81 Follow up

10-86 Pick up a rider at (location).

10-90 Officer welfare check.

10-97 Arrived at scene or location of dispatch.

10-98 Last assignment completed

Signal 30 Fatality.

Signal 76 Traffic collision without any injuries.

Signal 82 Traffic collision with injuries.

Signal 83 LPD vehicle involved in traffic collision.

Signal 87 Intoxicated pedestrian.

Signal 88 Intoxicated driver.

Signal 89 Hit and run traffic collision.

NAME YOUR SEDUCTION

Thank you for your interest in seductions to fulfill your life's dreams and make every day on earth more tolerable to your lifestyle.

The choices listed below will help us recommend an avenue for you to pursue palatable living that each one features:

Ceremonies and parades

With or without music

Choice of days for celebrations

Choice of years to celebrate

Option of females to join

Option to banish males for anything deemed an offense by the majority

Sporting events tolerated: A) Badminton; B) Curling; D) Water Boarding; E) Religious executions; F) Swinging sexual flings; G) Cliff diving; H) Spelunking; I) Sumo wrestling

Membership in small groups of less than 100 other people, groups of 1,000-5,000, conventions of 10,000-30,000, 50,000 to less than 100,000, Armies in excess of 100,000.

Preference of race or skin color of those surrounding you: A) Olive; B) Beige; C) Light brown; D) Dark brown; E) Red; F) Swarthy; G) Light black; H) Black black; I) Heinz variety

Choice of Republicans, Democrats, Independents or none

Choice of age group to connect to: A) 8-17: B) 18-28; C) 29-45; D) 46-65; E) 66-89; F) 91-death

Choice of listenable music preferred: A) Classical; B) Popular song; C) Jazz; D) Dixie; E) Ragtime; F) Be-Bop; G) Swing; H) Military; I) Rap; J) Country Western; K) Religious; L) Any kind; M) None

Choice of apparel: A) Uniform; B) Military; C)Medical; D) Puerile; E) Monastic; F) Flamboyant; G) Modest; H) Semi-nude; I) Persian; J) Aborigine; K) Regal; L) Saintly; M) Neanderthal; N) Nothing at all

Choice of funeral desired: A) Ronald Reaganesque; B) High ceremony in a cathedral with professional choir and famous cleric presiding; C) Cortege with at least twenty-five (25) vehicles; D) Mixed races attending dressed in mouse-gray clothing; E) Cremation; F) Lighted flame on a funeral pyre with my spouse floating down the Mississippi or any other nearby major river; G) None.

ASSESSMENT

From the eleven (11) choices you elected from the options available, our jury of evaluators have determined that you should seek out any of the 35,000 religions available to satisfy the selections that most conform to the content of the choices you made.

Thank you for your input and contributions from the American Psychiatric Association where your name and selections will be profiled in our April edition. We would like to illustrate our report with a photo of you. Expect a call from our photographer to arrange an appointment at your convenience.

FAMOUS COMMENTS FROM GUESS WHO?

I don't think being a minority makes you a victim of anything except numbers. The only things I can think of that are truly discriminatory are things like the United Negro College Fund, JET Magazine, Black Entertainment Television, and Miss Black America. Try to have things like The United Caucasian College Fund, Cloud Magazine, White Entertainment Television, or Miss White America, and see what happens. Jesse Jackson will be knocking down your door.

Guns do not make you a killer. I think killing makes you a killer. You can kill someone with a baseball bat or a car, but no one is trying to ban you from driving to a baseball game.

I believe they are called Boy Scouts for a reason, which is why there are no girls allowed. Girls belong in Girl Scouts! Are you listening Martha Burke?

I feel if you think homosexuality is wrong, it is not a phobia, it is an opinion.

I have the right NOT to be tolerant of others because they are different, weird, or tick me off.

When 70% of the people who get arrested are black, that is not racial profiling, it is the Law of Probability.

I believe if you are selling me a milkshake, a pack of cigarettes, a newspaper or a hotel room, you must do it in English. As a matter of fact, if you want to be an American citizen, you should have to speak English.

My father and grandfather didn't die in vain so you can leave the countries you were born in to come over and disrespect ours.

I think the police should have every right to shoot you if you threaten them after they tell you to stop. If you can't understand the word "freeze" or "stop" in English, see the above lines.

I don't think that just because you were not born in this country, you are qualified for any special loan programs, government-sponsored bank loans or tax breaks, etc., so you can open a hotel, a coffee shop, trinket store, or any other business.

We did not go to the aid of certain foreign countries and risk our lives in wars to defend their freedoms, so that decades later they could come over here and tell us our Constitution is a living document and open to their interpretations.

I don't hate the rich. I don't pity the poor.

I know pro wrestling is fake, but so are movies and television. That doesn't stop you from watching them.

I think Bill Gates has every right to keep every penny he made and to make more. If it ticks you off, go and invent the next operating system that's better, and put your name on the building.

It doesn't take a whole village to raise a child right, but it does take a parent to stand up to the kid and say "NO" when necessary.

I think tattoos and piercings are fine if you want them, but please don't pretend they are a political statement. And please, stay at home until those new lip ring heals.I don't want to look at your ugly infected mouth as you serve me French Fries.

I am sick of "Political Correctness." I know a lot of black people, and not a single one of them was born in Africa, so how can they be 'African-Americans'? Besides, Africa is a continent. I don't go around saying I am a Continental-American because my great, great, great, great, great, great grandfather was from Europe. I am proud to be from America and nowhere else.

And if you don't like my point of view, tough!

Those who view CBS' television program 60 MINUTES regularly probably recognize the sometimes cranky rhetoric of Andy Rooney whose comments have been a bookend to the popular Sunday evening show for decades.

CURIOSITIES

Francis Gary Powers, 1929-1977, was the American CIA pilot whose high-flying U2 spy plane was shot down (according to the Soviet Union by one of its ground-to-air missiles)) in 1960 over the Soviet Union while on his 24th mission to photograph that country's secret military installations and other important intelligence sites that could possibly create a future threat to the United States. That the U2 aircraft could fly at some 90,000 feet and beyond the range of any Soviet anti-aircraft weapons at the time, had allowed the U.S. spy plane to fly brazenly over the Soviet Union, and other countries of interest, since 1956. Loaded with high-definition aerial cameras that provided extreme clarity and detail, the U2 always brought a bonanza of information for the CIA wherever it flew.

Powers was selected for the mission after flying other secret flights for the CIA.

At the time his aircraft exploded, Powers was unable to trigger a self-destruct mechanism of his plane before parachuting to safety and being captured by Soviet KGB police. The U2 crashed almost intact, with most of its secret technology revealed. He was tried in a Soviet court, found guilty of spying, and sentenced to ten years in prison (three years of imprisonment followed by seven years at hard labor.)

On February 10, 1962, the United States did a prison exchange with the Soviets, trading Francis Gary Powers (and a student, Frederic Pryor) for the U. S. releases of

Soviet spy KGB Colonel Vilyam Fisher (aka Rudolph Abel) at the Glienicke Bridge in Berlin, Germany.

At the time of this international incident, President Dwight Eisenhower had issued a CIA cover story that turned out to be patently false, and he had to later admit the existence of such an airplane and the reconnaissance mission (Eisenhower originally said the aircraft was a "weather plane") that it had provided for the U.S. security interests. That it set back peace talks between the United States and the Soviet Union for years became obvious.

The story that was released later maintained that the U2 had been launched from a U.S. Peshawar Airbase in Pakistan.

Several years later this author was watching a Public Broadcasting Station in Pittsburgh (WQED) on a program that dealt with Gary Francis Powers U2 spy plane blown up over the Soviet Union while on a reconnaissance mission. The source of the story came from Sweden. It documented in detail about a remote airbase routinely permitted by Sweden to provide the U. S. a secret airport for refueling and servicing a U2 high-altitude flight prior to mission flights without mentioning the target country for the flyover.

The gist of the story had to do with an airport mechanic who worked at the secret airport who had been discovered to be a Soviet agent. It was further learned after his arrest that he had placed an explosive device in the rear end of the aircraft with a timer set to trigger some critical hours into the U2's flight. The program showed footage of the man from capture to the trial that followed. Found guilty, the agent was sentenced to fifteen years in a Swedish prison.

Original news that the U2 was launched from Pakistan didn't make it to the press. The distance from Pakistan to the Soviet Union's target area is some 3,200 miles; the distance from Sweden to the same Soviet target area is some 400 air miles. Logistically, it doesn't make sense to provide fuel to fly 3,200 miles to the Soviet border, and then have to fly another 2,000-6,000 reconnaissance miles, let alone land safely (which it had 23 times before) at an unknown base (never revealed) taxes credulity. It does make sense, however, to originate flying from Sweden to the target area and land at a U.S. base in Pakistan. The difference of fuel consumption for the flight from Sweden to Pakistan tells a story all by itself.

No investigative reporter or any news whatsoever of this lopsided account of what brought down Gary Francis Power's aircraft made the front (or back) pages of America's newspapers.

No challenge was ever made to the Swedish television account of the U2 airplane exploding in the air. There was never any proof provided that the Soviet Union had developed a missile that could reach the altitude that the U2 flew. What was known after the U2's crash was that the aircraft had an explosion in the tail end of the plane, the very location that was revealed by the Soviet spy to Swedish authorities of where he had placed the bomb when on trial.

There was never any acknowledgment or proof whatsoever forthcoming after the incident that the Soviets had, in fact, a ground-to-air missile capable of reaching the altitude that was the realm of the U2 spy plane. The United States simply believed the phony claim of the Soviet Union, and that was that. At no time after the incident was there any mention of such a missile even being test-fired that could substantiate that country's high altitude weapon.

Upon return to the United States after the prisoner exchange, Powers was quizzed in detail by Congress about his actions during the U2 crash.

Powers death was the result of piloting a news helicopter in southern California where a mysterious fuel shortage was blamed on his plummeting to earth with a fellow crew member. A faulty fuel gauge and a mechanic's work on it was the story pedaled to the press. More than a few people blamed it on other suspicious or nefarious circumstances.

Few people know that Canadian singer and songwriter, Paul Anka, wrote the tune "My Way" dedicated to summing up the career arrogance of Frank Sinatra, America's most popular singer during the mid-20th century. The lyrics are de facto descriptive of the disdain the entertainer treated reporters and subordinates alike.

Sinatra's handful of wives and girlfriends bore witness to the egotistical attitude he manifested when married to them, one exacerbated by his unending habit of constantly listening *only* to his own recordings and nothing else while they were married. The singer also had a volatile reputation of blowing up over the most trivial observations that he encountered almost on a daily basis. On one occasion, entering his home office, he went berserk over discovering an orange telephone had been installed on his desk, yanking it off the top and throwing it against a wall, yelling expletives at his staff.

When karaoke parties and similar events swept into bars and taverns in the latter half of the 20th century, Sinatra's angry version of "My Way" became the most predominant popular choice of males electing to seize a microphone and bellowing out their own version of the song – in tune, or usually out of tune. Sung out-of-tune, karaoke singers can provide manifold miseries for those having to suffer listening to the awful strains of wannabes grasping the mike. Nevertheless, people line up at karaoke bars to express their version of music chosen from a catalogue of favorites that whit their interest, and invite the rush of performing among fellow singers waiting for their moment in the wings.

The talent that shows up for karaoke nights can be wonderful, and draw huge crowds that benefit business owners. On the other hand, bad performances by people who expect to sing multiple times without surrendering the microphone can cause anger from those waiting their turn. In some cases, fights will break out, and in some countries, followed by a killing of the particularly bad performer. The song that has occasioned such deadly behavior more than any, was "My Way." It has become known as "My Way killing" in a certain part of the world where the population treats karaoke songfests akin to a fanatical religion.

In the Philippines the incidents of karaoke killings of men singing their version of "My Way" by others who are offended by the guy's voice, style, and ability to maintain in-tune vocal melody have caused authorities to label such murders in a category unto itself known as "My Way killings."

The Sinatra song has long baffled Filipinos to wonder what has caused such an outbreak of animosity among karaoke contestants to choose this favorite, and just what triggers such violence from an audience that would entail such displeasure to kill performer(s) whose version offended some in the bar crowd to commit such crimes.

It got so bad in the that country that the Sinatra hit was banned from karaoke bars to halt the criminal activity that no one could unravel the rationale for killing someone. It is no secret in the Philippines that the people take extraordinary pride in their natural ability for lyric singing, which, in turn, may explain why they may be vulnerable to take vital measures against anyone whose performance they find grossly substandard let alone offensive.

Truth to tell, most killings of karaoke singers were the result of those who sang loudly and out of tune, prompting people to laugh or jeer.

Pastime parties and social outings for the Filipinos invariably include karaoke songfests, and the prolific posting of outdoor sidewalk karaoke stalls throughout the country tempt passersby an opportunity to indulge solo singing in the open air to savor their appetite to exercise their vocal chords.

In that part of the world, karaoke bars are more abundant where similar races seem to have adopted this songfest activity. In Malaysia, a singer who refused to surrender his microphone to another waiting hopeful was stabbed to death for his hogging it. In another case, a man in Thailand was so offended by a neighbor's outdoor karaoke fest and a singer's version of a John Denver tune *(Take Me Home Country Roads)*, that he killed eight of the partygoers.

In the USA, such violent reactions to singer's renditions of their favorites at karaoke bars seem petty. Fights are more venial, a punch in the nose here, a kick in the ass there, and some obscene gestures and guttural words to the offender seem to satisfy most angry gestures aimed toward offending song performances.

Challenges to "step outside" to settle grievances could easily be on the horizon.

DATES OF DISASTERS AND DELIVERANCE

American history books have traditionally noted and published the positive aspects of how the United States of America developed from its earliest settlements to its current era of existence.

Book publishers of American history have always been keenly aware of how their accounts of history appeal to government officials who select and decide which company's version they want to buy and teach to the nation's children, adolescents, and even universities. It is no secret among historians that specialize in truthful fact-finding that history books have omitted or soft-pedaled any negative aspects of American governmental acts, misdeeds, or outright crimes against humanity.

As a refresher course of notable dates of infamy that have escaped inclusion in our history, the following list is rendered along with deliverance attempts to right such wrongs.

1619 – Slaves were introduced and delivered to American colonial shores, most from the Nigerian area of Africa.

1772 – On June 22, 1772, Lord Chief Justice Mansfield declared slavery illegal in England and all of its colonies and territories. The colonies in America refused to free their slaves, and a war broke out between England and its settlement abroad which was won by the colonial states in 1781. [This omission of fact, that the war was fought over slavery, has never been mentioned in U. S. history books.]

1865 – Thanks to President Abraham Lincoln and a congress composed of Northern states, slavery in America was outlawed by the Thirteenth Amendment.

1920 – American women of all races were permitted to vote. Even though giving birth to the men that deemed them incompetent to make intelligent choices, a woman prevailed but only after the Nineteenth Amendment was passed in 1919.

1942 – After declaring war against Japan and Germany in December, 1941, President Franklin Delano Roosevelt in an Executive Order decided in February of 1942 that some 127,000 Americans of Japanese descent should be force-collected and interned in concentration camps scattered around the country in military-style barracks (without interior walls), surrounded by barbed-wired walls and turrets manned by security guards. Given a month to dispose of any property or businesses, or face confiscation by the government after that deadline, the Japanese Americans were then allowed to carry no more than two suitcases of possessions aboard whatever bus or train was provided them for transport to the twenty-seven encampments constructed in remote areas of unusable land across the vast stretches of the mid-west and west. These included hot arid deserts, swamps, deforested plains void of fertile soil, and far removed from any populated towns and cities. By mid-1944, Roosevelt realized that these Japanese Americans posed no threat to the country, and freed the tens of thousands of them to disperse wherever they wanted to relocate in their country of choice. Without ownership of anything or any jobs or means to make a living, this disaster of the first magnitude seemed to escape history's opinion and reputation of the President. No German-Americans living in the United States were considered a threat to America's WW II effort or warranted internment of any kind during the 4½ year conflict.

1948 – President Harry Truman integrated the military services, permitting Americans of all races to serve side by side wherever they may be needed.

1965 – The Civil Rights act of 1965 declared that black Americans now had the rights and privileges that white Americans always had.

1967 – After a Supreme Court Decision, 9-0, (*Loving vs. Virginia*) people of different races were permitted to marry one another. Seventeen (17) states had heretofore criminalized it. They were Texas, Arkansas, Mississippi, Missouri, Louisiana, Alabama, Florida, Georgia, Tennessee, North Carolina, South Carolina, Virginia, West Virginia, Kentucky, New Jersey, Delaware, and Oklahoma.

1986 – President Ronald Reagan decided that any survivors of the American Japanese that were interned in concentration camps should be awarded an average $30,000 for their trouble. The amount was determined by the ages of survivors, most in their 70's and 80's that were deemed not to need excessive amounts of cash in their end-of-life years.

2000 – The United States Supreme Court elected George W. Bush President by a 5-4 decision, even though he had garnered 2,000,000 fewer popular votes than his adversary, Albert Gore. When Justice Antonin Scalia was questioned about why the Supreme Court snatched the suit illegally from Florida's Supreme Court, Scalia's answer was, "Get over it."

2003 – The United States President George W. Bush declared a pre-emptive war against Iraq on the specious and false premise that it had weapons of mass destruction that posed a threat to America. Thousands of American military troops died as a result of this historically mistaken judgment.

CONGRESSIONAL ROUGH & TUMBLE

A funny thing happened after the presidential election of 2008 when a half-white male, *nee Barack Obama,* was chosen to occupy The White House (pun intended.)

Enmities between Democrats and Republicans came out of the woodwork *en masse,* with nasty accusations on both sides that grew exponentially as President Obama's promise to "change" America began to take form, albeit after a shaky start after almost a year that witnessed both political parties resembling and oil and water's refusing to integrate.

The rhetorical tone of each party's reaction to bills introduced in Congress grew intemperate to their proposals, often including personal snipes at the person who proposed them.

That *Health Care* was the first item on Obama's agenda became a nuclear issue was an understatement. After discussing the myriad programs that ultimately were contained in the controversial 2,900-page bill, the noteworthy changes also included some unsavory ones, things that had to be included to reach a minimum consensus for the Democratic majority to pass under the noses of belligerent Republicans. It was during the process of enumerating these changes to the collective House and the Senate chambers that shouts of "You lie!", "Baby killer", "Hell no!" disturbed the traditional decorum demanded by this exalted body of legislators.

Worse was the unapologetic behavior of those (Republicans) that uttered them.

This is not to say that instances of elected representatives of this exalted body expressing its ire were rare in its history since conception. Check these out, according to history:

- In 1798, Republican Rep. Matthew Lyon, taking umbrage at nasty remarks of his war record by fellow Rep. Roger Griswald, spit a hocker in Griswald's face. A fortnight later, Griswald hit Lyon with a cane, and then had to fend off Lyon returning blows to his body from a pair of fire tongs.

- 1837: Rep. Bailie Peyton was so offended by testimony being given by a former federal bank director, Reuben Whitney, at a committee investigation that Peyton yelled at him, "You shan't say a word while you are in this room; if you do, I will put you to death."

- 1845: Rep. Edward Black came up behind Rep. Joshua Giddings while he was making a speech and whupped him in the back of his head with a cane. At this point a burly Rep. William Hammett seized Black, flung him over his shoulder and carried him out like a bag of flour (according to one report from John Quincy Adams' memoir of the event.)

- 1856: Rep. Preston Brooks was so upset about Sen. Charles Sumner's castigating remarks about his pro-slavery cousin Sen. Andrew Butler, that he went on the Senate floor and beat Sumner senseless, inabling the man to return to the Senate for three years.

- 1902: Sen. John McLaurin accused his fellow Carolinian Senator Benjamin Tillman of telling a "willful, malicious, and deliberate lie." The accusation got McLaurin a solid punch in the nose by Tillman.

- 1964: Republican Sen. Strom Thurmond, standing outside of a committee room, was attempting to frustrate a quorum forming from arriving colleagues to consider the nomination of a Civil Rights Community Relations Service candidate, when he spotted Democratic pro civil-rights activist Sen. Ralph Yarborough entering the room. The two senators engaged in a wrestling match before being restrained by other committee men.

- 1970: Sen. George McGovern exposed his opposition to the Vietnam War by taking to the Senate floor and accusing the venerable body by declaring, "This chamber reeks of blood!"

- 1985: Disputed elections brought out the worst of the losers especially in Indiana when House Democrat Frank McCloskey was awarded the 1984 election winner over Republican Rep. Bob McEwen. McCloskey won in a party-line vote orchestrated by Democratic Speaker of the House Tip O'Neil. McEwen told O'Neil, "You know how to win votes the old-fashioned way – you steal them." Republican Rep. Newt Gingrich maintained the Democrats were a "leadership of thugs."

- 2004: Vice President Dick Cheney, as President of the Senate, never permitted the decorum of the Senate chamber to influence his choice of words or behavior. When Democratic Sen. Patrick Leahy inquired about Cheney's ties to Haliburton where he was CEO of the giant company for five years, Cheney told him to "go fuck yourself."

UNCLE SAM NEEDS YOU! NOW!
WHO ARE THESE CONGRESSMEN?

In 2010, American voters who had confidence in the country's 435 Congressmen and 100 Senators had sunk to a dismal 12% approval level. Democrats, Republicans, and Independents were in turmoil with each other, blaming opposition parties for preventing passage of all but the most critical acts they needed to stay in existence.

Being hypercritical of Congress was nothing new. The writer Samuel Clemens, a/k/a Mark Twain, in the 19th century tweaked its efficiency mercilessly during his lifetime. This began a skein of humorists that followed him in excoriating certain members individually by revealing their quirks and corruption that have morphed into the 21st Century.

Collectively, citizens knew next to nothing about just who these lawmakers were except that they had elected 435 people to the House of Representatives for two-year terms, and 100 Senators for six-year terms in office.

In September of 2010, *The American Legion Magazine* decided to unveil statistics of these lawmakers, some that had reputations for being effete individually, and constipated collectively. Its revelations were eye-opening, to say the least. With the help of a Congressional Research Service report, it paints quite a jigsaw picture of the careers and educational backgrounds of those that compose this lawmaking body.

- The average age of members of both Houses of Congress: 58.2 years
- Average length of service for Representatives: 11 years
- Average length of service for Senators: 12.9 years
- Number of women in the House of Representatives: 76
- Number of women in the Senate: 17
- Number of physicians: 16
- Number of dentists: 2
- Number of ministers: 4
- Number of former governors: 13
- Number of former mayors: 38
- Number of former state legislators: 268
- Number of former congressional staffers: 115
- Number of former White House staffers/White House Fellows: 12
- Number of former sheriffs: 4
- Number of former police officers: 4
- Number of former state troopers: 2
- Number of former physicists: 3
- Number of chemists: 1
- Number of engineers: 6
- Number of former Major League Baseball players: 1
- Number of former National Football League players: 1
- Number of former pilots of Marine 1: 1
- Number of former astronauts: 1
- Number of former naval aviators: 1
- Number of former commanders of an aircraft carrier group: 1

A total of 122 members of Congress have served in the military dating from World War II up to wars in Iraq and Afghanistan. Three representatives and one senator are graduates of the U.S. Military Academy, and two representatives are graduates of the U.S. Naval Academy.

Twenty-seven representatives and one senator have no degree beyond a high-school diploma, 83 representatives and 17 senators hold master's degrees, 168 representatives and 57 senators hold law degrees, 24 representatives hold doctorates, and three senators and two representatives were Rhode Scholars.

Twelve representatives and one senator were born outside the United States, whose places of birth include Cuba, Mexico, Taiwan, India, Japan, Pakistan, Peru, Canada, Vietnam and the Netherlands.

WHAT DON'T YOU WANT TO KNOW

Only the United States and Japan, among civilized nations of the world, still have the death penalty for convicted criminals. The uniqueness of Japan's execution process by *hanging* includes features that diminish its methodology.

Without any warning whatsoever, the prisoner is suddenly escorted into an empty room with three solid walls and one wall with a glass viewing area for those witnesses to the execution. On the floor is a rectangle outlined in red paint for the condemned person to stand that constitutes a trap door that is released simultaneously by three executioners. Three ropes are connected to one wall, only one of which triggers the trap door mechanism when the order to initiate the execution is given. None of the three assigned to pull the ropes know which one of the trio actually send the convict into eternity.

Family and relatives of the condemned are never notified of the prisoner's time of death and location of the execution (Japan has eight such death chambers) until after it has occurred.

As a humanitarian gesture by the Japanese government and a prelude to the convict's hanging, he is served a meal of his/her? Favorite food.

Death penalties are usually meted out within two years of conviction, and no appeals are permitted the condemned once a death sentence has been issued.

The United States allows individual states a choice in method of execution, some even permitting the condemned to pick his/her choice of how to end one's life on earth. The usual ones offered are electrocution, chemical cocktails, gas chamber, and firing squad (Utah only.)

The average time for an execution to take place after sentencing can average 24 years and cost the government (us taxpayers) some $2,400,000. Since the discovery of DNA evidence in 1953, a horror factor has entered the equation of possible innocence thanks to high-tech methods that have exonerated dozens of prisoners who have been wrongfully convicted.

Certain states have had to be dragged kicking and screaming into using DNA evidence to determine whether the conviction might be overturned. Texas and Illinois lead the pack in wrongful convictions as a result of DNA tests or confessions from other convicts. Illinois alone revealed that it had wrongfully executed 16 innocent prisoners in the past decade as a result of DNA evidence and confessions of convicts that was unearthed by facts from attorneys of *The Innocence Project,* a program started in the 1990's by volunteer groups across the country composed of lawyers and law students. Some judges along the way succeeded to quash DNA requests to establish possible innocence in re-opening cases that were highly questionable by the legal community. Illinois has subsequently put a moratorium on the death penalty.

Few people know that there are more than 35,000 religions in the world today. And, that all but a handful were invented by male human beings over the millennia.

Little or no involvement by females participated in roles other than promoting the sects and cults proselytized by men.

History has revealed that there were four major religions from which spin-offs and splinter groups formed some 15,000 years ago: *Buddhism, Taoism, Hinduism,* and *Judaism.*

For every birth of a religion, the framer(s) pleaded that an extra-worldly spirit initiated their special power, usually via a vision from wherever, that galvanized them to get out whatever message they wanted to purvey to people who were mesmerized by the charisma and personality of who was promoting it (of course, after having been chosen by the deity of choice who had an agenda that had to be adopted "to be saved.")

The problem with so many religions was trying to justify the very plurality of them. The rationale could not withstand philosophical scrutiny of any of them. Of course, philosophy being the ultimate science of logic and reason stood in the way of discounting the presence of a deity, spirit, god, hallucination, or the some fifty names given to whatever spirit was claimed to be the source of the religion and whatever agenda it professed and promoted.

Religions prey on the ignorance of people to investigate whatever sect is seeking their obeisance. Preachers, ministers, imams, and people with extraordinary gifts of oratory are well aware of their influence on the masses whose education suffers from the wherewithal of trying to make a living. They know it's easier to "go with the flow" than challenge tenets of a religion claiming lofty principles when limited and bereft of even the basics of education.

A real religion buster came out in September, 2010, when the intellectually influential British scientist (mathematics and physicist) Stephen Hawking, (1942-) physically and vocally debilitated by a neuro-muscular dystrophy that had progressed over the years leaving him almost completely paralyzed, wrote a scholarly treatise debunking all religions whose faith was contingent on the existence of a "God" or a namesake indicating such a spiritual supreme being as the rationale for embracing their doctrines. His argument was based simply on proving that the *"big bang"* previous theory was replaced by factual discoveries of its very existence, and that through a progression of time over eons galaxies, stars, planets, and creatures have evolved, and that no spiritual deity had any involvement whatsoever in the transformations that sprang from this monumental event.

Stephen Hawking is universally acknowledged as the world's singular intellectual without peer in a field where he stands alone in scientific credibility above all others.

Leave it to one religion to abscond with the letters "BC" and "AD."

"Before Caesar" and "After the Lord" (Latin translation of A.D. [Ad Dominum]) referred to Julius Caesar who was considered a *god,* and referred to as *Lord* during his reign over the Roman Empire. When the Roman Empire collapsed circa 300-400 AD, guess which religion snatched the famous BC and AD from under the ruins of one of the most famous empires in the world. BC became "before Christ" and AD became "after the Lord", a title stolen from Rome's greatest Leader.

In 1920, Russian surgeon, Serge Voronoff, working in France, made headlines by performing the first monkey-to man testicle transplant as an enhancement and cure for men suffering from erectile dysfunction. The news set off a rash of other animal testicular transplants by Voronoff with two of his associates, goats being the favorite transplant choice for gonads.

Famous people who were born bastards constitute a *Who's Who* of history. Other than *Cain* and *Able*, of "Bible fame", famous sons of Adam and Eve, if you believe, the short list includes:

Alexander the Great, William the Conqueror, Leonardo da Vinci, Michaelangelo, Fidel Castro, Alexander Hamilton, Louis Armstrong, Ted Bundy, Oprah Winfrey, Cesare Borgia (son of Pope Alexander VI), Ella Fitzgerald, Adolf Schickelgruber (Hitler), - well, you get the idea.

In 1857, Dred Scott and his spouse brought suit against the wife of a doctor who owned the couple, maintaining the doctor promised their freedom as slaves when he died. Upon the physician's death, though, his wife balked at this decision, saying that Scott and his wife were also part of her property. The case, *Scott vs. Sandford,* was dismissed by the U.S. Supreme Court issuing a statement that only citizens of the United States could bring suit in this country – and the Scotts, being slaves, were denied their claim.

This was one of many justifications that brought about the country's 14th Amendment to the Constitution, July

9, 1868. Actually, the Civil Rights Act of 1866 granted citizenship to all persons born in the United States. It was included in the 1868 14ᵗʰ Amendment along with voting rights for all males born in this country – including blacks.

The curious thing about ratifying this Amendment that required ¾ of the states (28 of 37) to embrace it, was the initial count showing 16 states, mostly southern confederate ones, against it. Political pressure was brought to bear on enough of them, using questionably illegal tactics, to reach the 28 needed to pass the Amendment. Those tactics today remain the bone in the throat of the states that had confirmation stuffed down their craws.

Female suffrage in the United States had to wait until 1920 to exercise their voting rights. Early excuses (by male lawmakers) included fickle behavior and the weakness of women deciding important issues that kept them out of consideration from such a constitutional right until the 19ᵗʰ Amendment was passed and ratified in 1920. That females bore sons that ultimately denigrated their mothers' ability to choose wise choices in running this country is evidence of the profound ignorance so many of our forebears brought to the table in this nation's history.

DON'T EVEN GO THERE
SMORGASBORD

POLITICAL CORRECTNESS

Political Correctness, otherwise known as "everything is relative gone amuck", began in early times when it was taught in schools indicated that there are no absolutes where human activity is concerned. On the other side of the argument, there was a "school" that carried "absoluteness" to the extreme. Lost in all this effort was using common sense.

At Texas A & M University, it initiated an annual contest calling for the most appropriate definition of a contemporary term. In 2010, the term "Political Correctness" was chosen for examination to reach the closest reality of matching what these twin words conveyed to actual perception by those who heard it incorporated into so many media speeches and publications.

And the winner was . . .

"Political Correctness is a doctrine, fostered by a delusional, illogical minority, and rabidly promoted by an unscrupulous mainstream media, which holds forth the proposition that it is entirely possible to pick up a piece of shit by the clean end."

A SEX STORY

The sex story of the century began in 1953 when the team of Drs. Francis Crick and James Watson announced they had discovered the human genome configuration consisted of a double helix containing *deoxyribonucleic acid* (DNA), the biological instruction that makes each species unique. This startling event also enabled scientists an opportunity to then delve into the makeup of the role of what each single human genome controlled in the physiology of human beings.

With some 20,000 genomes incorporated in every person, the DNA of a single genome made it possible to locate the ones that determined the color of one's hair, the color of one's eyes, the pallor of one's skin, et cetera, et cetera, et cetera. And of course, it also revealed manifold evidence of one's sex and sexual orientation.

In the years that followed, scientists began the tedious process of investigating just what each of the 20,000+ genomes in the human body influenced and controlled. It was the entrepreneurial American biologist Dr. J. Craig Venter who was the first scientist to sequence the human genome in 2001, all 20,000+ of them in a six-billion-letter) genome – his own. It took him some three month to complete, and he shocked the medical scientific world when he made his epoch announcement in 2001.

Revelations began to pour out in science journals of genomes that revealed good news and bad news that depicted one's vulnerability to certain diseases, size and shape of bodily features, and a myriad of revelations connected to the history of the genomes that one inherited from one's past familial connections. Cost at the time for the curious to have their fortune told by a complete genome screening was $100,000. Needless to say, few people that could afford such an operation were not inclined to know what life had in store for them, good news or bad news.

DNA revelations led to a more startling reality when it came to human sexual orientations. Up to the middle of the 20th Century, *heterosexuality* was considered to be the only normal universal sexual orientation. Anything other than that was considered a psychosis, deviant, sub-normal, unlawful, punishable by imprisonment or death in many countries, condemned by most religions, and recognized by most medical authorities to be a physical and psychological condition that had a cure.

By 1964, medical scientists had discovered the genome that revealed *homosexuality* was real, valid, and unchangeable. This didn't mean that it was overnight accepted science by the world, certain countries, most religions, and the great majority of people who had grown up with the utter belief of its being a basic human malady.

In the years that followed, more shocking news came out that *bisexuality* also qualified as a sexual orientation. Then came the inclusion of *transsexual* and *transgendered* orientations. In 1993, yet another orientation was included: *asexual,* (persons who have no attraction to either sex.)

By the arrival of the 21st Century, a slow acceptance of persons having any one of these six sexual orientations began to manifest itself in people running for political office, those working in government and the public sector, and certain progressive countries throughout the world where religion's influence had waned.

In short, it took a scientific discovery of the first magnitude in the last half of the 20ᵗʰ Century for mankind around the world to discover just who exactly they were.

By 2010, the American Psychiatric Association, the American Psychological Association, the American Counseling Association, the National Association of Social Workers in the USA, the Royal College of Psychiatrists, and the American Psychological Association all maintained there is no sound scientific evidence that sexual orientation can be changed.

So there!

BEEF UP THE GRIEF!

A career that women have had a lock on for hundreds, if not thousands of years, were hired hands to provide professional mourners at funerals. That is not to say their work didn't have its problems with their male counterparts who found the practice demeaning, opportunistic, insincere, let alone mercenary.

History provides many examples of laws and rules banning such provocative examples of phony grief:

- 6ᵗʰ Century B.C.: Greek Legislator Solon institute curbs against the use of professional mourners
- 4ᵗʰ Century B.C.: Plato forbids hired mourners in his Laws
- 4ᵗʰ Century: Saint John Chrysostom derides the use of "hired women as mourners to make the mourning more intense, to fan the fires of grief."

- 17th Century: Irish church forbids the hiring of professional mourners
- 18th Century: Archbishop of Cashel prohibits "all unnatural screams and shrieks, and fictitious cries and elegies at wakes, together with the savage custom of howling and bawling at funerals"

Professional mourners were widely used in ancient Greece, Rome, and the Middle East. It continued through the middle Ages, and to some countries, even to the present day. Many professional mourners saw themselves as integral and a crucial part of the grief process. They also considered themselves as hired event planners.

The idea of paying for grief practitioners made many people uncomfortable, and accusations of opportunism, insincerity, and mercenary motives surfaced wherever the practice prevailed. On the other hand, countries such as Spain's Jews in the 14th Century used the hired mourner as a coordinator of grief more than metaphorical by accompanying her wailing with a rhythm-setting tambourine.

By the late middle Ages, the church stepped into the fray and looked down on the use of professional mourners maintaining the thought of heaven should be enough to satisfy the grieving parties, and excessive lamentation by mourners indicated a lack of belief in a happy afterlife.

Throughout the ages, grieving was considered more of a women's thing and a province that involved female members of a household. Some psychiatrists maintain that women have an inborn sensitivity to grief more than men. In ancient times, the only opportunity that they had to be heard was via the funerary ceremony.

Some historians have even suggested that banishing ancient professional mourners with laws and prohibitions was simply sexist: they simply did not want to encourage women using their voices as a prelude to power.

SUNDRY RUMINATIONS
WEAR AND WHEREFORE OF UNDERWEAR

The earliest evidence of men wearing anything that could be construed as underwear was discovered in 1991 when a group of mountaineers hiking through the Tyrolean Alps stumbled upon the frozen remains of a man believed to have lived some 5,300 years ago. The bits of clothing on the body included a leather loincloth, establishing the precedent that the *loincloth* clearly was the antecedent of men's underwear.

When the archeologist Howard Carter discovered the tomb of Egyptian Pharaoh Tutankhamen in 1922, a detailed examination of the young mummy (19 years old at death) revealed that he had been adorned with no less than 145 loincloths apparently to sustain him in the time to come in his afterlife. The isosceles triangular-shaped loincloth had strings attached to each tip to be worn with one of the triangles draped down across the buttocks, then fed through the legs to the front by its string, and inserted over the tied strings of the other two triangles whose strings were wrapped around the waist.

When the loincloth was covered by a robe or a skirt, the loincloth became *underwear.*

As late as 1835, the loincloth was still being used as underwear by shepherds in Southwestern France.

One thing is for sure, men's anatomy always dictated the shape of his underclothes.

By the middle Ages, undergarments came into use to protect the body from the elements and from outer garments; also to protect the outer garments from the body. Toward the end of the 14th century, the codpiece came into fashion, known as the *braguette* in French, and the *brachetta* in Italian. Worn above the stockings, it was a utilitarian flap men used to cover their genitalia, often doubling as a pocket for keys or small personal items. It was often padded for comfort as well as serving esthetically sexually to garner notice and possible envy in social circles. The most prominent codpiece of the 16th century was that of King Henry VIII, an exaggerated prominence that could probably accommodate a penile erection. His daughter, Queen Elizabeth assumed the English throne in 1558, and began a fashion change that diminished the use and form of the codpiece by feminizing men's apparel. It was gone by the end of Elizabeth's reign in 1603, being replaced by a vertical opening concealed in folds of fabric.

Armor in the 16th century followed fashion trends, and many suits of armor included the codpiece as a reflection of those trends.

The convenience of the codpiece was the opening it provided for urination without removing other pieces of clothing. It used buttons, snaps, or laces to quickly facilitate voiding as necessary – particularly when one had too much mead to drink.

The codpiece, however, didn't really disappear altogether. It is still used today by stage performers in modern era performances in costumes for ballet, rock music and metal musicians and in the leather subculture.

Throughout the middle ages to the present, men sought underwear that would not bulge, bind, gap, chafe or sag. It should be something that did not shrink in the wash, and when hung out to dry, would not attract enemy fire.

The early trend began with full "long john" underwear (with a flap in the back for bowel movements), knee high elastic shorts with a vertical frontal flap (sometimes a horizontal one), to a boxer type (designed from use by professional boxers), from products made from cotton Dacron, nylon, spandex, and artificial fabrics that promoted comfort over fashion.

For men wearing skirts, kilts, or other parade-use ceremonial garb, underwear is not traditional, if only because normal bodily functions can complicate the mission at hand which usually involves elimination of bodily fluids or solids.

And speaking of kilts, a color photograph of Queen Elizabeth 2nd, published in 2010, showed her seated next to a bagpiper wearing kilts at a British ceremonial event. The photographer took the frontal picture of the two from ground level, showing the Queen sitting properly in her usual royal style. The low angle of the photo not only captured the bagpiper's open kilt and his lack of underwear, he was also noticeably uncircumcised.

In the 1800's, people referred to men's underwear as *nether integuments*. [One wonders where in the etymology of words gave birth to this designation of bodily garments.] Undershirts for men became popular as blotters for underarm sweat were needed to fend off any visible fabric stains, particularly of expensive garments worn by the wealthy or military hierarchy in parades or official ceremonies, especially in warm weather.

The T-shirt model of underwear came into being during the reign of England's Queen Victoria in the 1800's. In a visit to the British Royal Navy, an officer feared that the sight of male hairy armpits would be unsuitable for the Queen's royal eyes, ordered that sleeves be sewn onto the soldiers' heavy woolen undershirts.

The first appearance of the combined undershirt and drawers was in 1876 when the B.V.D. was born by its manufacturer Bradley, Voorhees & Day.

The *Jockey* brief made its debut in 1935 at Chicago's famed Marshall Field store. First month's sales of the elastic-banded underwear was some 12,000 packages, and then zoomed to 30,000 in the following month.

But the monumental change in men's underwear showed up in the 1980's when designer Calvin Klein introduced his product with his name prominently incorporated in the waistband of his jockey-type shorts.

An event that sent undershirt sales into a nosedive occurred in a 1934 film starring "King of Hollywood" Clark Gable and Claudette Colbert: *It Happened One Night*. In a bedroom scene showing a close-up of Gable leering sexily at his co-star, the camera showed Gable slowly taking off his shirt to reveal – horrors – no undershirt! It was the first time in movies that a man other than Tarzan went bare-chested in a film. Suddenly, overnight, T-shirt sales took a tailspin since Clark Gable was everyman's ideal of what manhood stood for. It took years before the T-shirt recovered some modicum of popularity along with the sleeveless tank top.

HEAVENLY VOICES

In the last two decades of the 20th Century, a scandal of epoch magnitude was slowly beginning to unravel within the Roman Catholic religion that revealed sexual involvement of its priests, bishops, and even cardinals with youths from families of its faithful.

At first glance it seemed that the stories of pedophilia concerned local parishes in pocket areas of the United States, Boston in particular, where Cardinal Bernard Law managed to envelop himself in a massive cover-up of how he handled parish priests who had histories of flagrant sexual contact with young boys they victimized under the guise of religious mentoring.

When rumors of such deviancy began to have truthful origins, the clerics under Cardinal Law's auspices were transferred quickly to other parishes in a kind of musical chairs of the guilty to mitigate, if not conceal, the wholesale deviancy that had begun to sully the Catholic Church's image among its faithful. Cardinal Law's clumsy imperious attempt to discount the immensity of the scandal soon reached the Vatican in Rome, and he was recalled there to spend the rest of his life ministering to a remote basilica in the boondocks of Italy.

The virus of this emerging story of similar pederasty in other cities of the country slowly began to take root in the daily news to uncover a vast network of how other Catholic officials had been doing the same thing as Boston's now infamous cleric and subsequent reaction by Popes and their close Vatican assistants around the world. The scandal had become universal, with some revelations in foreign countries began and surpassed even the most grievous that filled the newspapers, magazines, and television stories and dominated the news that had leaked out in the United States.

The lawsuits that followed on these predator priests and dioceses in the 1980's, 1990's, and even into the 21st Century ended up with dozens of bankruptcies of prominent Catholic congregations almost non-stop. $billions of settlement dollars changed hands when the admissions that surfaced in courts compelled heretofore sexual secrets to become public knowledge.

Hidden in the Roman Catholic's historical past, however, that never received the damning universal press that its priestly pederasts received in the 20th and 21st centuries, was a sexual mutilation of young boys, seven to nine years old, with extraordinary soprano voices before the onset of puberty. It involved the Church's papacy's desire to include choirs of these unusual voices, *heavenly voices,* so to speak, that could enhance attendances and reputations at this religion's legendary cathedrals of worship – in Germany, but especially in Italy. The act of castrating pre-pubescent youths whose vocal range often achieved three octaves, especially in the upper reaches, captured the attention of the Vatican and popes who deemed it justifiable (in the sight of God, of course) to use them as ethereal choirs in the prominent churches and chapels of significance, especially in Rome, home of the Vatican. To achieve the assemblage of these choirs, a systematic program was instituted to select young boys with soprano and alto voices that could reach the upper vocal registers of sound that often eclipsed those of the best female opera singers. [The Roman Catholic religion had traditionally always forbidden women to speak, let alone sing, in its churches.]

To achieve long-range voice stability in selecting these youths, their emasculation included removal or mutilation of their testicles to maintain the permanency of such ability to reach the upper ranges in singing the hymns during Catholic religious services.

These specially chosen youths at such a tender age designated for emasculation became known as *castrato* (singular) or *castrati* (plural.)

Historically the practice of assembling these choirs of *castrati,* the chosen male children often donated to church officials by parents of the youths, often used the rationale as the privilege of having been selected to dedicating their lives to the *Glory of God.*

Many catholic families actively relinquished their young sons to this vocal assembly to achieve status within the papacy itself. Those that were reluctant could not bring themselves to deny any request by the Church's hierarchy of Vatican representatives.

As mentioned previously, the voices of women in Catholic Church services had been banned for centuries, justified by interpretations from select phrases of the Bible used as proof of God's wishes for his faithful on earth.

Again, historically, the Roman Catholic hierarchy had always condemned the use of music in its churches and cathedrals until the mid-seventh century when the advances of the organ galvanized a maverick bishop from Western Europe to install one in his cathedral. The sudden influx of new faithful drawn to the music was so overwhelming and abundant, that the papacy quickly reversed itself, and a new source of attracting people (and revenue, of course) spawned a revolution of immense recruitment in church congregations.

The introduction of the organ's *heavenly* sounds created by composers whose efforts were readily encouraged and patronized by church officials began an era of culture of a magnitude few could ever have imagined coming from a steadily growing religious movement.

With the advent of church music came the introduction of choirs to supplement the grandeur effect of the constant development of the organ. Male singers began to appear, something new that also increased new converts to the faith. When youthful boys added another dimension of using higher vocal registers in the soprano range, choirs of just the very young got the attention of popes and other church officials that presented yet another dimension that drew more converts to attend the increasing ceremonial events on the Catholic Church's calendar.

The problem that arose, however, was the turnover of these youngsters once they reach puberty, and their voices changed to the lower registers. A need for establishing a permanent choir of *heavenly* voices was solved in the late16th Century when Pope Sixtus V issued a papal bull in 1589 approving the recruitment of *castrati* for the choir of St. Peter's basilica in Rome. It was the sweetness of the *castrati* voices that appealed to his legitimizing the mutilization of the children, and all for the glory of God, of course.

First use of *castrati* choirs were employed in the late 1550's in the chapel choir of the Duke of Ferrara. This followed in1574 in Germany at its court chapel in Munich, 1599 in the Sistine Chapel of the Vatican,

1610 in Wurtemburg, Germany, and 1637 in Vienna, Austria.

Almost all of the youths chosen for these choirs came from Italy, with probably none of them giving consent to what was going to happen to them as eunuchs in the removal of their gonads.

Typical physical effects of youthful castration was manifested by longer growth of both the arms and legs, and a more robust chest capacity which enhanced their ability to reach higher notes and sustain them longer than the average person.

Several historical accounts exist depicting the methodology of disabling and/or removing youth's testicles. One involved soaking the boy's scrotum in a tub of hot water and squeezing the organs with increased pressure to the point of dissolving them, possibly after the victim was drugged. Other methods were undergoing the screams of victims as their genitals were knifed open and physical slicing and removal of the two organs. Some barbers got into the act, even advertising castrations being available in their shops. Reports of deaths of these youngsters undergoing these amputations ranged from an astonishing 10% to 80% depending on the skill of the practitioners.

Just because these male children underwent emasculation didn't necessarily mean they would be acceptable to any professional youthful choir. Most of them were rejected because the quality of their voices did not develop in the positive ways anticipated by those who initiated their mutilation, left on their own to find some kind of purpose or employment in life. [Only 1% of the *castrati* candidates were ever selected for inclusions in church choirs, a horrific statistic of the first magnitude.] Many sought jobs in the world of opera or other menial work they could find as essentially outcasts of their community.

Some of the *castrati* became famous throughout the next 3½ centuries as singers in operas or on their own as vocal anomalies giving concerts that displayed their extraordinary range of pitch and sonic volume.

It was the Sistine Chapel that employed only the best of them in its choir as late as the 20th century. That practice was stopped in 1903 by Pope Pius X who banned any *new castrati* admitted to the choir of the Sistine Chapel. Those that remained had their employment end in 1928 according to Church records.

Estimates of three to five thousand boys *per year* in Italy alone were castrated during the 17th and 18th centuries, and as mentioned, only 1% of them were ever admitted for inclusion in papal choirs, and still fewer were selected to perform only in the grandeur of the Sistine Chapel.

It took the Roman Catholic Pope John Paul II (1978-2005) until 1994 to acknowledge the horrific mistake and misery the Church caused the famous Catholic astronomers Copernicus and Galileo for insisting the *sun was geocentric* to our universe (as opposed to the Catholic Church's centuries earlier endorsement of Thomas Aquinas' declaration that the *earth* was geocentric) ordering them to house arrest for the duration of their lives. They were just too famous to be burned at the stake that was common to others that had the temerity to challenge Church doctrine.

As for the *castrati* and its origin, involvement, and employment of them for 3½ centuries: Not one word, effort, or even consideration of having initiated and participated in the most dastardly criminal acts of history was uttered from the Roman Catholic Church Papacy, or deemed worthy of a public apology to the world's faithful despite petitions made world-wide in 2003 and 2007, and also as of the year 2011.

The immensity of this indelible stain on this religion's historical credibility can never be erased.

CROSSES TO BEAR

Celebrity Trash
Gated Cemeteries
Fat Chefs Promoting Healthy Foods
All Pharmaceutical Advertising
Brainless Columnists
Handguns in Schools
Ignorant Rich
Wacko Religions
Presidential Candidates with Multiple Wives
Deep-fried Southern Politicians
Brain-injury Sports
Medical Students That Graduated in the Bottom
Half of Their Class - Call Me "Doctor"
Anybody Having Multiple Husbands
Powerhouse Churches
70-Year-Old Wannabe Presidents
Rap Singers – the Penultimate Oxymoron
Dick Cheney
"You Can Trust Me" Liars
An SUV in Front of You
A SUV Behind You
Refreshment Prices at Sporting Events
Lottery Tickets One Digit Away from Winners
Political Pinocchio's
Clerical Child Molesters
Celestial Junkyards
Price of Super Bowl Tickets
Halliburton
Bernie Madoffs in the World
Flat Tires in Heavy Traffic
Eye-smarting Perfumes
Flat Beer

Donald Rumsfeld
Unwieldy Saran Wrap
Human Fertilizers
Neighbors with Kudzu Lawns
Middle-East Religions
Soda Pop Energy Drinks
Television Meteorologists
The Donald

SO YOU WANNA BE A CHEF

The seductive ads that culinary schools boast in television commercials and print advertising specifically target teenagers approaching high-school graduation that haven't the foggiest idea of what career they want to pursue after escaping the schoolroom.

Having abandoned any thought of college, if only because their grades were insufficient to gain admission, or the enormity of tuition costs was a downer, the thought of attending a culinary institute has mass appeal to young males and females wondering what their future might hold for them.

The attractiveness of not having to perform to any certain grade level while attending such schools and no student ever fails is an appealing inducement for enrollment in these for-profit schools. There is also a reputation to be gained by one's peers for working in an environment that has a veneer of respectability in life – after all, food is the sustaining ingredient that every human being relies on forever whether s/he likes it or not.

Restaurants are traditionally not vulnerable to the unemployment variables of industry that seem to be cyclical throughout the world. After all, everyone has to eat something, and the proliferations of eateries have always had a history of immunity from the vagaries of business trends regardless of economic roller-coaster cycles.

The sheer appeal of becoming a chef and knowing how to prepare food in a gazillion ways includes being the envy of an army of friends, relatives, and neighbors wherever one chooses to live. This fact is not lost on culinary school promoters who employ a host of compelling reasons why choosing a career in the highly respectable field of food preparation can lead to the always available manifold job opportunities in major hotels, resorts, corporate kitchens, and possibly (with luck via connections) the White House.

The tuition charged by culinary schools is not too different from some colleges and universities, and obtaining loans to pay for them are not as elusive as college students often find a stumbling block to enter, let alone pay for them.

The advantage that these for-profit culinary schools or other named "Institutes" of learning manual trades purvey is an ability to finance the fees via the wealthy company investors that are in fact loan officers for the corporate schools that they own. School officials make it easy to sign-up students for tuition costs usually for two-year terms to earn a "degree" or certificate of accomplishment. That such certificate of achievement are meaningless from such for-profit schools when applying a job upon "graduation" is never mentioned in the schools promotional literature or in the initial interview with students. Tuition amounts ranging from $32,000 to $42,000 for such two-year school terms is dollar-for-dollar almost identical to what the annual tuition a student attending a four-year college or university pays for his/her education.

Missing in this whole picture of courses advocating culinary school experience are the major cities in the country that offer Community College classes that compete with the for-profit schools in the subject matter taught at a fraction of the fees charged by the independent institutes owned by private corporations.

Also missing from the for-profit culinary schools are the names and employment histories of the faculty teaching the courses described in their promotional literature. Faculty reputations to induce student enrollment is rarely, if any, influence to attend one's choice of which for-profit "academy" to start one's career in restaurant-related professions.

To give some perspective to what kind of wages are paid to those working in food preparation, some eye-opening pay scales were released in 2011 in some of the country's prime newspapers.

ENTRY LEVEL CHEF: referred to as *Commis Chef.* Under the training of more experienced chefs, they work in the kitchen peeling vegetables, setting out cookware, and generally cleaning the kitchen. Top salary for the Commis Chef is $20,000 a year (roughly $10/hour.)

LINE COOK: often referred to as *Chef de Partie.* They work in one area of the kitchen preparing foods. The top salary of a Line Cook is $30,000 ($15/hour.)

PASTRY CHEF: they specialize in creation of pastries and desserts. They work their way up from bakers to pastry cooks to pastry chefs. Average annual salary of a salaried Pastry Chef is $50,000 or $15/hour for part-time chefs.

SOUS CHEF: they work their way up as assistants to the executive chef. They are trained in most areas of the kitchen, and not only cook, but become administrators who create work schedules, resolve customer problems, and are in charge of the kitchen in the absence of the executive chef. The average annual salary of a Sous Chef is $40,000 (roughly $20/hour.)

EXECUTIVE CHEF: he doesn't do much cooking, is more of a manager, hiring other chefs, and planning menus. It is his recipes and vision that create the personality and reputation of a restaurant. The average annual salary of an Executive Chef is around $70,000, but a highly-talented elite one can warrant much higher wages.

For those who want to learn a business career *while getting paid for it in the restaurant business,* a start can always begin as a dish-washer if only to see how a kitchen functions. Showing an avid interest in advancing to a fry-cook, then a line cook, and whatever other cooking specialties are available, a person can advance over the years while getting paid (not necessarily handsome wages) to a point where other job offers in the field are more financially rewarding. The advantage of this kind of career selection is avoiding the heavy costs of tuition payback.

Students who choose to enroll in for-profit "Institutes, Academies, or fancy-sounding French-name sobriquets" rarely envision what's involved with tuition loans that could take them into mid-life to pay them off.

Misinformation of the pay scales usually coupled with fraudulent advice of demand for jobs in this field rendered by schools' enrollment counselors is usually only realized when the "graduates" find themselves out in the world finding only entry-level wages offered them that often burst their bubble of what they contemplated when choosing a career in food preparation.

The high percentage of students opting to pursue careers in the culinary field that dropped out in the early stages after committing a healthy chunk of enrollment dollars got the attention of the Federal Government in 2011. It began investigation of fraudulent business practices of dozens of companies nationwide that had discovered easy profits with a minimum investment in promoting appealing careers to youths as well as middle-agers seeking some means of making a living. It was the failure of the small percentage of "graduates" from these for-profit corporate schools that finally got the attention of the nations Attorney Generals to investigate them.

Two careers pedaled by these for-profit schools whose records had particularly high failure rates were programs in the culinary arts and jobs as medical assistants.

PRIESTS, PEDERASTY,
AND THE CATHOLIC CHURCH

The flood of Catholic pedophile priest revelations of the late 20th and early 21st centuries came out of the woodwork from all over the globe after such scandals were unearthed in the United States in the 1990's, particularly in Boston. Shocking stories that began to appear in newspapers were akin to seepage from a leaking dike that flowed uncontrollably from a dam that grew exponentially to a flood of complaints from hemispheres around the world.

Only when investigators unearthed documents that tied the Vatican directly to suppressing reports of child sexual abuse around the globe, and manipulation of pedophile priests, bishops, and yes, cardinals, in transfers to other dioceses within countries, continents, and even to the Vatican itself , was the enormity of the scandal revealed.

In just about every country in the world, child sexual molestation is labeled a criminal act and subject to physical punishment for the guilty.

The Roman Catholic Church has always recognized human acts, however egregious, as "sins", *venial* or *mortal,* contingent on what the Church arbitrarily wishes to name them. Removal of the consequences of committing them, and forgiveness of the mental burden of the guilty who committed the act(s), requires penance and prayer, particularly reported in person to an ordained priest in person or in confidential booths in what the Church refers to as confessionals. According to the Church, there is no act so evil that it cannot be forgiven in a confessional by a repentant sinner.

With the inundation of growing reports of sexual molestation from Catholic clergy from an outpouring of men and women in their senior years, the sheer numbers of them demanded investigations from church officials. At first, Catholic spokesmen pooh-poohed the incidence of them, then attempted to divert attention to how it handled the priests involved, and at a last resort transferred them out of the country where the act(s) were committed. When the criminal courts of countries brought charges against an offending cleric, the Church fought to relinquish any records of an incident, citing confidentiality and exemption from such investigations.

While daily newspapers, magazines, and television continued reporting new scandals with more and more frequency, none of them delved into the why and wherefore that could have precipitated such prevailing sexual deviance by the Catholic clergy. The answer was there all the time and it was missed in headlines around the world.

The Catholic confessional, where people were compelled to tell the priest sitting in judgment of them of their "sins", listened to a gamut of stories involving sexual acts with words that could stimulate a prelate, especially after hearing similar revelations of people lined up to admit to "sins." The very nature of listening to sundry sexual experiences from the confessors, one after another, couldn't help but trigger a latent response to clerics who were supposed to suppress their own temptations after listening to sinful descriptions of penitents whispering their most grievous faults to them. The therapeutic effects of personally divulging one's faults, however serious, was not missed by the Catholic church in employing this exercise as a regimen to bond its faithful to the religion. Never mind that the cleric hearing the confession need not have the intellectual credentials to advise the supplicant akin to a psychiatrist or psychologist trained in dealing with human deficiencies, however serious they may be. It was the act of confessing that labeled human beings fallible and only the Church could remedy and wipe their sins away with frequent visits to the confessional booth. That such confessions could foster and induce criminal acts by the clerics sitting in judgment of the "sins" of the confessors was almost a given in light of the nature of what was exchanged between priest and "sinner."

The very nature that the Catholic Church recruited its priests from the ranks of single males, as early as eleven and twelve-year-olds, via special "retreats", was employed by the religion's hierarchy for centuries. Seminaries were very appealing to males whose sexual orientation attracted them to other males. That homosexual and bi-sexual orientations and their origins went physically unexplored until the latter half of the 20th century was an unfortunate circumstance, but advantageous to a religion that capitalized on human sexual frailties to attract young men into the ranks of serving as priests. The attraction of vestments, clerical garb, and high ceremony featuring inspiring music, incense, parades, communal disks of bread, wine, and security of a lifetime were hard to resist for youths approaching adulthood. The additional prestige that clerical recruiters used to induce them to seminaries was the high praise they would receive from their families, relatives, and even friends who automatically put them on an intellectual level that was deceptive to truth and reality. That this very concept could later result in mental anguish for priests who realized how hollow the whole choice of vocation had become evolved into the broken lives who left the priesthood, used clerical garb to satisfy sexual urges of a perverted nature, or lived out their lives quietly acknowledging, but accepting, their fate of a youthful decision that seemed so right at the time they made it.

The Church assisted any of its clerical ranks that chose to leave the fold of Mother Church in a manner that included a certain shame akin to a prodigal son leaving a life of truth and redemption. Ex-priests seemed to be branded in an unflattering manner once the news of their former life became public knowledge.

That the unique feature of the confessional booth with all of its transfers of "sins" between confessors and priests could be the root of errant clerics exposed to the worst of sexual deviances is no wonder that such behavior could have resulted in the multitude of molestations by the very clergy whose everyday life could have been exposed to the very acts they performed on their faithful – and very young and innocent faithful at that.

[Author's note: He was molested by a Catholic priest visiting St. James Church in Wilkinsburg, Pennsylvania, in June 1946, to recruit boys 11-13 years of age for seminary training by way of a "retreat" he then conducted at St. Vincent College in Latrobe, Pennsylvania. It was at this "retreat" where the act occurred.]

BIRTH OF RELIGIONS

From 900 BC to 200 BC, four traditions arose in four different parts of the world, each representing a new approach to the sacred: *Confucianism and Taoism* in China; *Hinduism and Buddhism* in India; *Monotheism in Israel;* and *Philosophical Rationalism* in Greece.

While all these traditions had their own particular historical precursors, and most would have offspring (including Christianity and Islam in the case of Judaism), each one acquired its distinctive and classical formation during this age.

The common thread running through these traditions was the fact that all of them "took the diffuse and variegated order of earlier religion and tried to unify it under a transcendent supreme principle." That principle could be a *supreme creator God* or *some unified principles of order, like the Tao;* or the endless cycle of *samaras,* the *Hindu and Sikh concept of reincarnation or rebirth*; or escape into the *Buddha's nirvana.*

MY NAME IS OTA BENGA

I was from the Belgian Congo brought to America in 1904 by a noted African explorer, Samuel Verner, and first presented on display at the St. Louis World's Fair where I was exhibited with other pygmies as "emblematic savages" along with other strange people in its anthropology wing, influenced by some people called "Darwinism and racism." Later I was given a permanent home at the Bronx Zoo whose founding director was William Hornaday, famous for devoting his life to prevent the extinction and disappearance of animal species in America, but especially Africa. I became a resident there as its first exhibit of a human being as a pygmy. Born in 1881, I was 4' 11" tall, about 23 years of age at the time, and weighed 103 lbs. Even though displayed to the public as a boy, I had actually been married twice. My first wife had been kidnapped by a hostile tribe, and my second wife had died from a poisonous snake bite. At the Bronx Zoo I was put on permanent display in the monkey house, caged with companions of a parrot and an orangutan named Dohong. Zoo Director Hornaday considered me a wild beast that evidenced little difference between a wild animal and a little black man. Verner's interest in bringing me to the U.S. was somewhat more complex, but my body shape and size akin to an orangutan, and the fact that we both grinned in the same way when pleased influenced him convincingly.

Brought over from Africa as a companion to a "fine young chimpanzee" (Verner's description) we were housed in the zoo's Primate House. Hornaday described me as "a genuine African Pygmy belonging to a sub-race miscalled "the dwarfs." "Ota Benga is a well-developed little man, with a good head, bright eyes and a pleasing countenance. He is not hairy or covered with the downy felt described by some explorers. He's happiest at work making something with his hands."

Eminent scientists at the time considered blacks to be evolutionary inferior to Caucasians, but caging one in a zoo produced much publicity. In 1974, author William Bridges, in his book, Gathering of Animals: An Unconventional History of the New York Zoological Society, mentioned "The Pygmy worked – or played- with the animals in the cage, naturally, and the spectacle of a black man in a cage gave a Times reporter the springboard for a story that worked up a storm of protest among negro ministers in the city. Their indignation was made to Mayor George B. McClelland, but he refused to take action."

Some whites also became concerned about the 'caged negro'. According to one author, part of the concern was because the "men of the cloth feared ... that the Benga exhibition might be used to prove the Darwinian theory of evolution." The objections were often vague, as in the words of the New York Times of September 9, 1906:

"The exhibition was that of a human being in a monkey cage. The human being happened to be a Bushman, one of a race that scientists do not rate high in the human scale, but to the average nonscientific person in the crowd of sightseers there was something that Benga doesn't think very deeply. If he did it isn't very likely that he was very proud of himself when he woke in the morning and found himself under the same roof with the orangutans (sic) and a monkey, for that is where he really is."

The Times article created a variety of opinions and created many protests and the threat of legal action. As a consequence the zoo director finally acquiesced and 'allowed the pygmy out of his cage', then dressed Ota Benga in a white suit who then spent most of his days walking the grounds of the zoo, often with large crowds following him, and returned to the monkey house only to sleep at night.

Being treated as a curiosity, mocked and made fun of by visitors, eventually caused Benga to being mobbed by curiosity tourists and mean children, resulting in a letter from Zoo Director Hornaday that revealed new problems that the situation had caused.

"Of course we have not exhibited him (Benga) in the cage since the trouble began. Since dictating the above, we have had a great time with Ota Benga. He procured a carving knife from the feeding room of the monkey house,and went around the Park flourishing it in a most alarming manner, and for a longtime refused to give it up. Eventually it was taken away from him."

"Shortly after that he went to the soda fountain near the Bird House to get some soda, and because he was refused the soda he got into a great rage... This led to a great fracas. He fought like a tiger, and it took three men to get him back to the monkey house. He has struck a number of visitors, and has raised 'Cain' generally.

The pygmy later made a little bow and some arrows and began shooting at zoo visitors who he found particularly obnoxious. 'After he wounded a few gawkers, he had to leave the Zoological Park for good.' The New York Times of September 18, 1906, described the problem:

"There were 40,000 visitors to the park on Sunday. Nearly every man, woman and child of this crowd made for the monkey house to see the star attraction in the house the wild man from Africa. They chased him about the grounds all day, howling, jeering, and yelling. Some of them poked him in the ribs, others tripped him up, all laughed at him."

After Ota Benga left the zoo, he was able to find sympathetic care at a succession of institutions and with several sympathetic individuals. But he was never able to shed his 'freak' label. Employed in a tobacco factory in Lynchburg, Virginia, Ota Benga grew increasingly depressed, hostile, irrational and forlorn. Concluding that he would never be able to return to his native land, in 1916 Benga committed suicide by shooting himself with a borrowed pistol.

The young Negro had been brought to Lynchburg by some kindly disposed person, and was placed in the Virginia Theological Seminary and College, where for several years he labored to demonstrate to his benefactors that he did not possess the power of learning, and some three years later he quit the school and went to work as a laborer. After leaving college Ota lived at a 'colored home' near the school earning his livelihood working as a laborer in a tobacco factory. Hornaday later suggested 'his suicide was committed because the burden became so heavy that the young negro secured a revolver belonging to the woman with whom he lived, went to the cow stable and there sent a bullet through his heart, ending his life.'